KU-015-839

QUEEN'S PROGRESS

A Kit Marlowe Mystery

M.J. Trow

CRÈME de la CRIME

This first world edition published 2018
in Great Britain and the USA by
Crème de la Crime, an imprint of
SEVERN HOUSE PUBLISHERS LTD of
Eardley House, 4 Uxbridge Street, London W8 7SY
Trade paperback edition first published
in Great Britain and the USA 2018 by
SEVERN HOUSE PUBLISHERS LTD

Copyright © 2018 by M.J. Trow and Maryanne Coleman.

All rights reserved including the right of
reproduction in whole or in part in any form.
The moral right of the author has been asserted.

British Library Cataloguing in Publication Data
A CIP catalogue record for this title is available from the British Library.

ISBN-13: 978-1-78029-104-8 (cased)
ISBN-13: 978-1-78029-586-2 (trade paper)
ISBN-13: 978-1-78010-966-4 (e-book)

This is a work of fiction. Names, characters, places and incidents
are either the product of the author's imagination or are used fictitiously.
Except where actual historical events and characters are being described
for the storyline of this novel, all situations in this publication are
fictitious and any resemblance to actual persons, living or dead,
business establishments, events or locales is purely coincidental.

All Severn House titles are printed on acid-free paper.

Severn House Publishers support the Forest Stewardship Council™ [FSC™],
the leading international forest certification organisation. All our titles that
are printed on FSC certified paper carry the FSC logo.

Typeset by Palimpsest Book Production Ltd.,
Falkirk, Stirlingshire, Scotland.
Printed and bound in Great Britain by
TJ International, Padstow, Cornwall.

QUEEN'S PROGRESS

528 648 76 0

A Selection of Recent Titles by M.J. Trow

The Kit Marlowe Series

DARK ENTRY *
SILENT COURT *
WITCH HAMMER *
SCORPIONS' NEST *
CRIMSON ROSE *
TRAITOR'S STORM *
SECRET WORLD *
ELEVENTH HOUR *
QUEEN'S PROGRESS *

The Grand & Batchelor Series

THE BLUE AND THE GREY *
THE CIRCLE *
THE ANGEL *
THE ISLAND *

The Inspector Lestrade Series

LESTRADE AND THE KISS OF HORUS
LESTRADE AND THE DEVIL'S OWN
LESTRADE AND THE GIANT RAT OF SUMATRA

The Peter Maxwell Series

MAXWELL'S ISLAND
MAXWELL'S CROSSING
MAXWELL'S RETURN
MAXWELL'S ACADEMY

* *available from Severn House*

ONE

The flames of his torch flickered on the rough stone. Spiders scurried from the light, rats scuttled from the soft padding of his footfalls. This was a kingdom of darkness, a realm of silence. He had no business here, this man from the air, this refugee from the sun. Yet, here he was. And he had every business here.

A door loomed ahead of him at the end of the passage, ancient oak thick with webs, its studs rough with rust. He slid the dagger from the small of his back, the lethal blade flashing silver in the guttering torchlight. He tapped its tip against the metal. A padlock. How apt. And he found himself smiling. One twist of the steel and the old iron gave way, cracking loudly in that silence. He put his hand to the door, then his shoulder, and it swung wide under his weight, the hinges growling with anger at the intrusion of this stranger.

He held his torch high, taking in the small chamber that lay before him. There was a crucifix set high in the far wall, nails driven anew through the Lord's hands to anchor it to the crumbling masonry. There was a table, oak again and covered in cobwebs, dense and complex as damask. An inkwell – empty now save for rainbow echoes of the ink it once held caked around its mouth – held a quill, its feathers frowsty with age. He touched it and it disintegrated, dissolving into dust. At the far end of the table stood a chair. And on the chair, sitting watching him, a man. He had been dead for years, all life gone, all light extinguished. His hands stretched out ahead of him, as if he had been about to rise when something had stopped him.

The intruder rested his torch in the iron bracket and bent to peer at the keeper of the chamber. He wore full armour, rust-brown and obsolete, the spiky work of the master smiths of Augsburg, the rivets no longer holding the plates, the hinges welded with the passing of the years. Over the breastplate, below the corrupted mass of mail, the tabard had lost its colour, but he knew the heraldry like he knew his own face. The quarters of Diencourt and Holand, the silvered bars of Rotherfield and the snarling lion of Burell. He glanced down. There it was, on the ankle now, the once plump calf long withered to nothing letting it fall from the knee, the faded blue of the garter. Evil to him who evil thinks. He smiled. The time of evil was nearly at an end. It had been a long time coming, but justice would prevail and God would be in his Heaven again.

He probed with his dagger, lifting the metal chain of office that still lay across the shoulders of the dead man. He stooped to look into that face. It was not human now, a mask of death with holes for eyes and the brown teeth jagged in the jaw. The hair was home to the spiders, white straw wild over the shoulders. He glanced down to the table where the rats had long ago gnawed the fingers and left the parchment, rolled and old, to the dust of the ages. His dagger tip clinked against the silver lupellus, the wolf-dog at the apex of the chain. He snatched it, ripping it from the dead man's breast. This was what he had come for. This would be his talisman in the days that lay ahead. It was a trinket, nothing more. But its power was immense. He could feel it as he took the torch again, feel it as he eased the door back, closing the dead man again in the utter blackness of his tomb. Feel it as he made for the light, for the world he was about to change forever.

'Have you actually met the Queen, Marlowe?' Robert Cecil was asking. Mr Secretary was now Sir Robert, a member of Her Majesty's Privy Council and a married man. But he still had to look up to everybody. A careless nursemaid had dropped him as a child and his back was crooked, his feet wayward and his gait clumsy.

'No, Sir Robert. I have not had that exquisite pleasure.'

Cecil looked at the man at the far end of the table with those penetrating hazel eyes of his. He was Christopher Marlowe, the scholar, an alumnus of Corpus Christi in the increasingly Puritan town of Cambridge. That was good. He was also the Muses' Darling, all fire and air, the playwright who had dared God out of his Heaven. That was not so good. And he was, on the third side of the coin that few men even knew existed, Francis Walsingham's man, a projectioner of cunning, an agent of Her Majesty as elusive as quicksilver. For all he was now the Queen's Spymaster, Robert Cecil couldn't read a man like Kit Marlowe.

'Well, I doubt you will now,' he said, 'but she has a job for you nonetheless.'

'I am flattered, sir,' Marlowe said, his face a mask of theatricality when he wanted it to be, 'but I fear I must decline.'

Cecil jerked his head back and looked at Marlowe with basilisk's eyes. A taller man would have leapt to his feet, but Cecil stayed in his chair; to rise would merely accentuate his little stature and he would have to look up to Marlowe all the more. 'Decline?' he repeated. 'Why?'

'I have chained myself to Master Henslowe at the Rose,' Marlowe told him. 'I owe him a play.'

'Really?' Cecil sneered. 'What is it this time?'

Marlowe smiled. He wasn't about to share his genius with the Queen's Imp, Walsingham's successor or no. 'It's a rewrite of *Ralph Roister Doister*,' he said, folding his arms. 'Long overdue, I think you'll agree.'

'If I knew a rat's fart about the drama, Marlowe, I probably would. But that's precisely why you're here.'

'It is?'

Cecil sighed and rang a small silver bell on the table in front of him. 'Won't you have a seat, Marlowe?' A liveried flunkey appeared from nowhere, in the crimson of Her Majesty. 'Claret? A sweetmeat or two?'

Marlowe shook his head, smiling. He was in a declining mood this morning. Cecil clicked his fingers and the flunkey disappeared. The Spymaster looked out of his Whitehall window, his eyes following the road that ran like an arrow to Westminster, the abbey's turrets a pale grey in the morning sun, the bulk of St Stephen's Hall looming behind it like a thundercloud. 'Her Majesty,' he said, 'is going on another Progress this summer. She was with my father at Theobald's last month, but her plans for July are rather more extensive.'

Marlowe frowned. He knew, as all men knew, about the

Queen's Progresses. They were the stuff of legend; Gloriana, conqueror of Spain's mighty Armada, riding in pomp at the head of a glittering and adoring procession. She rode a horse as white as milk, her robes all cloth of gold, with rings on her fingers and bells on her toes. It was as though Cecil was reading Marlowe's mind. 'She shall have music wherever she goes,' he said.

Kit Marlowe had the voice of an angel, soaring to the fan-vaulted ceiling of the great cathedral at Canterbury, carrying the genius of Byrd and Tallis to the ear of God above. He laughed. 'Surely, Her Majesty can do better than me as choirmaster,' he said.

'Don't be flippant, Marlowe.' Cecil wasn't laughing. He wasn't even smiling. 'Whatever you've heard about the royal Progresses, they are as carefully orchestrated as a galliard. Or perhaps, more accurately, as any of the Duke of Parma's battle plans. On the surface, you'll be going ahead of her to arrange for revels – masques, music, fireworks, a few laughs. She particularly likes it when people fall over, so it doesn't need anything too sophisticated in that line. But, in reality . . .'

Reality. Marlowe was the man who had conjured the love affair of Dido and Aeneas. He had invented the Scythian shepherd, the limping Tamburlaine. He had crafted Barabas, the Jew of Malta. He had even summoned the Devil in *Dr Faustus*. What did he know of reality? Yet he felt the hilt of the dagger just between his back and his chair. He knew all about reality. And more than all the Hells of Faustus, it frightened him every time.

'In reality?' He couldn't leave it there.

Cecil narrowed his eyes. He knew how highly Francis Walsingham had rated Marlowe. He was a man to trust, he said, with his life, the life of the Queen, the life of England. But Walsingham was dead, laid to rest with Philip Sydney and marked with a simple inscription in wood. Wood that would rot, as Walsingham rotted in Paul's. Secretary Cecil smiled. 'You know, at Theobald's last month, my father offered the Queen his resignation.'

'He did?'

Cecil's father was Burghley, the grand old man who had guarded England now it seemed for ever. Whether reading Aeschylus from the saddle of a donkey, screaming at Francis Drake, restraining the Queen from her more dangerous dalliances, Burghley had been the rock of ages. 'He's getting on,' Cecil said. 'The eyes are going, the gout's slowing him down. He's seventy, for God's sake. Know what she said?'

Marlowe shook his head.

'Asked him if he wanted to become a hermit,' Cecil shook his head. 'Told him he was – and I quote – "the chief pillar of the welfare of England".'

'That's more or less true, isn't it?' Marlowe asked.

'Politics is a young man's game, Marlowe. You and I, we're players, albeit at different levels. The only way the Queen is going to grow old disgracefully is if younger hands hold her, catch her if she falls. The King of Spain still lives and he's fanatic enough to launch another thousand ships against us. The Duke of Parma still holds the Netherlands, whatever those Dutch peasants like to think.'

'I understand that the Earl of Essex was to lead an expedition against him.'

Cecil blinked. That news was not widespread. Perhaps old Walsingham had been right to put his faith in Marlowe. 'Never trust a man whose beard is a different colour from his hair, Marlowe – one of the first things my father taught me. No, Essex is a hawk, a warmonger. We need peace right now – doves around the throne.'

There was a pause. 'Then again,' the new Spymaster went on, 'there's the Pope.'

'Ah.'

'Nicolo Sfonrati – Gregory XIV to you. Prone to outbursts of hysterical laughter, I'll grant you – they say he giggled his way through his coronation – but he's sharp as a tack and he sides with Spain. You know he excommunicated Henry of Navarre?'

'No!' Marlowe was as outraged as a man could be who didn't give a damn about a man's soul.

'As I live and breathe. More importantly to us, the Bull against the queen still stands. God knows how many killers the Holy See has at their command.'

'You think there'll be another attempt on the Queen's life?'

'The Progresses are always the problem.' Cecil gnawed his lip. 'My father talked the Queen out of them in recent years, but she's determined anew. Wants to meet her people, be assured they love her after all. Last year went well. Lady Russell's girls looked after Her Majesty at Bisham Abbey and Julius Caesar gave her an outfit of silver cloth that must have cost him half his revenue. Stupid name he may have, but you can't question the man's loyalty.'

'And this year?'

Cecil sighed and rolled his eyes upwards. 'There you have it,' he said. 'She'll open the bout at Farnham, then hit the Montagues at Cowdray. Then it's Petworth, Chichester and Titchfield. They'll all try to outdo each other, of course, with fireworks and fanfares, lakes and bloody fountains. It never ceases to amaze me how much cash the aristocracy have lying about. We aren't taxing them enough.'

'Do you have any reason, Sir Robert, to doubt the loyalty of any of Her Majesty's hosts?'

'You've hit the proverbial nail on the head, there, Marlowe. I have none. Who'd have thought that Judas would betray Jesus? Or Peter deny that he knew him? But it happened. Your task will be to go ahead of Her Majesty, snoop, check the lie of the land. All discreet, of course, all under cover. *But,*' and Cecil leaned forward, standing with his heels on the stretcher of his chair, leaning on his knuckles until it hurt and he sat back down again with a bump, 'you will report to me regularly. If a Papist farts within a day's ride of the Queen's itinerary, I want to know about it. Understood?'

'Understood,' Marlowe said.

'Your cover will be entertainment for Her Majesty. Officially, you're working for Edmund Tilney, the Master of the Revels. I'll get the necessary paperwork for you. What'll you need? Five stout lads? Ten?'

'One.'

'One?' Cecil repeated. He liked a man who didn't make excessive demands on the Privy purse, but this seemed a little *too* cheese-paring.

'If I'm to lay on masques, I'll need a stage manager. I'll take the best I know. His name's Tom Sledd.'

Tom Sledd struck a posture in front of the polished tin mirror, aiming for regal, yet man of the people; deserving, yet humble. It involved a lot of repositioning of legs and arms but eventually he could do it without falling over. He moved nearer and tilted the tin towards the light. Time to concentrate on the expression; if a picture could paint a thousand words, then how much more could he express with a tilt of the eyebrow, a curl of the lip. He looked towards the left-hand corner of the ceiling as he had seen Ned Alleyn do as the ladies swooned over him, then swivelled his eyes to check the effect. No, too soulful; the Queen would run a mile. Or perhaps not – Tom Sledd was, if not as handsome as some, certainly well muscled, and he turned a comely calf, one of Gloriana's favourite body parts, if rumours were to be believed. Hadn't she elevated Sir Christopher Hatton just because he was the finest dancer in England? He looked towards the right, downwards, tilting his shoulder and sliding forward his opposite leg; again, he swivelled his eyes to see the effect and immediately fell over, feeling giddy and not a little nauseous. It might work for Richard Burbage, but falling flat on your face in front of the Queen was no way to get a knighthood. He had too much hair to ape Will Shaxsper, so there was no point in even trying.

He peered again into the mirror; this dull old thing was worse than useless, but it was no good wishing for Venetian glass and silver in Henslowe's Rose. Did he look like a man who could manage masques for the Queen? He couldn't tell – his Meg always told him he was handsome, but what else would a wife say? Impatient with himself, he turned his back on the mirror and faced into the small space of his workroom. The floor was ankle deep in wood shavings, laced with the odd crust and lost playbill, the walls gone forever behind leaning flats from plays from long ago. He wondered how much he would be able to take with him; Marlowe's message had been typically Marlovian but he got the gist. 'Tell Henslowe you're burying your grandame. We're off on a

Progress; masques, people falling over, a bit with a dog.' No dates. No details. Just endless possibilities.

He bowed low, doffing an imaginary hat and sweeping an imaginary cloak out behind him, taking care that it didn't get entangled in his imaginary rapier glinting at his hip. Pitching his voice just a tad higher than his normal register and putting a plum firmly in his mouth, he announced, 'Arise, Sir Thomas, Baron Sledd of Sleddshire.'

'Ma'am,' he muttered in his normal voice, 'Thou art too kind.'

He had swept so low in his bow that his head was touching the knee of his extravagantly extended left leg. He saw a movement behind him out of the corner of his eye and focused slowly on what might be causing it. Had his cloak been anything but imaginary, it could have been that. Had his rapier been actual steel instead of light and air, it could have been that. But no. It was neither.

'Something to tell me, Master Sledd?' asked Philip Henslowe.

TWO

Since Robert Cecil wasn't paying for men, the least he could do was to lay on horseflesh. Marlowe's chestnut had Flanders blood, gentle eyes and two white stockings. It could outpace Sledd's roan but that was intentional. Robert Cecil had grown up surrounded by power, at Hatfield, at Theobalds, now in Whitehall. Men like him understood the need for hierarchy. Rich men lived in castles, or at least moated manor houses. Poor men didn't have a pot to piss in. It was the natural order of things. Whoever this Tom Sledd was, he was Marlowe's man; give him a nag and let him think himself lucky he wasn't walking.

Behind the pair as they trotted through the Surrey sunshine, leaving the smoke and stench of London behind, Sledd hauled the rein of a packhorse, laden with struts of wood, coils of rope and a yardstick. A swatch of velvets dangled from the saddlebow, worth more than horse and saddle put together.

Ralph Roister Doister had left Marlowe's head as soon as the words had left his lips. When he was a boy, not yet at the King's School in Canterbury, the taverns of the town were agog with the ghastly news from Europe. The Protestants of Paris had been butchered in an orgy of killing, slaughtered by a female monster whose name was whispered in the Star and the Shepherd's Crook. She was Catherine de Medici, an Italian who ruled France, and she ate babies for breakfast. She had ordered an entire church congregation to be rounded up in a city square and she had sat, gurgling with delight as her minions sauntered along the kneeling, praying victims, cutting their throats so that the cobbles ran with blood. And it had to be true – all the Huguenot weavers along the Stour knew it for a fact.

It had not been a fit subject for a pot boy at an inn, but such things could not be hidden. One man in particular, Marlowe remembered, had looked him up and down and said,

'These are troubled times, boy. When you grow up and grow old, as you will, another generation will be there, asking you if there ever was a massacre in Paris.' The man had moved closer, pressing his nose against Marlowe's so that the beer on his breath filled the air. 'And you tell them,' he growled, 'Tell them for those of us who won't still be around then. You tell them, yes; there was.'

And the massacre in Paris was in his head now, the screams and the oaths, the clash of steel and the sudden awfulness of death. It all seemed so incongruous on this late May morning, the sun already high, the shade of the new leaves dappling the grass. He glanced across at Sledd. The man was no country bumpkin but he had a stalk of grass between his teeth and chewed the end of it, like the rangy cattle they trotted past.

A hunting horn brought them both up sharp and they reined in. The packhorse ambled to a grateful stop with a creak of harness and ungreased wheel. Ahead of them, the ground sloped away down to a lake, dark and brooding under a fringe of firs, and horsemen were cantering across the meadow, their animals sending up clouds of dust. Had it ever rained in this country, Marlowe wondered.

There were shouts and whistles, the jingle of bits and bridle bells. 'There!' Sledd shouted. From the knot of horsemen, a hawk sliced the air like an arrow, thudding into a wood pigeon that squawked once and tumbled to the ground in a wild spray of blood and flying feather.

'Hawks and doves,' Marlowe murmured, but Sledd didn't hear him.

'That's a fine bird, Kit,' he said as the kestrel scythed in a wide arc and circled back to the gloved wrist of its keeper.

'It was,' said Marlowe. He was looking at the broken pigeon, still trying to flap on the ground. He nudged the chestnut forward and slid from the saddle. For an instant, he cradled the dying bird, smoothing the ruffled feathers and looking into its eye, misted with pain. Then, quickly and without a sound, he broke its neck.

'Oi!' A shout made him turn and a trio of beaters with snapping dogs on leashes were hurrying over to him. 'What're you doing? That's Mistress Blanche's bird, that is.'

'I rather fancy it's nobody's bird now,' Marlowe said, holding the pigeon out towards them, its head dangling from his palm.

'You're trespassing,' another beater said. 'This is private land.'

Marlowe looked at the three. They bristled with weapons, cudgels and knives stuffed into belts over their brigandines. One had a bow slung over his shoulder, his quiver stuffed with goose-feather arrows. 'Is this the estate of Sir Walter Middleham?'

'It is,' the first man said. 'And you've no right to be on it.'

Marlowe reached into his purse and held up the Queen's cypher, letting the silver flash in the sun. 'Recognize this, lickspittle?' he asked.

The man blinked. Any Englishman born, and a good few foreigners too, knew that cypher, the dragon and the greyhound flanking the arms of England and France. There was a thud of hoofs and the whinny of a horse and a woman cantered over the hillside, hauling her reins within feet of Marlowe. Her grey snorted and shook its head, sending flecks of foam through the air.

'What's the trouble here, Fitch?'

The spokesman of the three tugged off his pickadil and nodded briefly. 'These two are trespassing, my lady. That one,' he pointed at Marlowe, 'just broke your bird's neck.'

The woman looked down at the handsome stranger in the black velvet, with a dead pigeon in one hand and the queen's cypher in the other. The sheen on his sleeve and the sheen of the dead bird's feathers made a pretty sight, his liquid eyes more so.

'Not my bird, Fitch,' she said, raising an eyebrow. 'Just one of God's creatures that ran out of luck.'

Another rider joined her, a thin, rather pale boy with freckles. 'What's going on?' His voice was petulant, and if Marlowe had been asked to guess he would have said, and rightly, that this was the son of the house, and not half the man his sister was at that.

'Don't fret yourself, brother,' the woman said. 'This gentleman has done one of God's creatures a kindness. I am waiting for him to introduce himself.'

Marlowe threw the bird to Fitch and swept off his plumed hat, bowing low. 'Christopher Marlowe, my lady,' he said. 'At your service. And this is my man, Thomas Sledd.'

Tom Sledd had never really thought of himself as anybody's man, not even Kit Marlowe's, but it was too early in the day to rattle cages and to remind everybody that Tom is as good as his master. He too doffed his cap.

'Master Marlowe,' the woman's face softened and she gave a tinkling laugh. 'You're Master Tilney's man – the Master of the Revels.'

Tom Sledd couldn't help smirking. It was Marlowe's turn to be placed in the straitjacket of hierarchy. It actually made no sense – Edmund Tilney had the discernment of a bedpan. What the Queen's Master of Revels knew about drama could be written on a pinhead, around the feet of the dancing angels. But nevertheless, in this mad world of Gloriana, he *was* Marlowe's master and no mistake.

'That I am,' Marlowe said, and only Tom Sledd could hear the hidden message in his tone. 'And you are?'

She laughed again. 'I am Blanche Middleham,' she said. She nodded at the pale youth. 'My brother James.'

Marlowe bowed again but the simp in the saddle barely moved.

'We must be getting back,' he said to his sister. 'Grandfather . . .'

Blanche held up her hand. 'Master Marlowe has ridden far,' she said, taking up her reins and patting the grey's neck. 'The least we can do is make him welcome. James, be a darling and ride to the Hall, will you? Tell Mason we have a guest for the foreseeable future. And tell him to find an outhouse for his man.'

Tom Sledd frowned. Two days ago, he was looking forward to a knighthood, the Queen's rapier tickling his shoulder. Now, he was Marlowe's man, consigned to sleeping with the hogs.

'I—' he began, but Marlowe cut him off.

'Delighted,' he said. 'And thank you, Master Middleham.'

The boy snorted and wheeled his horse away. Blanche leaned low over her horse's neck. 'Better go with him, Fitch. You know how badly he rides when he's in a temper.'

There were rumbled guffaws all round and Lady Blanche adjusted her hat, placing the peacock plum just *so* at a jaunty angle on her pale golden hair. 'Will you ride with me, Master Marlowe?' she asked. 'I want to show you the lake.'

'The lake?' Tom Sledd was lacing his best doublet. No expense had been spared at Farnham Hall that night. It was not every summer that the Queen came to Henry of Blois' castle and graced the Middlehams with her Presence. And the Queen's man deserved the best too, so dinner had been announced. 'The bloody lake?' He said it again, because clearly Marlowe hadn't heard him. He was slipping a small sheathed dagger up his sleeve.

'You were there,' Marlowe reminded him, 'when Lady Blanche was planning the masque.'

The stage manager stopped wrestling with the points. Why couldn't gentlemen use buttons like everybody else? 'Yes, I was *there*,' he said, his voice rising as it always did when he was annoyed. 'But Lady Blanche was so taken with you, she delivered everything at a whisper, about an inch from your ear. Did you notice that? Only, *I* did, because I couldn't hear a bloody word.'

Marlowe chuckled. 'Ladies don't shout, Tom,' he said. 'It's beneath them.' He frowned suddenly. 'Taken with me? Was she?'

'Plain as the nose on your face,' Sledd said, restarting the tying, having dried his sweating fingers on the seat of his venetians. 'Quite a looker too, if you ask me.'

'I didn't.' Marlowe was rummaging for his gloves. 'I thought married men such as yourself had no eye for another.'

'I can look, if I don't touch.' Master Sledd knew the leeway he was allowed. 'But, no, well, I mean . . . You could do all right there, Kit. Her grandfather seems to own half of Hampshire and she's got an arse on her like—'

'I bow to your judgement, Thomas,' Marlowe said, firmly. 'But that's not why we're here, is it? For me to settle my pension plan.'

'Er . . . no.' Sledd frowned, realizing he had overstepped some kind of mark; though precisely what that mark was, he wasn't sure. 'No, indeed.'

'We are here to provide entertainment for Her Majesty. Ten barges on the lake, filled with water nymphs, three fountains, a magic grotto, suitably lit with torches for the evening. Oh, and at least thirty musicians, heavy on the flutes and hautbois.' He leaned over and closed Tom Sledd's gaping mouth with a gentle finger. It was hard to stay annoyed with him for long; the man carried the ghost of the boy on his shoulder and he had never had a mean thought in his life. He was a rare bird in theatreland indeed. 'Any problems with that?'

The theatre manager shook his head. 'No, no problem with that.' He was all at sea when he was out of London, but he couldn't imagine that this arse-end of the country was exactly filled with lads who could double as water nymphs, or with musicians who could do more than make rough music with the tongs and the bones. There were few problems on a stage he couldn't fix; perhaps this would be the same. Muttering, he wandered off, his hands up before his face, squaring off lakes, fountains and grottoes in the air, trailing still unfastened laces.

Marlowe smiled and watched him go. The more Tom was immersed in his staging, the less likely he would be to notice if there was skulduggery afoot. And that would all be to the good. Although Tom Sledd was no more loose-lipped than the next man, and less so than many, he tended to wear his emotions across his face and that wouldn't help at all. No – let him plan his fountains and his nymphs and, who knew, he might even succeed.

Farnham Hall was large, draughty and had seen much better days. The great keep had been built by Henry of Blois, the Bishop of Winchester, in the days when Stephen fought Matilda for the crown of England. A vicious, war-torn land it was then, a time to hide behind tons of stone and mortar, to take refuge behind walls. But that was then. The days of Gloriana, or so Lord Burghley said, had brought light and freedom and peace. Nobody built castles any more, if only because the Queen's cannon could knock them down like skittles. The Hall that the Middlehams had built in the days of King Hal lay below it, pretentious in its own way, with half-timbering and new brick, a gateway out of proportion to the wings and a half-hearted fountain of the Italian style playing before it. No one used the keep any more, except the pigs that rooted in the tangled mass of ivy and willowherb that all but choked the old stones, snuffling and snorting where Henry of Blois once kept his court.

Trestles had been set up in the banqueting hall, and candles were spaced frugally along them, leaving many of the diners more or less in the dark. Somewhere in the gloom, Marlowe knew, Tom Sledd would be rubbing shoulders with the lesser tenants of the estate. It had taken some doing, but he had finally managed to explain to the steward that Tom was not his manservant, that he should not be lodged in a stable somewhere. It had been touch and go until he had eventually made it clear that no room for him, no masque for the Queen. After that, it had been more or less plain sailing. The room he had been given was not wonderful, but it was inside the house and had an actual bed in it, rather than a few bales of straw. The mattress was lumpy, the hangings full of cobwebs and – according to Tom at least – several bats, whose baleful twitterings could just be heard over the rustle of the rats in the wainscoting. But, as Marlowe had told him he should be, he was grateful for small mercies.

Marlowe was at the top table with the family and some of the more important tenants of the estate, primarily those who paid the rent on time, a small and honoured clique. He was between Blanche and her grandfather, a man so old and crumpled he looked as though he had been left out in the rain. Although his clothes were rich and sumptuous, they came from an earlier time and also seemed to have been made for a much bigger man. The old man's head emerged from the elaborate ruff and velvet ruching like a tortoise from its shell, his eyes small and rheumy, his skull clearly visible beneath the skin straining over his temples. He had been introduced by his granddaughter in what Marlowe thought was an unnecessarily perfunctory manner – 'Grandfather,' she had announced with an airy wave of her hand as the scion of the house was eased into his seat by two burly retainers. Marlowe had bowed and smiled but the response was disappointing. The only emotion that the old man showed was when the food began to arrive, and then there was a glint in his sunken eye.

Wheaten loaves were distributed down the table by serving maids and they were followed by kitchen boys bearing tureens. Each guest, whether they wanted it or not, was served with a ladleful of what Marlowe's nose told him was hare, so very gamey that the smell was on the edge of repulsive rather than pleasant. The old man nudged the playwright in the ribs with a razor-sharp elbow.

'Pass the bread,' he grated. 'I must sop the gravy if I am to eat tonight. This hare has bones in it that no hare has in its body. It's rat, rat, say . . .' He subsided back into his clothes a little further, furtive eyes flashing left and right.

Marlowe reached for the loaf in front of him but his wrist was gripped in Blanche's muscular fist.

'Who is that bread for, Master Marlowe?' she hissed.

'Umm . . .' Marlowe was in a cleft stick. It seemed so impolite to refer to the old man as 'grandfather' and yet, what else was he to call him, as he had not been introduced. He settled for a gesture to his left.

She grabbed the bread from him and leaned forward, glaring at the old man. 'Grandfather,' she snapped. 'How many times must you be told? White bread gives you bad dreams. Not to mention wind.' She smiled like a basilisk at Marlowe. 'Poor, dear old soul,' she gushed. 'He forgets he isn't twenty any more.' She leaned forward again. 'Your gruel will be along shortly, Grandfather,' she screamed at the top of her voice. 'Your gruel. Along shortly.' She turned again to Marlowe, sitting wide eyed and stunned by having her scream in his ear. 'Poor lamb,' she said, 'deaf as a stile. But a dear old soul, of course. James and I would be lost without him.' She turned around and clicked her fingers at a serving boy, who approached at a fawning crouch.

'Yes, Mistress Blanche?'

'Were you the fool who gave the hare to the Master?'

The boy shook his head, but she cuffed him on the ear even so.

'Take it away and bring his gruel.' She turned back to Marlowe. 'Imbecile!' she said. He assumed that she meant the lad, but was not absolutely sure. He turned back to the chelonian on his left. He was running his finger around the edge of the pool of gravy on his plate, where a scum of grease was already forming. With a quivering hand, he raised the glutinous digit to his mouth, but by the time it got there, all but a trace had gone, flying off in all directions and going who knew where. Marlowe, looking down onto his own plate and noticing some alien gobbets, pushed his hare away and decided that hunger was the better part of valour.

The elbow hit him in the ribs again, exactly on the spot still stinging from the time before. He leaned across slightly. He didn't need another lesson to tell him that Blanche would be best left out of any communications he had with the Master of Farnham.

'When the fish comes round, laddie,' he grated in Marlowe's ear, 'push a bit to the side of your plate so I can pick at it.' Marlowe reflected that he had rarely had such an appetizing request. 'But scrape the ginger off it. It makes me cough and *she'll* know I'm eating it.'

Marlowe would have given his right arm to make sure the old creature didn't cough at the table, so nodded his acquiescence. 'Perhaps the fish disagrees . . .' but he got no further.

'Disagrees?' the old man spat. 'Disagrees? I have the constitution of an ox, an ox, I tell you. They're trying to kill me, that's what it is. Starve me out. My boy,' and his eyes filled with tears, 'my boy, their father, he's spinning in his grave if he can see how they treat me.'

The maids and lads were doing the rounds again and clearing away the platters. An enormous fish of dubious ancestry was brought round next, covered in powdered ginger in a layer so thick it filled the air with pungent dust as the food was ladled anyhow in front of the guests. When the clatter of spoons had stopped and the fish lay balefully on everyone's plate, as if daring them to try it, the old man spoke again, taking up where he had left off.

'My boy, my Edmund, he died and left me with . . .' his eyes swivelled in their sockets towards where his grandchildren were sitting, off to Marlowe's right. 'The boys're not so bad, I suppose. Weak. Snivelling. Sneaky. But not so bad. But

Blanche . . .' His head sank into his ruff until his chin disappeared, his petulant lower lip resting on the grubby linen.
'Blanche . . . she's the spawn of Beelzebub, laddie, mark my
words.'

Marlowe was adept at table talk. He had shared a board
with everyone from scholars in their cups to almost the highest
in the land and had rarely found himself as out of his depth
as he was right now. True, he hadn't taken to Mistress Blanche
Middleham, but spawn of Beelzebub? That seemed a bit strong.
He opened his mouth to try and steer the conversation into
less choppy waters.

'But that's enough about my family,' the old man suddenly
said. 'Where's my bit of fish? Make sure there's no ginger
on it, mind.' He extended a crabbed and filthy finger and
rummaged on Marlowe's plate. 'There's a good bit, look.
Tender and plump. I can suck on that.' He manoeuvred it to
the edge of the platter and scooped it up with his spoon.
At the third attempt, he got some of it into his mouth,
distributing the rest up Marlowe's sleeve, where bits of it
got caught in the embroidery.

Blanche laid a firm hand on the poet's other arm. 'Is
Grandfather being a nuisance?' she asked, modulating her
voice for Company. 'He can be a touch garrulous, sometimes.
A dear, sweet old soul, of course, who we love to death,
naturally. But . . . what has he been talking about, could you
tell me?'

'Oh, this and that.' Marlowe smiled at her as he pushed the
fish away. Somehow, he just didn't feel hungry.

The fingers resting on his arm grew tense, digging in
between the tendons above the wrist. 'No, really, Master
Marlowe. What *has* he been talking about? It's important that
he doesn't exert himself. His man will have to know, in case
it stops him settling, you know. If he gets excited, he doesn't
sleep. And that means we're all awake.'

'Food,' Marlowe smiled. 'Family. The usual table talk.'

She looked at him with a gimlet stare. 'Food. Family. I see.
Anything specific?'

Marlowe began to feel as if he were between the Devil and
the deep blue sea. On one side he had a mad old man in a

frenzy of flying fish. On the other, Lucrezia Borgia, though
nothing like as amusing and cultured. He prised her fingers
from his wrist with difficulty. 'Your grandfather has been
telling me about Edmund,' he said, paraphrasing and culling
for the benefit of politeness.

'Edmund?' Her voice could have frozen over the lake in
one instant. 'And anything more?'

'No. Just that. And how he enjoys a nice bit of fish . . .'

'Fish?' Her shrill voice almost punctured his eardrum and
made faces down all the trestles swim upwards in alarm under
their guttering candles. '*Fish*?' She stood up and swooped
around behind Marlowe's chair and tilted her grandfather's
head back so the starched ruff crackled. With expert fingers,
she scooped out the fish from his mouth, throwing the noisome
results behind her to be lost in the rushes on the floor.
'Grandfather!' she screamed into his upturned face. 'You know
you can't eat fish. Bones.'

The old man stared at her, struggling free from her grasp
and staggering to his feet. In an instant, he had snatched
up his goblet and held it aloft in a shaking hand. 'A toast!'
he shouted in his strongest voice, 'to our friends in the
North.'

'Our friends . . .' a few of those tenants nearest to him
raised their cups and echoed the old man's sentiment, though
they had no idea what he was talking about and their voices
trailed away.

Furious, Blanche clicked her fingers, and this time two burly
men unpeeled themselves from the shadows and took her
grandfather, one under each arm and half marched, half carried
him from the room. The old man looked a little bemused, but
not outraged. This – or something like it – had clearly happened
before.

The room was silent for a moment until a lute player, tucked
away in a corner, struck a rather desperate chord and the chatter
began again.

Blanche sat once more on Marlowe's right and looked down
at his plate, smeared with fish and ginger and looking far from
appetising. 'Sorry about that,' she smiled. 'He gets confused,
poor dear. But you're not eating, Master Marlowe,' she added,

gaily. 'Dig in. Dig in. You'll need all your strength for planning my masque.'

Marlowe was no actor, he would be the first to agree, but somehow he managed to give a good performance of a man enjoying a bit of unrecognizable fish covered in powder until her attention mercifully went elsewhere.

He looked around him as the fish congealed further. He looked into the rafters, hanging with cobwebs like linen. The plaster was softly flaking from the walls and gently added to the dust covering the fish. The windows were grimy and let little light in. In short, Farnham Hall had seen better days. It wasn't that it was old and venerable, it was just middle-aged and tired. It hadn't had love from its owners in many a long year and it wore its sadness like a shroud. Marlowe raised his glass an inch and silently toasted the ghosts of the place, who crowded above his head, silently weeping.

Tom Sledd was helping Marlowe out of his boots later in his room and regaling him with the details of his meal. Marlowe had one foot on the man's behind and it was hard not to give him a kick and send him flying.

'I'll have to see if the cook will give me the recipe for the chicken,' he said, hauling on the buskin. 'I tried to work out the spices. I have never tasted anything quite like it. Spicy, but very creamy, somehow. It was . . .' he licked his lips as he gave a final tug and the boot came loose.

'Tom.' Marlowe hadn't meant to sound so terse, but his empty stomach gave him little option. 'Must you?'

The stage manager turned round, the soft calf's leather draped over his arm. 'Did you not enjoy the chicken?' He sounded staggered that such could be the case. 'It was delicious.'

'I daresay it was,' Marlowe agreed, proffering his other foot. 'I didn't have chicken. On the top table, we had . . .' he paused as his gorge rose, 'some very old hare and a fish. I really don't want to talk about it.'

Sledd shrugged and grabbed his friend's ankle. 'That's a shame. It was—'

'Delicious. I know. And what about your company? Amusing, was it? Good conversation? Jolly japes?'

Sledd smiled to himself. It wasn't usual for him to have come off best by such a wide margin. 'Very enjoyable, yes, since you ask. Everyone is looking forward to the masque. And of course, you know how the ladies flock to anyone who knows Ned Alleyn. His fame goes before him, that's for sure.'

'Even here? Don't tell him, for the sake of our peace. He will never let us forget it.'

'They hadn't heard of Shaxsper, though.'

'Well, that's a mercy.' Marlowe pushed with his stockinged foot on Sledd's rear and the boot slid off. 'I'm glad you had a good time, Tom. I'm sorry to be a curmudgeon. Hunger will do that to a man. And perhaps it wasn't helped by the company.'

Tom Sledd shrugged. 'Mistress Blanche seems comely enough.' He winked at Marlowe.

'Comely is as comely does, Tom. Her treatment of her grandfather was not something she should show as her public face. She shouldn't do it in private, but she made him look old and foolish in front of his tenants and his servants. It was cruel.'

'Well . . .' Tom Sledd suffered under the yoke of a tyrannical mother-in-law whose mind was not all it once had been, so he could see both sides. 'Perhaps he tries her beyond what she can bear.'

'She doesn't have to bear it, does she?' Marlowe was unlacing his doublet and venetians. His bed was not much softer than Tom Sledd's and the hangings, if richer, were no cleaner but, even so, it looked tempting. Perhaps sleep would soothe his angry, empty stomach. 'He has a man for that. And she has servants galore.'

'Not that galore,' Sledd said, as the arbiter of the gossip. 'Most of the serving wenches and all but one of the lads had been brought in for the meal from the farms and cottages. Usually Mistress Blanche has a very small household. She's trying to train them up before the Queen arrives.'

'She has a mountain to climb if tonight was anything to go by. Did you notice any nymph material amongst them?'

'There were a few well-turned calves,' the stage manager said, nodding. He could never quite stop looking for more walking gentlemen, a habit which had sometimes brought him to the brink of a broken nose, if not worse. He suddenly yawned and stretched. 'I'm for bed, I think. A heavy meal . . .' He lowered his arms and looked contrite. 'Sorry.'

'*Ego te absolvo*,' Marlowe said, in a parody of Rome extending two fingers. 'Now get out; you are beginning to look rather delicious and I don't want to deliver you back to Meg with a bite taken out of your thigh.' He threw a stocking at him for good measure. 'I'll see you by the lake in the morning, to work out where we can start and how much of Mistress Blanche's vision we can deliver.'

'Oh!' Tom Sledd's face lit up. 'Do you mean we can choose what to do?'

'Within reason,' Marlowe acknowledged. 'The Queen does like a bit of pomp, as we all know.'

'I can do *pomp*,' Sledd said. 'But can I do pomp without fountains and nymphs, that's my question.'

Marlowe smiled and shooed him out of the room. 'We'll see, Tom, we'll see. For now, my empty stomach and I would like to get some rest.'

'Good night, then.' Tom Sledd was not looking forward to his walk through bat-haunted corridors and stairways to his room and was putting off the evil hour.

'Good night, sweet Thomas; may flights of angels sing you to your rest.'

They looked at each other – sometimes, a good line just popped out from nowhere.

'Jot that down, Thomas, will you? I can use that somewhere, I'm sure. Now, good *night*!' And with that, Marlowe blew out the candle and pulled the damp and slightly musty bedding up to his chin and closed his eyes resolutely against the dark.

Hours passed, punctuated by the whispering of mice under the bed and worse in the dark corners of the ceiling. The curtains at the window didn't quite meet in the middle and a ghostly line showed their inadequacy where a sliver of moon-light poked its fingers across the floor. As soon as Tom Sledd had left, closing the door behind him with exaggerated care, Marlowe had sprung wide awake. He closed his eyes and told himself to sleep. He counted sheep and then, when that didn't work, a host of other animals, becoming more and more exotic as the night wore wearily on. When he had reduced himself to counting tortoises, which looked increasingly like Sir Walter Middleham but a little faster on their feet, he admitted defeat and swung his legs over the side of the bed and groped on the nightstand for his stump of candle. Blanche Middleham's frugal housekeeping meant that beeswax candles were kept for high days and holy days – here in the bedrooms, tallow was the order of the day and, soon after the click of the flint, the room was heavy with the smell of roasting meat. Marlowe usually disliked the smell of tallow candles but never more so than now – it brought to mind huge, glistening sides of beef, running with juices, accompanied by hunks of bread, still warm from the baker's paddle, with an ebony crust speckled with sea salt and caraway. There was nothing to be done now – even if he blew it out at once, the smell would last until dawn. He padded across the floor, trying to ignore the skittering of tiny feet dashing out of the way as he made his way to the window. Perhaps some fresh air would help.

He flung the curtains wide and opened the window with a creak of hinges fit to wake the dead. The night air was still, cool and welcoming after the fug of the hall and the dusty confines of the bedchamber. He leaned out, listening to the silence that wasn't silence, the click and hum of the countryside going about its business in the dark. He could hear, over a far distant horizon, the lowing of a cow mourning for its calf, the cry of an owl and the squeal of its prey, its life cut short in a flurry of feather and talon. He could hear the rustle of birds in the ivy which cloaked the wall beside his head, the faint cheep of a sleepy sparrow making him smile in spite of himself. From the hulking shadow of the keep which hung like a thunderhead over Farnham Hall, he heard the chitter of bats and the ring of a footfall. Briefly, a flash of candlelight shone in a bright rectangle across the mossy stones of the quadrangle two storeys below. An urgent whisper from inside the room brought whoever was abroad scurrying across the flags and the door was shut, leaving a bright patch to float before Marlowe's tired eyes. No doubt a maidservant sneaking in a lover; it wasn't the first time and no doubt it would not be the

last that the Hall had been the unwitting host to such a thing.
Suddenly, sleep came to Marlowe, sweeping down from the
moonlit sky like a living thing and perching on his shoulder,
muttering sweet lullabies in his ear. Leaving the window open,
he turned back to his bed and, leaning over to blow out his
candle, slept.

THREE

'Master Marlowe! Master Marlowe! Wake up!'

In his dream, Marlowe was being shaken by the shoulder and some huge, golden creature was shouting in his ear. He put up a hand to fend it off and it sank, as it seemed, wrist deep in some warm and cloying morass. He shook his head and muttered, trying to make the dream go away, but it would not leave him alone.

'Master Marlowe! Wake up, I say.'

This time, he opened his eyes and squinted up at the creature. It had a halo of light around its head, which was enormous and ringed with snakes, all writhing around its face, snapping at him and shouting.

'Wha . . .? Who are you? What's going on?'

'Master Marlowe, for the love of God, wake up! Wake up!'

The creature resolved itself into Blanche Middleham, leaning over him and dripping her candle onto his pillow. His hand seemed to be embedded between her breasts, breaking from the confines of her nightgown. He hastily withdrew it and struggled upright. He shook his head and was awake.

'Mistress Blanche,' he said, clearing his throat. 'What is it? What *time* is it?'

'Dawn, dawn or thereabouts,' she said, testily. 'It's Grandfather.'

'What is? Is he choking? Disappeared?' There seemed to be so many things that could be wrong with the old man, from what he had seen so far.

'No.' She stood upright and turned modestly aside so that Marlowe could clamber out of the clutches of her fourth-best feather bed and assume some nether clothing. 'No. I'm afraid it's worse than that, Master Marlowe. I'm afraid he's dead.'

Halfway into his venetians, Marlowe was brought up short. 'Dead? What happened? Was he taken ill?'

'No,' she said, short and to the point. 'He has just been

found out in the grounds. Dead, broken, at the foot of the battlements. Excuse me if I sound cold, Master Marlowe. I am of course distraught, that the dear old soul . . .' she made a sound which was suspiciously like the one Richard Burbage made, usually in about Act Two, Scene Four, to show how distressed he was about something '. . . that the dear old soul should meet his Maker alone and in such a place.'

There was a mutual silence, caused by surprise on Marlowe's part at least. Then she turned back to him, oblivious to the fact he was still only half dressed.

'Hurry, Master Marlowe, if you please. We must go to poor Grandfather.'

Marlowe paused in tucking in his shirt. 'Why me?' he asked. It was true that he was a good choice in such a circumstance, but how did she know that?

'I need a man by my side, sir, and James is certainly not the one I would choose. He will only go to pieces and, really, I am only holding myself together by the merest thread as it is. The others are servants and it does not do to show emotion in front of them.'

Marlowe looked at her face in the candlelight. Not a thread so much as a hawser thick enough to hold back the *Pelican* at the very least, but he always tried to give a lady the benefit of the doubt whenever he could, so he grabbed for his cloak and wrapped it around him against the chill of dawn. Slipping his feet into his shoes, waiting at the side of the bed for the day which was not yet here, he extended an arm towards his bedroom door.

'After you, Mistress Blanche,' he said. 'Shall we go and bring your grandfather home, with all due respect as he deserves?'

'Thank you.' She bowed and went out into the corridor beyond, lit with a faint silvery light from the pre-dawn sky. 'Grandfather liked you. He would be glad for you to help him now.'

'I am here to be of service,' Marlowe muttered.

'Poor dear Grandfather. He was so looking forward to seeing Her Majesty beneath his roof.'

Privately, Marlowe thought that it was now unlikely that

the Queen would ever cross this threshold now, but said nothing. If the woman was really upset and just hid it very well, it would serve nothing to make things worse at this point. And he was a gentleman, when all was said and done.

The old man lay on the grass cropped short by the Middleham sheep. He was wearing his nightshirt, and his nightcap lay some feet away, caught on a thorn bush by the wind of his fall. The great, silent keep loomed above him, brooding guiltily, as if it had crushed the old man with its presence, blocking out the sun and killing the light.

Instinctively, Marlowe knelt by the corpse, turning the face to the wall.

'Don't touch him!' Blanche screamed, her face red and angry and her eyes wet with tears which might even have been sorrow.

Marlowe stood up and grabbed her shoulders. 'Madam!' he said, then, softer, 'Mistress Blanche, I have experience in these matters.'

She blinked away her tears but didn't attempt to back away. 'What matters?'

Marlowe looked down at the frail body, the legs twisted at an impossible angle, the neck clearly broken. 'Sudden death,' he said.

Blanche Middleham straightened, in command once again. Around the body, in the still early light of the May morning, the household had collected. Mason, her steward, stood grimly at their head, frowning at what was left of the old master. There was Cook and her women, the maids of all work and the stable lads. They were still tumbling out of their stalls, all straw and horse liniment, buckling belts and tying points.

'Mason,' Blanche said, 'get your people about their business. Fires. Breakfast.'

'Very good, m'lady.' Mason moved among the servants, nodding, murmuring, patting the shoulders of sobbing girls and even closing the gaping mouth of a harness boy, who had never seen a dead man before.

In the end, there were only four of them at the foot of the keep.

'Mistress Blanche,' Marlowe said, 'If you would care
to . . .' He nodded in the direction of the others.

'I have no intention of leaving this spot, sir,' she said. 'Tell
me what happened.'

Marlowe looked across at Tom Sledd, who had now joined
them, sleep in his eyes and cobweb in his hair, and motioned
him to check the ramparts forty feet above. The stage
manager, as used as any Londoner to picking his way through
pig-shit, hopped over the wicket fence and made for the
spiral steps that wound their way up the nearest drum tower.
While Blanche looked on, Marlowe set to work. There was
blood on the sloping stones of the buttress a little above his
head, dark and congealed. The old man's skull would have
hit that on his way down from the battlements, and the impact
had made him bounce away to where he lay now. Marlowe
checked the man's skin – cold as the grave. His hands and
feet were stiffening already in the way that dead men's
extremities do. It would spread next to his arms and legs
until he was as rigid as a board. Marlowe turned the head
again, gently, hearing the telltale click of a vertebra displaced.
The whole of the left side of the head and face was a mass
of dark blood, congealing down the neck and spattering the
dingy linen of the nightshirt. Marlowe took the stiff fingers in
his hands and checked the nails. Filthy, certainly, but no
obvious signs of a fight. The old man was covered in bruises,
but how long they had darkened his skin was impossible to
tell.

Marlowe straightened, glancing up momentarily to see Tom
Sledd briefly peering down from the embrasure above.

'Well?' Blanche spoke for the first time in minutes.

'How well could your grandfather move about, Mistress
Blanche?' Marlowe asked. 'I only saw him sitting down last
night – and being helped out by your servants.'

'If you mean could he ride to hounds or handle a lance at
the tilt; no, of course not. But he walked well enough, given
time. Just from room to room.'

'Why would he be in the keep at night?' Marlowe asked.

'My grandfather, Master Marlowe, was in his second child-
hood – you cannot have helped but notice that at dinner. Sans

eyes, sans teeth, sans everything. As for his nocturnal ramblings, you'll have to ask Ledbetter.'

'Ledbetter?'

'His man.'

'Wasn't he here?' Marlowe asked, 'a moment ago?'

Blanche frowned. 'No,' she said. 'No, I don't believe he was.'

Tom Sledd had rejoined the trio by this time, shaking his head in response to Marlowe's raised eyebrow.

'Can we take him now?' Blanche asked. 'He should be in his chapel, at rest. I have arrangements to make.'

'Of course, madam,' Marlowe half bowed. He noticed Mason hovering under the archway that led to the Hall and the man scurried over at Blanche's clicked fingers. 'I shall of course recommend that Her Majesty progress elsewhere.' He held his breath – if his guess had been correct, Mistress Blanche Middleham would not take that suggestion well.

'What?' Blanche stood stock still as if she had been pole-axed, and Marlowe gave himself a metaphorical pat on the back.

'We cannot intrude on your grief, madam,' Marlowe said. 'Her Majesty will understand.'

'Nonsense!' Blanche all but screamed. 'The shame of it. If you think that mad old bastard is going to . . . No, sir. I will not accept it.'

'But . . .'

'There *are* no buts, Master Marlowe,' Blanche snapped. 'The Queen's visit will go ahead as planned. You and your man there will spend however long it takes to finalize the plans and I will bring in the carpenters and builders. Never let it be said that a Middleham's misfortune stood in the way of progress.'

And she was gone.

'Anything, Tom?' Marlowe asked, moving away from the scene of death as Mason's people began lifting the body onto a bier. The old man's arms trailed over the sides and his head lolled back.

'If you mean, did anybody leave a shoe behind, or a pickadil with their name on it, no. But . . .'

Marlowe smiled to himself. He had been right to refuse Cecil's offer of ten stout lads. He had Tom Sledd.

'It's five feet from the rampart walk to the top of the embrasure; four more to the merlons. Grandpa there would have had to climb five feet to throw himself off. And as for the chance of slipping by accident . . . well, there *is* no chance.'

'Suicide, then?' Marlowe murmured, out of earshot of the others, 'five foot climb or no, while the balance of his mind was disturbed.' That wouldn't have surprised him at all, considering the way the old man was being treated. At the very least, he was starving to death.

'Or murder, Kit,' Tom said as they wandered away. 'Let's not forget that possibility.'

'Let's not,' Marlowe nodded. He held the man's arm and pulled him closer. 'Look around you, Thomas,' he said, dropping his voice to a mutter. 'Who's missing?'

Tom Sledd blinked. He didn't actually *know* anybody at Farnham Hall, still less who might not be there. He grinned at Marlowe. This was one of those conundrums, those little philosophized puzzles that University Wits set each other. But Tom Sledd had never been to University. His alma mater were the smock alleys of London, the Bridewell and the Clink. His tutors had been the cutpurses and the Winchester geese who robbed the unsuspecting gulls who came to town, with eyes as bulging as their purses. His professor had been Ned Sledd, actor, manager; all things to all men, but a father to the little-boy-lost with the pretty face and the fluting voice. He gave it a moment's further thought, then shook his head. 'Don't know. Give up.'

'One Ledbetter,' Marlowe said. 'The old man's man. *And*, that perfect host of the genial company, Mistress Blanche's brother, James. You would think, with his grandfather dead, the walking pustule would come running, wouldn't you? You find the man. I'll take the pustule.'

No one had seen Ned Ledbetter since he had put the old man to bed the previous night. Tom Sledd found him eventually, sitting on the little wooden jetty that jutted into the lake. It was evening now and the gnats of early summer danced their galliards in the warm breeze that rustled the willows trailing the lake's edge.

'Bad business, this.' Tom Sledd sat down beside the man. Ned Ledbetter was forty, perhaps more, with patient eyes and short-cropped hair. He wore a fustian doublet with the Middleham eagle sewn to the left sleeve. His face was drawn and pale, exuding sorrow.

'Who are you?' he frowned.

'Tom Sledd.' He held out his hand. 'On the Queen's business.'

'Oh, the Progress.' Ledbetter's grip was firm. 'Fat chance of that now.'

'Yes, it's a pity. How long have you been in the Middlehams' service?'

'Man and boy,' Ledbetter said. 'Not here, though. On their estates in the North.'

'And the old man?'

'Sir Walter? Master Edmund appointed me to watch him, back in the day.'

'Edmund is . . .?'

'Was,' Ledbetter corrected him, throwing a desultory stone into the darkening water and watching the ripples spread. 'Master Edmund went of the sweating sickness . . . oh, must be five years ago now. His wife too.'

'So Mistress Blanche is mistress now?' Sledd liked to leave no stone unturned. Attention to detail was his middle name, as everyone at the Rose knew only too well.

Ledbetter shook his head. 'No,' he said. 'Arthur is the master here, her brother.'

'I thought the brother was James.'

'Ah, that's the other brother,' Ledbetter explained. 'No, Arthur is the eldest of the three. Master Arthur, Mistress Blanche and Master James. And some others, along the way, died. Arthur's away in London. The Exchange or some such.'

'What happened to Sir Walter?' Tom Sledd had made enough small talk. Time to cut to the chase.

Ledbetter shook his head. 'Damned if I know,' he murmured. 'I settled him down as usual.'

'Where are his chambers?'

'East wing,' Ledbetter said. 'Next to the dairy.'

'What time was this?'

Ledbetter frowned. 'Why all these questions?' he asked.

'I told you.' Sledd found a stone to throw as well. It plopped into the water and the ripples spread, as ripples and rumours will. 'I'm here on the Queen's business. An unexplained death . . .'

'Unexplained?' the manservant repeated. 'How do you mean?'

'How old was Sir Walter?' Sledd asked.

'Seventy-two. Three,' Ledbetter told him. 'I'm not exactly sure.'

'Fall over much did he, the old man?'

'He *could* be a bit unsteady,' Ledbetter remembered.

'Unsteady enough to climb five feet onto an embrasure and slip off, having managed a spiral staircase of forty-two risers?' Tom Sledd had counted every one of those steps that morning and even his young legs were aching by the last. 'You see what I mean about an unexplained death?' he said.

'What are you saying?' Ledbetter frowned. He didn't like the way this conversation was going.

'What *I'm* saying doesn't matter in the scheme of things,' the stage manager said. 'It's what *you* say that counts. Where do you sleep?'

'In the East Wing; I . . . look, I loved that old man. The last time I saw him, he was lying half asleep in his bed. When I next saw him . . .'

'Yes?'

Ledbetter turned to look out over the lake. 'When I next saw him, he was dead. At the foot of the keep wall.'

'And where have you been all day?'

'Here,' Ledbetter said simply. 'I couldn't stand it. Everybody fussing and clucking. He was an embarrassment to them all, that's the way of it. Mistress Blanche would have had him chained to a wall if she'd had her way. Master James would have fed him to the pigs and not turned a hair. He liked to wander the keep, the old man. Took him a while to get there, but we'd help him up; he said it reminded him of the past and gave a promise of the days to come.'

'What about Master Arthur?'

'He's the only one who gave the poor old bastard the time of day. I hope Mason's sent for him; sent him word.'

'Tell me, Master Ledbetter.' Sledd looked sideways at the man. 'Do you mean that? That Master James wouldn't care if old Sir Walter lived or died?'

'What's all the fuss?' James Middleham was teasing the goshawk in the mews as daylight faded. He threw a dead chick to the bird, rattling its chains on the cross-perch, watching its prey with deadly eyes.

'I can see,' murmured Marlowe, 'that you're mortified by your grandfather's death.'

James Middleham spun to face him, his eyebrow arched. 'We Middlehams are not known for gushing sentiment,' he said, 'and certainly not in the presence of a writer of plays.'

Marlowe looked a little surprised.

'Oh, yes, Marlowe. I know who you are. You may well work for the Master of the Revels but you are a common scribbler at heart. I wonder our Puritan friends haven't burned you as an idolater.'

'Well,' Marlowe smiled, 'it's early days. We didn't see you this morning, with your grandfather, I mean.'

'No, I've been hunting.' James Middleham watched as the hawk tore red strips from the chick's dangling body, tiny feathers twirling, circling and falling to the floor around its perch. 'There *are* priorities.' He caught Marlowe's look of cold disapproval. 'Oh, don't worry. I'll be along later to the chapel, to pay my last respects. Now, if there's nothing else . . .'

There *was* nothing else. Marlowe could cheerfully have felled the repellent lad, but if he was looking for a murderer – which he was – he didn't believe that James Middleham was his man. He seemed too indifferent to bother. The candles were guttering in the little chapel of Farnham Hall that night and it was Marlowe, not James, who had come to pay his last respects. That was not *quite* true. Marlowe had actually come to see what else old Walter Middleham could tell him about his last walk on the battlements.

The body lay in a shroud, tied at the neck and ankles with

a linen hood to cover the ghastly wound to the old man's head. The women who do had stripped him and washed away the blood as best they could. Herbs were placed in a neat posy in the man's folded hands and his jaw was bound up. For someone who had fallen headlong from a battlement, he looked remarkably peaceful, his eyes closed, his lips shut fast on his Peter's penny. A candle burned at his head and his feet. To the casual observer, Walter Middleham was just an old man who was waiting for the grave after the midwives had finished with him. Such women had helped him into the world; now they had helped him out of it.

Marlowe carefully checked the old man's arms and legs. The body was limp now, the stiffness of death having left him, and in the candlelight the bruising of lividity looked black and evil, as if the old man's frame were rotting already on its way to Hell. He *could* have been grabbed by the forearm and the ankle, swung across brawny shoulders and hurled to his death. Alternatively, he could have been hoisted onto the slippery wall of the embrasure and simply pushed. In any case, after his rough handling of the night before, when he was dragged from his platter, greasy and hungry, any bruising that was there would not help a jot.

A faint footfall behind him made the man turn, his hand already on the dagger hilt in the small of his back.

'Mistress Blanche.' Marlowe relaxed and bowed.

'You know, don't you?' she said. She was wearing her cloak fastened at the neck with a sprig of rosemary pinned to the front. She threw back her hood and looked at him.

'What do I know?' he asked her.

She looked at him, the candlelight dancing in the darkness of his eyes. 'That we Middlehams are of the old faith. And that Grandfather killed himself.'

Marlowe had no need to look around the chapel for confirmation. There was an ivory crucifix on the far wall and incense smouldered in a niche in the corner, smothering the smell of the herbs on the old man's breast and at his granddaughter's throat. Saints, painted in ochre and sage, glowered from the walls. There was no Puritan whitewash here, no cold harshness of the Presbyterian, the Calvinist or the Lutheran. Even the middle way of Elizabeth's Church of England had never got much further than the porch.

'Do I know that?' he asked.

She closed to him. 'Master Marlowe,' she said, her face and voice softer than he had seen and heard so far. 'We live in dangerous times. Should Lord Burghley hear of this—'

'Then the Queen would not come calling,' he finished the sentence for her.

'And I care nothing for that,' she said. 'This morning, I pretended that it would be a shameful thing; the reputation of the Middlehams and so on.'

'Whereas . . .?'

'Whereas,' she sighed, annoyed that this man was making her spell it out, 'in reality, we cannot betray our faith. We have too much to lose. The Almighty has fixed His canon against self-slaughter.' She looked down at the sunken yellow-ness of the old man on his slab. 'I don't know if Grandfather's soul has found its way to Heaven with that stigma – I pray that it has. But for those of us who are left, we must wander for ever in Purgatory, the darkest of the limbos. To admit the old man's sin to the world would be too much. Master Marlowe . . .' She moved closer so that their eyes shone in the same candle glow and her hand was resting on his chest, '. . . can this secret be ours, at least until the Queen has come and gone? Perhaps even for ever?'

He looked at her, the earnest pleading in the eyes, the sorrow he had not seen before etched onto her face.

'Perhaps,' he said.

The next morning, Marlowe and Sledd went their separate ways. The playwright-projectioner had written a note for Robert Cecil and waxed it with the Queen's cypher. He told Blanche Middleham that the stage manager had gone in search of timber for his staging of the masque and had watched him canter away along the ridge of land to the east, bound for Whitehall and the Queen's imp.

'You will be mourning your grandfather,' Marlowe had said to her as he steadied the packhorse in the courtyard, 'and arranging his funeral. In the meantime . . .'

FOUR

In the meantime, Marlowe trotted southeast in the sunshine, the dust of his horse's hoofs trailing along behind him as he crossed the Devil's Jumps and negotiated the tricky path across the Punchbowl. The way was strewn with gorse bushes, needle-sharp among the pines, and the packhorse stumbled more than once on the stones of the road. Other than the sound that the animals made, the Punchbowl lay bathed in silence, mute testimony to Satan's handiwork that had gouged the land in some long-ago duel with God. It was noon before Marlowe rested, swinging down from the saddle and stretching his legs. In the distance, above the trees of Houndown Wood, he saw the gibbet creaking in the breeze and the crows circling it before swooping down to peck at the leather skin of the rotting wretch trapped in the iron frame. Another lost soul who had fallen foul of the Cecils.

Marlowe had not taken the breakfast bread and cheese on offer from Farnham; what with the ill-fare of the last couple of days, his stomach growled. Even the packhorse looked tasty and Marlowe was in need of an inn. The river Wey sparkled below him and, on the crest of a hill, a cluster of thatched cottages promised hospitality. Marlowe mounted again and made for it. The sign of the sun swung overhead and there was the sound of laughter from inside. He passed the reins to a pot boy and ducked under the low lintel.

After the heat of the ride, the inn was cool and dark and stank of old ale and pipe smoke. In the far corner, a game was in progress – Even and Odd, the rattle of the dice on timber worn smooth by roisterers down the years. Half a dozen men sat there, in their cups, snarling at each other and spitting on the floor as their luck ran.

Marlowe sat with his back to the wall and ordered ale and cheese. It would be a loud meal but, once taken, he could be on his way.

'Even and Odd, stranger?' one of the men called to him. 'Try your chances?'

Marlowe realized that one of the men was talking to him. He smiled and waved his hand, shaking his head at the same time.

'Why not?' The man's initial bonhomie had vanished and he was scowling now.

'I'm never lucky with dice,' Marlowe explained.

A larger man turned to face him. 'Perhaps he thinks our dice are false, Pip,' he said, tauntingly.

'Is that it, stranger?' The first man was on his feet now, swaying uncertainly. 'Flat six-aces, is it? Fullams? Light graviers, maybe?'

Kit Marlowe had diced away too many of his nights at the Mermaid and the other Hells along the river in London. He knew all the tricks of the trade – the dice with weighted corners, with long and short sides, the dice that always turned up three or four, the cinque-deuces and the barred cater-trays. He smiled again. 'I'm sure your dice are straight, gentlemen,' he said, 'but I've just come to break my fast.' His trencher had arrived and very good it looked too.

Pip was suddenly at his elbow, the others, their game forgotten in the prospect of greater sport, crowding round Marlowe's table.

'You'll find our cheese is the best in the land,' Pip said, looking down at the plate.

'I'm sure I will,' Marlowe said.

'But the bread,' another said, 'the bread needs a bit of salt.' And he upended the cellar so that its contents covered Marlowe's meal. There were guffaws and whoops of delight. Patiently, and with a smile still on his face, Marlowe lifted as much of the salt as he could onto the table and continued this among sneers and insults. Then he sampled the bread. He frowned and shook his head. Then he added more salt. It was Pip's turn to reach for the cellar but Marlowe was faster. He grabbed the man's codpiece and squeezed hard, forcing the oaf down to his knees. In the same instant, Marlowe's right hand flashed clear of the table and his dagger tip was forcing Pip's head back.

The laughter and the taunts had stopped. Pip's eyes bulged and watered as he fought the agonizing pain coursing through his body, like ice-cold lightning. He daren't move his head and knew that the dagger point had already punctured the skin under his beard.

'Thank your God you're cup-shotten, pizzle,' Marlowe growled in his ear, 'or you'd be dead by now. Landlord!' he shouted and a wary host reappeared, wiping nervous hands with a greasy apron. 'I trust this meal is on the house.'

'Oh, yessir,' the man blurted out, tugging his forelock. 'Yes, indeed.'

Marlowe jerked the knife away and, with a final wrench of Pip's testicles, let him roll to the floor, groaning and sobbing. The projectioner was on his feet. He pushed through the group and crossed to the table with the dice. He weighed the first pair in his hand. 'High fullam,' he said. He took the second pair and threw them. 'Quarters,' he said. 'It looks as though I was wrong, gentlemen. Your dice are false indeed. Where I come from, you'd be tied at the cart's tail for this.' He tossed the dagger in his hand and slid it home into the sheath at his back.

The men muttered among themselves, ignoring Pip at their feet, and watched Marlowe cross to the door.

'We don't know where you're from, roisterer,' one of them snarled, 'but we know where you're going,' and they rushed at him, knives glinting in the half-light of the inn.

Marlowe stepped aside as a blade bit into the timbers of the doorframe. He brought his knee up into its owner's groin and the man doubled up, falling out of the attack. That still left four of them and it was a long way to the pot boy, still clutching the reins of Marlowe's horses, with the rapier strapped there. The animals jittered at the noise as men tumbled out of the inn into the sunshine. One of them slashed the sleeve of Marlowe's doublet, missing the skin by a hair's breadth. Another tripped him, sending him flying to the dust. He rolled to his knees and felt the sickening crunch as another man's boot caught him on the side of the head. Dazed and with his vision reeling, he steadied himself to face the renewed attack.

'Here!' he heard a voice call, and his own sword was

sailing through the air towards him. He caught it and parried for his life, hacking a rough's knife out of his hand. Another swordsman stood over him, his rapier like none that Marlowe had ever seen, making lazy, expert circles in the noonday air.

The four men checked themselves. There was still no sign of Pip from inside the inn and now they were facing not one chancer, armed with a knife, but two, each with a sword. The newcomer spread his arms wide. 'Come on, lads,' he said. 'You outnumber us two to one. What are you waiting for?'

The men looked at each other, then licked their lips and sheathed their weapons before shambling back into the darkness beyond the inn door. They leaned against the trestle holding the ale barrels and looked out balefully, like ferrets from their burrow, little eyes glittering with malevolence.

'So,' the newcomer said. 'Discretion *is* the better part of valour. Are you well, sir?' He pointed to Marlowe's ripped sleeve.

'It's nothing a good tailor can't fix,' he said. 'I am grateful to you, Master . . .?'

'Norfolk.' The man sheathed his sword. 'John Norfolk, but my friends call me Jack. You?'

'Christopher Marlowe.' Marlowe was not as ready to share what his friends called him.

'Well, Christopher Marlowe,' they shook hands, 'I'd invite you in for a drink, but I am not too sure we'd be very welcome. I was going to wet my whistle here, but on second thoughts . . .'

'That sword,' Marlowe pointed to the many-barred hilt, 'what is that?'

'This little thing? It's called a schiavona. The Venetians use them to protect the Doge, I believe.'

'Is that where you bought it?'

'God, no. I won it in a dice game in St Giles. That's London, by the way.'

'I know it is, Master Norfolk. And I owe you a drink, at the very least. Will you ride with me?'

'Delighted.' Norfolk crossed to the stable yard to where his bay waited patiently. 'As long as you promise me, Master

Marlowe, that you won't pick a fight at the next inn we come to.'

Tom Sledd wouldn't deny it; despite his many years on the road when he was younger, he was only happy in London. Give him paving beneath his feet, the smell of the river, the cry of vendors in his ears and he was happy. In the country, the silence got him down. He smiled to himself as he sauntered across St James's and finally entered through the gates of the Palace of Whitehall. He wasn't as confident here as he was out in the street. This was Westminster, and only the Strand linked it with the city he knew and loved. The sounds of the city fell away as he walked gingerly across ancient flags, worn smooth with the scurrying feet of those who oiled the wheels of state. He stood and waited; he knew that a stranger would not be left alone for long here and so it proved.

'Can I help you?' The voice seemed forced through dry caverns where the sun had never shone. It fell, cold and unwelcoming, on Tom Sledd's eardrums and made him spin around. He hadn't heard a single sound as the man had approached him and it gave him a prickle of apprehension up his back as he realized that he could have been lying dead at the man's feet, a stiletto between his ribs, and be none the wiser.

He cleared his throat to give himself a moment for his heart to stop pumping madly. 'Yes,' he said, and pulled himself up a little straighter. Even so, his nose barely reached the other's breastbone. 'I am here on official business to see Sir Robert Cecil.'

The man in black bent at the waist and put his aristocratic nose an inch from Tom Sledd's snub. 'No,' he said simply, then turned and walked away.

'I have a note of hand here from Christopher Marlowe,' Sledd called, his voice echoing in the vast space.

The man stopped stalking away and turned slowly, as though worked by gears. 'You do?' He retraced his steps and held out his hand. 'May I?'

Tom Sledd clutched his purse with both hands. 'It is for the eyes of Sir Robert only,' he said, taking a step backwards.

The man in black raised an eyebrow. 'In that case, I bid

you good day.' He walked away again and then paused, but did not turn. A sinewy arm, with a pointing finger on the end of it extended from his side. 'The door is over there.' And he continued his steady walk.

'It is vitally important,' the stage manager said, but without much hope of being heard. A door opened in the panelling and the man disappeared behind it. So *that* was the trick! Somehow, seeing how it worked perked Tom Sledd up a lot and he stood his ground. He wasn't leaving until he saw Robert Cecil and that was that.

This time, the footfalls were very easy to spot, as they seemed to belong to a whole phalanx of men in hobnailed boots. Underlying the tramp of buskined feet was the occasional cry as from someone in pain. Tom Sledd recognized it well enough; it was the sound of a company of the Queen's Guard on the march. This could mean one of several things but only one sprang immediately to mind; the man in black had mustered a company to arrest, incarcerate, torture and eventually kill one Thomas Sledd, of Bankside. He stood transfixed as the tramping got closer and suddenly two enormous doors at the end of the hall were thrown open and the Guard marched in, halberds at the slope, the light flashing on their morions and breastplates. Tom Sledd was in their path and he closed his eyes and waited for the impact.

Instead of the feeling of nailed boots stamping down on his head and the scream of nerves stretched beyond enduring, there was a silence. Then a shuffling, followed by a voice from just level with the stage manager's armpit.

'Who are you?' it said, in the tone of one who was just asking.

Sledd opened his eyes. In front of him stood a small man, tiny by anyone's standards and Tom Sledd worked in the theatre, where all things were possible. He knew this was the man he sought, but he was at a loss as to how to go on. 'Umm . . . I am Thomas Sledd,' he said. Start with the simple things and work up seemed to be the best plan. 'I am here to see . . . umm . . . well, *you*, sir, on business from Christopher Marlowe.'

Cecil's right eye twitched a little but otherwise he showed

no sign that either name meant a thing to him. 'Marlowe, you say? I know no one of that name.'

The captain of the Guard stepped forward. 'Shall we remove him, sir?' the man asked.

Cecil raised a hand and his yard and a half stopped the six-foot guard in his tracks. 'No,' he said, 'no, let him stay. I will talk with him a while. Go and . . .' he waved a hand, 'do some manoeuvres or something useful. Come back later and we will continue.'

The men marched off, the drill sergeant calling incomprehensible instructions in the rear in a high voice.

Cecil looked around and then pointed to a bench against a wall. 'Shall we?' he said, and they went and sat down side by side. Cecil looked Sledd up and down. 'So, you are Kit Marlowe's man, are you? When he said he just needed one man I was expecting someone . . . bigger. Older.' His polite upbringing stopped him from adding 'More intelligent.'

'I am his stage manager, sir,' Sledd said, by way of explanation. 'He needs me for arranging the masques and such. I will call on local craftsmen if I need them, when the time comes to build stages and similar. Seamstresses too, for the costumes . . .' He noticed Cecil's eyes begin to glaze and was silent. He knew that not everyone had the same enthusiasms as he did.

Cecil blinked away his ennui. 'But you have a message for me, I expect,' he said.

'Yes, sir.' Sledd rummaged in his purse and fished out the letter.

Cecil skimmed it silently. 'You were there when this happened?' he asked at length.

'I did not witness it, sir, but I saw the body almost as soon as it was discovered. I examined the battlements from which Sir Walter fell.'

'And in your opinion?'

Tom Sledd almost burst with pride. He had just been asked his opinion by Sir Robert Cecil! 'Well . . . he was dead, sir.'

'Yes, yes,' Cecil drummed an irritated foot. All of the benches and chairs in the hall had been cut down so that his tiny legs could reach the floor. Everyone else was very uncomfortable, but what did he care? 'But dead as in murdered? Suicide? Accident?'

'In my opinion . . .' Tom Sledd could not help repeating the phrase, '. . . murder, sir.'

'Hmm, yes, that's what Marlowe thinks too. So – any idea who the murderer might be?'

This just got better. 'The old man was a favourite of the servants, sir. Not so much a favourite of his family.'

Cecil shot him an appraising glance. Perhaps there was a head on those shoulders after all. 'But further than that, you are not prepared to say?'

'No, sir.'

'Perhaps you're wise, Master Sledd. Now, what to do, that is the question. We could cancel the Queen's visit, but that may cause alarm . . . I will think on that. But meanwhile, and with no offence in the world intended, I think I will give Master Marlowe – and your good self, of course – some extra protection. Perhaps a contingent from the Guard?'

'I think that may be a little obvious, sir,' Sledd ventured to suggest. 'We are going in to places in the country, quite simple folk. A contingent of the Queen's Guard might alarm them.'

'You're very astute, Master Sledd, very astute indeed.'

'I spend a lot of time with Kit . . . er . . . Master Marlowe,' he said, by way of explanation.

'Indeed. Well, I believe I have a solution which will suit us all. When do you leave London and where are you off to next?'

'I was planning to rejoin Master Marlowe in Cowdray in two days' time.'

'Ah, yes, the Montagues. Then look for my man at Tyburn as you leave. You can't miss him.' Cecil slid down off the bench and gave a little chuckle. 'No, I don't think you will miss him but, if you are in any doubt, his name is Leonard Lyttleburye. But really, you will find him with no trouble.' Chuckling, Cecil made for the door. As he opened it, the sound of marching feet came through in a wave, shut off again as the door swung to. Tom Sledd followed him after a polite interval, swaggering a little. That had gone well. Very well indeed. Now all he needed was to avoid meeting Leonard

Lyttleburye and it would be perfect. Whistling through his teeth, he made his way through the thronged May streets to the river and the theatre. He'd tell his Meg and his baby all about it, but most of all he would tell them all at the Rose – the son of the Lord Chancellor of England had just asked him for his opinion.

The Blue Boar at Haslemere was altogether more welcoming than the Sun at the Punchbowl. There were no drunken oafs here, just a handful of merchants earnestly discussing the cost of a bushel of wheat, shaking their heads and wondering what the world was coming to. Marlowe and Norfolk sprawled on the benches in the little garden at the back of the building while a pot boy watered their grateful horses.

'I'm afraid I haven't been entirely honest with you, Master Marlowe.'

'Oh?' Marlowe was a projectioner of standing. For nearly seven years now, the length of a young man's apprenticeship, he had served Her Majesty. Suspicion was his middle name. Real people's lives were as dark and twisted as the characters he created for the stage, where all was smoke and mirrors. Tamburlaine the lame, Barabas the Jew, Faustus who worshipped the Devil, they all had their counterparts in life. What, Marlowe wondered, lay behind the mask of Norfolk's carefree banter, his easy smile?

'You see this?' Norfolk held out the cloth of his braided doublet. 'My horse? My sword?'

Marlowe nodded.

'All I have in the world.'

'I'm sorry,' Marlowe said. Money came easily to few men. While Sir Francis Walsingham had been his paymaster, the projectioner was comfortable. But Walsingham was dead, and everyone knew that he had died in penury because of the tight-fistedness of the Queen. Robert Cecil was no Francis Walsingham and Marlowe could not be sure of his next groat. As for the theatres . . . whoever knew a rich playwright?

'I am, as they say, a masterless man. I was wondering . . . well, to be blunt – can you give me a job?'

Marlowe laughed, sipping his ale. 'I told you, Master Norfolk, I am on the Queen's business for the Master of the Revels. But I am impressed that you ask for a job, not just a hand-out.'

'Neither a borrower nor a lender be, or so my old grandfather used to tell me. And he died in prison for debt, so he should know. But as far as your work for the Master of the Revels goes, you seem to be carrying out that difficult task all alone,' Norfolk observed. 'Surely, you need help? An amanuensis?'

'I have one,' Marlowe told him, 'who is away on business at the moment.' He saw that Norfolk looked a little crestfallen. 'What can you do?'

'I lose money at Odds and Evens. And lansquenet and primero and any other card game you care to name.'

'Can you draw?'

'Er . . . well, after a fashion.'

'How about carpentry? Can you knock a nail in, Master Norfolk?'

'I should think so.'

Marlowe was not impressed. Tom Sledd could conjure up a royal palace or a cathedral or a sepulchre with a few deft strokes of a brush. He could build them, too, with hammers and chisels, saws, and language that would make a harlot blush. On the other hand, Marlowe reflected, he just *may* owe Jack Norfolk his life. And Cecil may have been right. Perhaps he *did* need five stout lads, perhaps even ten. Sending Tom Sledd back to report to Whitehall was an inconvenience, but he could hardly send Norfolk to the heart of government on covert business. A third pair of hands to plot masques in such a situation might be useful.

'You'll have to travel as my man,' Marlowe said. 'You'll sleep with the servants, with the hogs if you have to; some of our hosts will not be generous – with the cost of entertaining the Queen on their shoulders already. You'll get board and lodgings and three pence a day. And, if I have need of your sword . . .'

'It's yours,' Norfolk said, 'and the arm behind it.'

He held out his hand. 'I'm grateful, Master Marlowe,' he

said. Marlowe took it. 'Better make that Kit, Jack,' he said, 'when we're alone, of course.'

Master Sackerson was laid out in a patch of sunshine, his belly sprinkled with sparse hair warming nicely. Every now and then, he gave a happy grunt and scratched himself voluptuously. Tom Sledd leaned over the wall of the Bear Pit and smiled down at the creature. What a life! Food, shelter, and love of a sort, from Philip Henslowe and everyone who knew him. He had claws but no teeth, huge muscles but a pleasant disposition; the world could do with more like Master Sackerson, thought the stage manager as he peeled himself away from the low wall and walked up the remaining slope to the wicket door of the Rose. He had only been away a few days, but it already seemed like a lifetime. He drew a deep breath and, pushing the door, walked into the fug of sawdust and hoof-glue, with a faint overlay of yesterday's audience and Ned Alleyn's perfume, a gift from an anonymous but grateful patron. Had he known the patron in question was one Oswyn Gasper of Clench Alley at the back of the theatre, he may have worn it with less panache, but it was hard to tell; Tom Sledd, who knew the donor well, smirked at the waft of it that entered his nostrils. It was good to be back.

He followed the sound of voices to the rooms at the back of the stage. Apart from Alleyn and Burbage when he got in quickly enough, all of the other actors, minor principals as well as walking gentlemen, shared the one large space with each other and the costumes for the current play and those past. Not many costumes survived intact from one production to another; Philip Henslowe was far too pernickety for that, checking every farthing spent with as much care as he counted every farthing taken on the door. But, as Marlowe had been heard to say on more than one occasion, the play was indeed the thing, so scissors and needles flew almost constantly as the seamstresses ruined their eyesight conjuring wonders from canvas, paint and a carefully positioned glass jewel by the light of guttering candles. Fortunately, as Marlowe was also wont to say, the audiences had the average intelligence of a sleeping baboon, so they wouldn't notice what the actors wore. The seamstresses pretended not to hear. In any case, for most of them, this wasn't their principal means of support, so Christopher Marlowe, for all his flashing eye and soft lip, could go and do whatever he liked to himself or indeed any member of his family, for all they cared.

If Tom Sledd had expected an ecstatic welcome, he would have been sorely disappointed. A few heads turned but, other than that, there was no discernible change in the level of conversation. Most of them, had they been asked, hadn't even noticed he had been away. He was always busy, always in the theatre, morning, noon and night, but rarely in one spot for long. It was therefore very easy for an actor, carpenter or other sundry Rose denizen to go for weeks without knowingly clapping eyes on the man.

Finally, someone noticed he was there and strolled over.

'Thomas.' Will Shaxsper clapped the man on the shoulder. 'You look puzzled. Can I help?'

'I . . . puzzled?'

'Well . . . let's say, a little dawcocked, then.'

Tom Sledd looked at the Warwickshire man a little askance. Was it just his three-day absence, or had the man's head grown even bigger, the brow more cliff-like, the petulant mouth more tucked and twisted under his little beard? He had certainly grown rather stranger in his behaviour, that was certain. 'What? I have no idea what that might mean.'

Shaxsper was discomfited and not a little annoyed. He had expected more from Sledd. 'Dawcocked. As in jackdaw. Idiot. Stupid fellow. It means puzzled, confused, perplexed, befuddled . . .'

Sledd was in no mood for wordplay. 'I know all the other words. I just have never heard . . . what was it again?'

'Dawcocked. It is a word I have coined myself. I sometimes think we put too much store by the old, well-known words and phrases which our grandfathers used. It amuses me to make up new ones.' The polished dome of his head reflected the candles of the toiling women and gave a rather mad glint to his eye.

Sledd edged away just an inch or two. 'Well, Will, that

sounds fascinating. But I'm only here for an hour or so, just checking everything is well until I get on my way again.'

Shaxsper decided not to take offence at Sledd's obvious lack of interest. After all, this man had influence with Henslowe and Marlowe and an actor and incipient playwright couldn't have too many friends with influence. He arranged his features into an interested and matey smile. 'Have you been away?' he said. 'I hadn't noticed.'

'No,' sighed the stage manager. 'You and everyone else. I've been on the road with Kit, planning some masques for the Queen's Progress.'

Suddenly, heads swivelled on shoulders, eyes flashed, mouths smiled. The Queen's Progress? Now that was something worth listening to.

'Except, of course,' Sledd lowered his voice, 'I can't tell you where or when, exactly. But, that's where I've been. And you'll never guess who I met this very morning.'

Shaxsper put a proprietorial arm around the stage manager's shoulder. The rest of the room retuned their ears to their conversation but resumed their nonversations with each other. There were some things more important than wagers and seduction, after all. 'By Royal Appointment' ranked among them. Even an argument about who had more lines in Act Four could easily wait a while. 'If you need any help, Thomas,' he purred, ignoring Sledd's last sentence, '*any* help at all, just ask me and I will be there. Where is *there*, by the way?'

'As I said,' and Sledd shrugged off the arm, 'I can't possibly tell you. But if I get . . . what was that word again?'

'What word?' Shaxsper had so many spinning in his head, how was he supposed to remember just one?

'Doorstepped. Is that it?'

'Oh! Dawcocked. Ha ha, yes. I see what you did there.'

'I think we'll manage, Will, if I'm honest. Most of the hosts have some . . . let's just say some very definite ideas about what they want. Nymphs. Fountains. Things of that nature.'

'I can do nymphs!' Shaxsper was clutching at straws. 'And shepherds.'

'I'm sure you can, Will.' Sledd patted his arm. 'I'm sure you can. But for now, I need to see Master Henslowe and then go home for a while. Don't forget, Meg and I have a new baby on the way and I need—'

'How many is that now?

'Just the two. Well, one and three-quarters, I suppose I should say.'

Shaxsper looked wise. 'We thought that when Anne was expecting our second.'

Tom Sledd waited for the rest of the sentence. He had definitely detected a significant pause.

'Twins,' Shaxsper said, in sepulchral tones. 'Things were never the same after that, if you follow my drift.' He looked up to the ceiling, blinking back tears. 'I miss them, sometimes. Especially Hamnet, my boy.' He put a sentimental arm across Sledd's shoulders again and, for the sake of paternal comradeship, Sledd let it stay. 'There's nothing like a son, Thomas,' the man from Warwickshire said, fighting a sob. 'Nothing like it.'

'We'll be pleased with either,' Sledd said, embarrassed. 'As long as it's healthy.' Shaxsper showed no sign of either cheering up or removing his arm. In fact, he had gone a stage further and had now turned his enormous brow into the crook of his arm and was weeping openly on Sledd's shoulder. Heads were turning and Sledd could see people slipping out of doors and away into the shadows. Shaxsper in paternal mood could be very trying. Soon, the two were alone and only Burbage, the usual recipient of Shaxsper's weeping, had patted Sledd on his unencumbered shoulder in silent understanding.

'Thank you,' Sledd had muttered to the actor's retreating back, 'Dick.' He absently patted the by now inconsolable actor/playwright on his back, muttering 'Ssshhh, there, there . . .' If nothing else, it was good practice for when the baby or babies arrived.

He was still there when Philip Henslowe came in on a wave of financial crisis, as he always did, an imaginary army of creditors in his wake.

'Where is everyone?' he yelled. 'I don't pay you to . . . ah.' He backed out, ignoring Sledd's rolling eye. 'I'll . . . nice to see you, Thomas, I just need . . . yes . . .'

And he was gone.

*   *   *

Eventually, Will Shaxsper stopped weeping. He wiped his eyes and blew his nose on a piece of hanging fabric Tom Sledd could only hope did not form part of his own clothing. He didn't want to know, so kept his hand from his sleeve cuff as he walked, happy to be going back to his Meg at last, along the side of the Thames. Summer was just around the corner and the smell of the river reinforced the message of the green buds and blossom, which shed its petals in white drifts from the May trees lining his path. The new father-to-be whistled as he walked and swiped at the weeds sprouting from the wall on his right with a careless hand. He could grow to like this life; half the time wandering the countryside and the other half in London. The best of both worlds indeed. Out of the corner of his eye, he saw someone approaching, and he instinctively stepped aside. He was no coward, but in London he had seen it proved time and time again that discretion was indeed the better part of valour. He looked down at his feet and kept walking, increasing his pace just a threat.

'Tom?' a voice said. 'Tom Sledd? Is that you?'

He looked up. After his less than overwhelming welcome at the theatre, it was good to hear someone pleased to see him.

'I thought it was you,' the man said. 'I haven't seen you for ages.'

Sledd thought fast. He knew the man before him, but bearing in mind his business, he wasn't sure whether to admit it. And yet, here and large as life, was Nicholas Faunt, spy extraordinary, greeting him like a long-lost brother. He decided to be friendly; you could never tell with someone as sneaky as Faunt quite what might be in his mind. 'Master Faunt!' he cried, with every semblance of surprised delight. 'How are you?'

Faunt shrugged and looked rueful. 'Well, since Sir Francis . . .'

Tom Sledd was instantly contrite. Of course! Nicholas Faunt had been banished, or as near as made no nevermind, once Robert Cecil had come to power. 'Yes, of course. I'm sorry . . .'

'No, no,' Faunt turned and fell into step with him. 'I do a little here, a little there, you know. And . . .' he gave a chuckle, 'a rich wife doesn't hurt, either. Though I do have to—' he lowered his voice to a man-of-the-world whisper – 'behave myself a little more than I used to.' He gave Sledd a nudge in the ribs. 'But I'm sure you know how that works, being a theatre man and all.'

The stage manager laughed. 'Oh, yes, indeed.' He wondered whether the spy was actually as bright as he had always supposed. Didn't he *know* all the women on stage were boys, in various stages of adolescence? If he didn't, they deserved rather more pats on the back than they routinely got, for jobs well done.

They walked in silence for a few more paces. 'So . . . how is Kit?' Faunt turned a dazzling smile on Sledd. He didn't smile often but, when he did, it was reminiscent of a crocodile on a sun-baked bank somewhere far, far away.

'I've just been travelling with him, since you ask,' Sledd said. He knew it was not meant to be gossiped about, but surely Nicholas Faunt was exempt.

'Have you?' Faunt slapped his own thigh with excitement. 'How wonderful. How is he?'

'He's well, very busy, but you know Master Marlowe.' Tom thought he should keep this conversation a little more formal. 'Writing, that kind of thing.'

'Writing . . . of course. Anything else, at all?'

Sledd slipped down the bank a little without even realizing how near to the smiling jaws he had got. 'Planning some masques, for the Queen. Exciting, really. I'm helping him with the stages, that kind of thing.'

Faunt spread his arms. 'And yet here you are, in London.'

'It's funny you should say that,' Sledd said, 'but we hit on tragedy almost at once.'

Faunt's face was now a picture of concern. 'Tragedy? Not personal, I hope.'

'No, no,' Sledd was quick to reassure him. 'No, it was all to do with the family we were visiting . . .' and slowly, painlessly, but completely, the crocodile ate Tom Sledd and his story and left not fin nor fur nor feather behind to tell the tale.

FIVE

They hanged men at Tyburn and had been doing it there for twenty years by the time Tom Sledd rode below the fatal tree. The stream had slowed to a crawl in this driest of springs and the reeds along its banks stood parched at the topmost ends, their mud-caked roots showing above the water. Today was not a hanging day, or Sledd could not have got himself or his horse as close to the tree as he had. It was still early morning and the ducks, still hoping for water to paddle in, were just stirring with the dawn. The dabchicks muddled in the trodden mud at the edge of the sluggish water, and Tom Sledd, still only a father of one, smiled to watch the babies aping their parents in the constant search for food.

There was no one about at first. Then a solitary milkmaid came tripping across the yellow grass from the fields to the west. Unless she was a mistress of disguise, she was not Leonard Lyttleburye. Sledd told himself he would wait for ten more minutes, and if Cecil's man did not show up, he would ride south without him. The girl bobbed under her yoke to Sledd, who, his Meg notwithstanding, was a fool for a pretty face and a well-turned ankle.

'Keep your mind on the job, now, Master Sledd.'

The voice made him turn so fast that he almost fell out of the saddle. A huge man, with a beard and hair to his shoulders, stood next to Sledd's horse, patting the animal's muzzle.

'Where did you come from?' Sledd managed to keep his voice down to a manly pitch.

'Under a gooseberry bush, my grandame told me. 'Course, the truth is a bit more complicated. I'm Leonard Lyttleburye.' He thrust a giant hand in Sledd's general direction and the stage manager winced as he took it.

'I thought you'd be . . . smaller,' he said.

'Don't let my size fool you, Master Sledd,' the giant said. His voice was pitched so low that it made ripples appear on the murky water. 'As I've just proved, I can blend for England.'

'Yes,' Sledd tried to smile, shaking some feeling back into his hand. 'I think blending is vital for what we had in mind.' He crouched low in the saddle. 'What did Sir Robert tell you, about the matter in hand, I mean?'

'Only that I was to take my orders from Master Marlowe. And, failing that, you.'

Sledd straightened. He liked the sound of that. He was Tom Sledd, for God's sake, stage manager at the Rose. The great playwright Christopher Marlowe called him friend. The great actor Ned Alleyn likewise. The great impresario Philip Henslowe called him . . . quite often. And, only yesterday, he had sat in Her Majesty's Palace of Whitehall, hobnobbing with Her Majesty's Spymaster. Of course, Leonard Lyttleburye took orders from him. It was simply proof of Sledd's impending greatness – the first step on a Jacob's ladder to fame and fortune.

'Have you a horse?' he asked.

'Of course,' Lyttleburye grinned. Then the grin vanished. 'Now, where did I leave it?'

The woman had tears in her eyes and she gripped Kit Marlowe's arm with determined, talon-like fingers. 'I can't tell you,' she sobbed, her words coming in choking gasps, 'I can't tell you what an honour this is. The Queen, God bless her, coming to stay under my roof. Mine.' Although she was only a tiny little thing, she had a grip like death. Marlowe could feel the sensation going in several of his fingers. He could look down on the crown of her head with room to spare, and yet he still couldn't undo her clutches. She was like a fragile bird, with jerky movements and a delicate face with large, frantic eyes; not a linnet in a cage, or a nightingale or wren, but more one of the smaller raptors – a merlin, possibly. She even had a pronounced overbite; it was uncanny.

'Actually, *mine*, Mrs B.,' the bear of a man behind her muttered, 'but let's not fall out over it. Where are you from, Marlowe?' The man was as huge as his wife was tiny, but for all his size he moved with ease and grace. He was so full of life that his hair and beard almost seemed to crack with an electric force and being near him was like riding the lightning.

'Originally, my lord,' Marlowe was delighted to be able to extricate himself from the woman, 'Canterbury. Currently, I lodge in Hog Lane, Norton Folgate.'

'Hog Lane?' the woman had grabbed his forearm again, looking up into his face. 'Anthony,' she turned back to her husband, 'Hog Lane. What a coincidence. Oh, it was meant to be!' She looked to Heaven and clapped her hands, releasing Marlowe yet again from her clutches.

'My sister-in-law owns property in Hog Lane, Marlowe,' Anthony Montague grunted. A lackey was buckling his left arm into a harness for the tilt and it wasn't going well. 'Gently, Bennett, that's my shield arm.'

'Sorry, my lord.'

'Do you know Mistress Francis Browne?' Lady Montague was pursuing Marlowe across the lawns at Cowdray Castle, her lapdogs yapping at her feet and stumbling over the grass. 'My sister?'

'Er . . . I have not had the pleasure, my lady,' Marlowe had to confess.

'But . . . why has she never mentioned you? I mean, a famous playwright living only a few doors away . . .'

Lord Montague sighed. 'Your sister doesn't actually *live* there, Mrs B.,' he said while Bennett adjusted the straps. 'She just owns the place. Bit of a rat-hole, Marlowe, I expect.'

'I like it, my lord,' Marlowe smiled. 'It's home, of a sort.'

'Yes, of course. An Englishman's home is his castle.' He glanced up at the mock turrets to his left. 'Literally, in the case of mine, of course. Tell me, how's old Tilney? I haven't seen him for years.'

'He's well, my lord,' Marlowe beamed, 'and sends you every good wish for you and yours.' He missed out the little fact that the last time he had met the Queen's Master of the Revels, he had blacked the man's eye over dramatic differences.

'Edmund Tilney!' Lady Montague's eyes flashed under her fringe of steel-grey hair. 'He always rather liked my volta.'

'Yes.' Lord Montague flexed his gauntlet-hinges to prove he was still young enough to move his fingers without the aid of external flunkeys, 'and you rather liked his, I seem to remember. Master Marlowe, go with her, will you, and see that she doesn't go completely Bess O'Bedlam over the garden party? She's talking about tables forty-eight yards long! I mean,' and he looked at the playwright with exasperation written all over his face, 'it's not normal, is it? Mrs B.,' he spoke to his wife sharply but clearly and using simple words. She was not an easy woman to manage, being considered by most who met her as a bit of a handful. 'I will lend Master Marlowe to you for precisely twenty minutes. After that, he and I will discuss boys' things. After all, Her Majesty isn't coming to coo over your table linen, she's coming to see a tournament. Blood and guts, eh, Marlowe?'

'I'm sure Her Majesty will approve of all she sees at Cowdray, my lord,' he smiled.

'Yes,' Montague sighed. 'You're a courtier all right. Twenty minutes, Mrs B. – then I'm sending Bennett here to save Marlowe's life.'

Jack Norfolk had not accompanied Marlowe up to the house. In accordance with his status, he walked the horses to the stables and made small talk with the ostlers, Montague men to a man.

'You won't find a better master this side of the Rother,' one told him.

'New money,' another said, 'knows what's like to be shoe-worn. Man of the people.'

'One of us,' a third chimed in, passing a water-ladle to Norfolk. 'No airs and graces. What's yours like?'

'My master?' Norfolk chuckled. 'So kind a lord. He's a playwright, you know. Famous.'

'Is he?' That was as far as intellectual curiosity went among the stable lads on the Cowdray estate of the Viscount Montague in the year of his Lord 1591.

Supper was excellent and the Rhenish flowed. Lord Montague regaled Marlowe with tales of Tilbury, where, as a Captain of

Horse, he had heard Her Majesty's speech to her troops as Philip's great Armada approached. Marlowe found himself reciting along silently, without moving his lips, of course; to do otherwise would not have been the action of a polite guest. But, after all, he had written it.

'I know I have the body but of a weak and feeble woman; but I have the heart and stomach of a king – aye, and a king of England too.' Montague sighed and looked into his goblet reminiscently, a tear in his eye.

'And to think,' Lady Montague broke in, 'she is coming here, under my roof.'

Montague rolled his eyes but said nothing.

'Master Marlowe, isn't it just *too* exciting?'

Marlowe could almost hear the jingle of the bells on her jesses and couldn't look at her; it would spoil the illusion to see just a little, brown-haired woman by his side.

'*How* long?' Jack Norfolk thought he must have misheard.

'Forty-eight yards,' Marlowe confirmed.

'Is she quite the full angel?' Norfolk had to ask.

'Just go through the motions, Jack, there's a good lad.'

And Norfolk shrugged, trudging off in the early morning light to measure out the dining area with Lord Montague's groundskeepers in tow.

Marlowe himself had other priorities. Montague had yielded nothing the day and night before. On the surface of it, he was a loyal Englishman, devoted to his Queen and country. But there were rumours in Whitehall, whispers among the Intelligencers who had once worked for Walsingham and now worked for Cecil. In Montague was a man who, like them all, was fed by Elizabeth, but maybe now was the cur that bit the hand that fed it. And, anyway, Marlowe was walking towards the sounds of combat.

The tilt yard was paced out already, hung with flags and ropes, although it would be weeks before the Queen arrived. Marlowe glanced back to the house and chuckled to himself. If Jack Norfolk had hoped to work out the guests' seating in relative peace, he would be disappointed; Lady Montague had joined him and Marlowe could see the diminutive woman fluttering around him, hands flapping with excitement, babbling about God-knew-what.

Anthony Montague sat his horse at the edge of the field, a goblet of wine in his hand and his legs encased in iron. In front of him two men, in full armour for the foot combat, slogged it out, halberd to halberd and toe to toe. They swayed together, their pole-axes glancing blows off helmets and pauldrons.

'Keep your guard up, Georgie!' Montague shouted. 'He's running rings round you!'

One of the duellists saluted him briskly, his face completely hidden by the ugly helmet. He swung himself forward and met the solid bulk of his opponent, who batted him aside. Montague pounded his high saddle in fury and muttered to Marlowe, 'Do you have children, Marlowe?'

'No, my lord.'

'Hmm,' Montague snorted. 'When you do, be sure you don't breed a goose. Actually, between you and me, I think young George is a changeling. He's no Browne. Hasn't even got the fire of his mother. Lower, you clod!' But the warning came too late and Georgie Browne found himself flat on his back, his halberd gone and a bruised mess where his ego had been.

'Hoo!' Montague called, giving tongue to the old cry that broke combatants up in the lists. He spurred his animal forward and he stooped to help the boy up. Georgie tilted back his visor and Marlowe saw that the boy was no more than fifteen or sixteen. 'We'll have words, boy, you and I,' Montague said. 'Her Majesty's rumoured to be in a knighting mood this summer. Give her a display like that and it won't be you feeling the rapier on your shoulder. Get yourself cleaned up.' Marlowe could see how Montague suspected a cuckoo in his nest. Young Georgie was pale and thin, with light eyes for which downcast seemed to be the only position. But for all his slightness, Marlowe could see muscles strung to twanging point in his neck; a young man on a sword edge, or he was no judge.

'Sorry, my lord,' Georgie's opponent raised his visor too, 'if I was too rough . . .'

'Pox on it, Shoesmith,' Montague growled. 'It's what I pay

you for. If the bastard Don comes back, they'll not be gentle with any of us, least of all wimps like this one.'

'Papa—' the boy began, but his father cut him short.

'We've a practice tournament here in two days' time,' he snarled. 'Unless you can make a better fist than that, you won't be in the field for Her Majesty. You can make cakes in the kitchen and show off the stumpwork with your mother,' and he wheeled his horse away.

Shoesmith replaced his halberd in the rack and unbuckled his helmet. He shrugged at Georgie and trudged off in his master's wake. The boy put his weapon back too and pulled off the heavy helmet, letting it fall to the ground.

'Master Browne?' Marlowe crossed to him. The boy looked even younger now that his auburn hair lay plastered to his forehead with sweat. He had a sprinkling of freckles over his nose and his pale eyes were full of tears of embarrassment and humiliation. Marlowe had not seen him at supper the night before, perhaps because he was hardly the apple of his father's eye. 'I am Christopher Marlowe, here on the Queen's business to arrange the revels for your parents. Can you spare me a minute?'

They sat side by side on the hay bales, sipping ale and munching bread. It had been a hard morning, but a worthwhile one, they both believed. Marlowe was more at home with a rapier and dagger, he had to admit, but as a boy he had swung a quarter-staff to good effect along the Stour at Canterbury. A halberd was a little different. And by the time the pair were taking their repast, he had passed on a world of knowledge to the lad.

'Of course,' Georgie said, 'I'll never be as good as Martin.'

'Martin?' Marlowe repeated. The name had not come up before.

'My brother,' Georgie moaned. 'My elder, bigger, better brother. Heir to all this.' The boy waved his arm in the direction of the park, where the land fell away into the sun of the South Downs and the deer herd grazed.

Marlowe smiled. He came from a family of girls. His only brother was much younger than he was and never a threat.

With a father like Anthony Montague – and he *did* have a father like him – what chance did this runt of the litter stand? 'Do you hate him?' the playwright asked.

Georgie thought for a moment. 'I used to,' he said. 'Martin was always beating me up, making sure I got the blame for things. Mama couldn't see it. Neither could Papa. The sun shone out of Martin's arse and I was just blinded by the light. Now . . .'

'Now that you're older,' Marlowe smiled.

'You're laughing at me, Master Marlowe,' Georgie said, a little boy lost in a man's world of steel and hard knocks and treachery wherever you looked.

'No,' the projectioner said, not wanting to hurt the boy's all-too-injured feelings for the world. 'Never that. It must be difficult, though, what with the Old Religion.'

Georgie gave a start and blinked. 'How . . . how did you know?'

Marlowe laughed. 'Your father is famous, Master Browne,' he said. 'Wasn't he at the trial of the Queen of Scots? As an impartial judge?'

'He was,' Georgie nodded. 'I was only little at the time, but I heard things . . .'

'Oh?'

Georgie gnawed his lip. 'Can I trust you, Master Marlowe? Papa has often told me not to talk to strange men.'

'Your papa is right,' Marlowe smiled, 'but we of the Faith must stick together.'

'You . . . you too?'

'I am from Canterbury, Master Browne,' he said. 'It was once – and for me, always will be – the beating heart of the Catholic Church in England.'

'Amen,' the boy said and crossed himself. He opened his mouth to say something else, but suddenly thought better of it. Whatever this man's faith, he worked for the Queen, the Jezebel of England. His papa – and his mama – had been right. There were some men too strange to talk to. The boy was on his feet. 'I'll try it, Master Marlowe,' he said, 'at the mock tournament. I'll try it.'

Marlowe stood up with him. 'Remember, Master Browne,'

he said. 'Right hand. Left hand. Your opponent will never see it coming.'

It was far into the afternoon that Marlowe saw him arrive. The playwright was standing in Lord Montague's library, dusty with unread tomes of the Puritan persuasion, and the thud of hoofs and the barking of dogs below made him turn to the window. A tall young man, slimmer and darker than his father, bigger and harder than his brother, swung out of the saddle as grooms rushed to hold his horse. Lady Montague was there, as always, kissing him and fussing. Marlowe saw her gesticulating to the library window and saw the young man looking up. Calmly and quietly, he began to focus on the tilt yard and the deer park. He pulled a sheet of parchment from his purse and studied it carefully.

He had barely counted to twenty in his head when the door crashed back and the young horseman strode in, pulling off his gloves. 'You, sir,' he said. 'What do you do there?'

'The Queen's business,' Marlowe said. 'And a good day to you, Master Browne. Er . . . it is Master Browne?'

'I am Martin Browne,' the man said. He flung his gloves onto a table and poured himself a goblet of Rhenish. 'You must be Marlowe, Tilney's man.'

'I suppose I must be,' Marlowe bowed.

'What are you doing in here?' Browne wanted to know, his brow knotted and his fists clenched at his sides, the goblet unlifted, the wine undrunk. Martin Browne was a man in whom anger and frustration were never far below the surface. A vein throbbed in his neck and Marlowe noticed it; it was not a good sign in one so young and he foretold an early grave for this one – by the hand of God, if not by a fellow man.

'Surveying your father's grounds,' Marlowe said.

'What? How?'

Marlowe held out the parchment scrap and Browne looked at it, frowning. 'This is Cowdray Castle,' he said, outraged. 'The plans of my father's house.'

'Quite,' Marlowe said, secretly rather surprised that this oaf recognized it. 'But it is a flat, two-dimensional depiction. It's not the same as seeing it in the flesh, as it were. The angles of the windows, the colour of the stones.' He breathed in the dust, the unique taint of leather books left alone to moulder for far too long. 'You have to see a place,' he said, 'and to smell it to truly know it. Don't you agree?'

Browne blinked. He had none of the happy enthusiasm of his mother, none of the wide-eyed innocence of his brother, not even the rough bonhomie of his father. Somehow, he was the embodiment of all the faults none of his family seemed to possess and Marlowe pitied him for it. 'What are you?' the heir to Cowdray snapped. 'Some damned poet?'

'Poet, certainly,' Marlowe smiled. 'Damned? Well, that remains to be seen.'

'Where did you get this?' Browne demanded to know, waving the paper in Marlowe's face.

'Whitehall,' the progress planner said. 'We have the ground plans – and a few projections – of every landed house in the country.'

'The Devil you say!' Browne blustered.

'Indeed I do,' Marlowe said. 'Are you bothered by this, Master Browne? Have you something to hide?'

Marlowe had not expected the young man to become any redder or more furious and yet, here he was, purple and posturing like a turkey cock. He closed to him, his jaw flexing, the vein now beating a mad tattoo. 'We Brownes – we Montagues – have nothing to hide, Marlowe. We serve the Queen, man, like all Her Majesty's loyal subjects. But . . .' he raised the paper and tore it slowly down the centre and then again and once more before letting the pieces fall to the floor, '*this* is going too far. I would rather the Master of the Revels and his lackeys didn't know every fart that flies at Cowdray. Wherever Mama has housed you, stay there. The library, the solar, the chapel, they're all out of bounds – d'you hear?'

'Of course,' Marlowe said, with a half-bow. 'Oh, and don't worry about that little accident there.' He pointed to the paper pieces scattered on the floor. 'We have plenty of copies in Whitehall.' He made for the door, then paused. 'Couldn't help noticing,' he said with a smile, 'that you have a first edition of Timothy Bright's *Characterie* there.' He pointed to a shelf.

'The finest annotation of the Puritan gospel ever written. Her
Majesty will be delighted.'

The library. The solar. The chapel. Those were the rooms that
Martin Browne had banned Marlowe from entering. Those
were the rooms where something was hidden from the light
of day. The man from the Office of the Queen's Revels had
already checked the books. Unless there was a secret catch
that revolved shelves or slid walls aside, there was nothing of
a sinister nature there. The solar would be full of family – Lord
Montague holding forth in his gruff way on anything under
the sun; his over-excitable wife rabbiting away about the
Progress; the sons ignoring each other with a nonchalance that
was almost palpable. Nothing would be gained there. That left
the chapel.

He waited until after dark, lying on his bed fully clothed,
his dagger ready for the sheath. He left the curtains of the bed
and of the window drawn back so that he could catch every
sound, watch the courtyard below emptying of its people and
growing quiet with the coming of the night. He heard the bolts
slide and rattle as Montague's servants locked the doors and
fastened the casements. The dog-handler was the last human
he saw, the master's hounds yelping and snapping at his heels
as he swore at them and disappeared into the kennels. Then
. . . silence.

Marlowe moved. The dagger was at his back and he wore
his black doublet to blend with the shadows. The door
opened quietly enough and he walked slowly, testing each
floorboard with a careful toe before putting his weight on
it. Montague's house servants served him well – each board
was firm and silent, though waxed enough to slip the unwary.
At the head of a stairs, a bad copy of the Queen's Armada
portrait stared out of its canvas, her sleeves unfeasibly huge,
her hair somebody else's, her hand on the world her admirers
claimed she owned. No, Marlowe smiled, remembering his
last conversation with Cecil, he had never met the Queen.
Yet, here he was, doing her bidding again, creeping along
a landing in a stranger's house, prying into another man's
secrets, putting his life on the line that separates good from

evil, night from day. A line that was not easy to tread, being the misty aurora of twilight and of dawn.

The dogs had gone. The servants and the house slept. Marlowe crept down the curve of the stairs, across the marble of the hall. The glimmer of the fading light through the windows shone briefly on the full harness of Lord Montague, the armour he had worn at Tilbury in the dark days of the invasion threat. But had that threat gone? A Papist king who ruled half the earth had launched not one, but two Armadas – who was to say he would not launch a third? And there were other ways by which it could be done. Threats to the nation's security, like troubles, came as spies more often than they came as battalions – a single knife, not a company of cannon.

He knew where the chapel was and he slipped down the side stairs and along the dark passageway. He was unsure of his footing here. He would not risk a light, so he felt his way along the walls. Most gentlemen in England had their chapels built openly, above ground, for the world to see. This one was buried in the bowels of the earth; dark, alien, forbidding. He found the door and eased its brass handle, using both hands to minimize the noise. A solitary candle stood on the altar, itself a simple wooden table covered in white linen. The walls too were white, the colour of virtue, the shade of the Puritan. The arms of England glinted dully overhead, below a single arch of brick, simple and unadorned. Could any church be lower than this one?

He stood facing the altar, listening intently. It was a whisper, no more, that rose to a mutter now and then, like distant voices on the wind. It could even be just the susurration of blood in the ear but then he smiled, recognizing the snatches of Latin. Lauds. The old habits died hard. And the whispers were coming from . . . his eyes swivelled to the right . . . behind the Arras tapestry, embroidered with its Garden of Eden and the fall of Adam.

In a single move, he wrenched the heavy fabric aside and pointed his dagger at the startled figure kneeling there.

'Forgive me, Father,' Marlowe said, 'for you have sinned.'

The man was on his feet, a Jesuit to the core, a rosary in his twitching fingers.

'This is more like it,' Marlowe smiled, taking in his surroundings. The Jesuit had been praying in an ante-chapel, tucked away from the false Puritanism next door. As priest holes went, it was surprisingly lavish, with an altar laden with brass crucifixes and chalices, the room heady with incense. The walls were covered in Biblical scenes and the crossed keys of Peter glinted in the candle flame. Overhead, the ceiling was fan-vaulted, crusty with the arms of Rome and of Montague, as though they were of the same family.

Marlowe focused on the priest. 'Who are you?' he asked.

'I could ask you the same question, sir.' The man stood his ground. Jesuits were made of stern stuff.

'I am here on the Queen's business,' Marlowe told him, 'which, in this instance, is to root out the cancer of Catholicism from the realm. Some of my colleagues have subtler methods, but I use this.' He prodded the man's throat with his blade tip. 'So, again – who are you?'

'Father Emilio,' the Jesuit said. 'Confessor to Lord Montague.'

Marlowe nodded and sheathed the dagger. Then he hopped up to sit on the altar.

'Blasphemer!' Emilio hissed in horror, crossing himself.

'Spare me, Idolater,' Marlowe said. 'All this,' he waved at the sacraments around him, 'is smoke and mirrors.'

'This is God's house,' the Jesuit insisted.

'No, it's Anthony Browne's house. Or it was until a moment ago.'

'What do you mean?'

'I doubt it will have escaped your notice, Master Jesuit, that there has been a reformation of the church of late. The Queen, may God keep her safe, is Governor of the Church of England. The man you follow is the Bishop of Rome – you see the imbalance there.' He raised one hand and lowered the other. 'Governor . . . Bishop . . . England . . . Rome . . . no comparison, really. Or are you one with your foreign master in the claim that Her Majesty is a bastard, the Jezebel?'

Emilio shook his head, but carefully. The ghost of the dagger still tickled his throat. 'You must not believe that Puritan propaganda, sir,' he said. 'I serve Lord Montague and he serves the Queen.'

'Ah,' Marlowe smiled, 'but that's the question, isn't it? *Does* Montague serve the Queen?'

'He does,' Emilio insisted. 'He was with her at Tilbury, as was I. It will be obvious to you, sir, that I follow Rome, but I do not follow Philip. I wish no ill to the Queen.'

'Montague backed the rebellion of the North,' Marlowe said, and suddenly, the toast of a dead grandfather leapt, unbidden, into his mind. 'Or our friends in the North.'

'Before my time,' the priest shrugged, 'and yours too, I'll wager.'

Marlowe laughed. 'I was somewhere between my hanging sleeves and my first hornbook.'

'The point I am making,' the Jesuit closed to him, willing the man to get off the altar, 'is that men change. From what I have heard, that rebellion took place in the dark days of the warring sisters, Mary and Elizabeth. Certain lords had ambitions, above their place. They paid for it with their lives.'

'So they did,' Marlowe knew, 'but I am here to see that nothing of the kind happens again. Your master in Rome still has a Bull against Elizabeth. She is a marked woman. Who is to say that you and Montague are not his instrument, merely awaiting the arrival of the Queen?'

The Jesuit looked deep into Marlowe's eyes. 'I have taken vows, sir,' he said quietly, 'to my God, to His Holiness, to Lord Montague. But first and foremost, I vowed to do no evil. I turn my hand against no man. Or woman. I beg you to believe that.'

Marlowe looked at him. How many good men still wore the trappings of Rome? And how many assassins hid behind Arras tapestries? He slid off the altar as the priest hurriedly re-set the crucifix and goblets. 'What I believe, Master Jesuit, is no concern of yours. But it will be to others. Prepare yourself.'

And he saw himself out.

SIX

The day of the mock tournament at Cowdray dawned bright and fair. Such clashes between armoured knights and the run of the lance had all but disappeared from the battlefields of Europe, replaced by the roar of cannon, belching smoke and fire, killing indiscriminately. An iron ball knows nothing of chivalry and honour. Old men clung to the old ways, remembering the gallantry of their youth, their crests dazzling in the sun, their sleeves rich with the flowing colours of their ladies. It was all long, long ago, but it was kept alive here at Cowdray and kept alive in the name of the Queen, who loved such things.

The servants and workers of the estate were up betimes, laying out trestle tables less grand than those Lady Montague dreamed of and carting tureens, trenchers and barrels of ale. From the country came the locals, the men, women and children of Lavington, Cocking, Ebernoe and Lickfold. The merchants came out in their carriages from Midhurst, bringing half the cellar of the Spread Eagle with them. Everyone wore their finest, according to the Queen's Sumptuary Laws, and everyone was determined to make it a holiday. No expense had been spared for this, a dummy run for the arrival of the Queen.

Marlowe and Norfolk had had little enough to do. The servant spent hours cloistered with the mistress, the master with the master, although it had to be admitted that what Marlowe knew about the laws of the lists could be written on a gnat's arse. Montague's steward, Hawtrey, was herald for the day, bright with the arms of Montague, quartered (illegally) with those of Her Majesty. Boys of the estate ran backwards and forwards, carrying helms with giant crests of painted wood and leather, tripping over swords and halberds.

There were to be four bouts – one foot combat and three passes of the lance – and the crowd grew in size and volume as the morning wore on. Marlowe was with young Georgie, watching as his squire buckled him into his armour.

'Greenwich,' he said to Marlowe by way of explanation. 'Papa insists we all wear English armour.'

'Quite right.' Marlowe winked at him. 'Who's your opponent?'

Georgie scowled. 'Alfred Lumley,' he said. 'His father has estates to the west. I feel such a fool.' He flicked at the solitary favour on his arm. 'Do you know whose this is?'

Marlowe shook his head.

'It's my mother's. What kind of knight only has his mother's favour on his arm, by all that's holy? Alfred Lumley will have half the women in the valley fighting to tie their kerchiefs on him.'

'How old is he?' Marlowe asked.

Georgie shrugged. 'Twenty? Twenty-one? I'm not sure.'

'More importantly, how tall is he?'

Georgie scowled again. 'Half a head taller than me,' he said.

Marlowe laughed. 'All to the good,' he said. 'He'll never see you coming. Look there,' he pointed to the pavilion that had been erected behind the palisade, glittering with heraldry. 'Under the sign of the portcullis. That's where I'll be. Watch for me – er . . . keeping an eye on Lumley, of course. Remember – right hand, left hand.'

He smiled, locked the boy's forearm with his own and felt the chill of the steel. He watched as Georgie marched away to the parade ground. Alfred Lumley crossed from the other end, encased in iron for foot combat, his halberd at the slope. From this distance, he looked twice Georgie's size. There was a roar and a cheer as both men took centre stage below the Cowdray pavilion. Marlowe negotiated his way through the throng, declining the ale and sweetmeats he was offered, and shuffled in below the standard with the portcullis. Lady Montague caught first his eye and then his arm with her usual paroxysmal grip. Marlowe looked around in vain for Norfolk, but the man had wisely vanished.

'Oh, Master Marlowe. He *will* be all right, won't he? My Georgie? It only seems the other day I was dandling him on my knee, and look at him now – a man almost full grown.'

'I daresay his opponent's mother is remembering something similar, my lady,' he said.

'Lettice Lumley?' The old girl's face hardened. 'That I doubt. There she is over there, the one with the look of a basilisk. Not a maternal bone in her body. And Arthur is *such* an oaf. Half the women in the valley . . . oh!'

A fanfare close at hand brought her up short and Anthony Montague pricked his horse with his spurs, trotting out onto the field with his steward in tow.

'Why have you come here?' Hawtrey bellowed in the time-honoured tradition, 'at this hour and this place?'

'We have come to do battle for the honour of Gloriana, our Queen,' the combatants chorused, as best they could above their beaver-rims.

'Gloriana smiles on you both,' Montague said and the pair wheeled their horses away. They reined in below the ladies in their pavilion, within Marlowe's earshot. 'God help us,' he heard Montague mutter, and Hawtrey raised his hand.

'Now,' the Lord of Cowdray murmured and Hawtrey's hand came down. Alfred Lumley swung his halberd, clashing on the staff of the younger lad, and pulled back. The fighters circled each other as the watching crowd whooped and whistled. Lumley came to the attack again, tapping the butt of Georgie's halberd before driving the flat of the steel head hard against the boy's shoulder. The power of the blow jolted Georgie and knocked the breath out of him. It was all Montague could do not to bury his face in his hands. Shoesmith was a good old warrior and trainer par excellence, but there were just some people beyond teaching. The result was going to be bloody.

'Come on, Browne!' Lumley snarled, his voice like gravel inside the helmet. 'People have come a long way to watch this. Put some spine into it, man!'

Stung by the insult, Georgie sprang forward, but his halberd flew high, bouncing off Lumley's pauldron and thudding into the dust of the arena. A roar and a groan made him realize how close he had come to losing the bout almost before it had started. He fought for breath now as Lumley came for him, raining blows like a blacksmith's hammer onto the anvil of his halberd, his shoulders, his head. His vision was reeling and he knew he was bleeding from a bitten lip. Where the Hell was Marlowe? He tried to focus beyond Lumley to the pavilion but, every time, his man whirled him around so that he had his back to the portcullis. He lost his footing and felt the blade of the halberd hack into his armpit, where the steel gave way to mail. He knew he was cut and he heard his mother scream.

'Anthony!' she shrieked. 'Stop them. This is not to the death!'

The Lord of Cowdray half turned in the saddle below her. 'As a man far greater than I once said, Mrs B., "Let the boy win his spurs." Leave it, woman.' And he turned back to the inevitable.

Down on one knee and in serious pain, his eyes full of tears and blood trickling over his mail, Georgie saw Marlowe's right hand in the air. He lunged, attacking high from the right and Lumley wasn't ready for it. Assuming the fight was all but over, he had relaxed a little too much and he paid the price. Georgie's halberd crunched on the helmet skull, bouncing off to cut the fixing straps from his pauldron and biting into the older boy's shoulder. It was Lumley's turn to drop to one knee, but Marlowe had not been trained in the school of chivalry and politeness. He had learned his weapon-play in the cobbled streets of Canterbury, honed in the dark alleys of London. No one asked – or gave – quarter there. His left hand was in the air and Georgie swung with his left, driving the halberd staff low against Lumley's leg. The man rolled sideways, his weapon gone from his grasp, gasping in the dust as the murderous halberd flashed over his face.

'Craven!' he had the presence to shout, and Hawtrey was racing his horse across the yard to break up the bout.

'Mother of God!' Montague bellowed. He turned to his wife again. 'Did you see that, Mrs B.? Did you see our boy?' And he cantered forward to dismount and take the quivering lad in his arms.

Marlowe, whose hands were back at his side now, couldn't help but smile when he saw Lady Montague mouthing to her rival across the pavilion, 'Oh, bad luck, Lettice!' A handful of younger ladies in the pavilion looked crestfallen.

The trumpets sounded again. The foot combat was only the warm-up; the main bouts were now to begin and Martin Browne featured in every one. Delighted though he was with the new-found mettle of his younger boy, Montague had long ago pinned all his hopes and fatherly pride in his eldest. Marlowe had to admit that he looked the part, walking his powerful chestnut before the adoring crowd. The ladies, even some of the shepherd girls, were throwing flowers at him, plucked from the hedgerows on their way to the tournament.

'Martin, darling,' Lady Montague still had tears in her eyes from the brilliance of little Georgie's performance. How manly and brave her Martin looked today. And not garlanded by the favours of every slut in the area, like the Lumley lout. 'Will you wear my colours today?'

In the temporary absence of a lady of his own – the husband had come home early and he was staying away for a while – Martin Browne was the essence of chivalry. 'My lady,' he bowed in the saddle, and lowered his lance for her to tie the blue scarf to it. The crowd went wild.

William Maskell was the first opponent, from the Maskell estate along the South Downs way, and he clattered into the field now. Hawtrey and Montague did the honours again, for form was everything and they retired from the field. For a moment, there was silence as the two men wheeled their horses to the opposing ends of the lists. The low barrier between them was hung with heraldry and both men knew the risks of that. Ride too close and you'll stumble into it, throwing your aim. Ride too wide and you'd miss your opponent altogether. Each man took his lance and held it aloft, waiting for Hawtrey's signal. When his flag came down, they rammed their spurs home, jamming the butts of their lances under their arms, locking the weapons into the rests that jutted from their breast-plates. The ground flew under their hoofs as the animals found their stride. They had just reached the gallop when they collided, the shock echoing around the walls of Cowdray. Maskell's lance flew high, Browne's hit squarely on the man's curved shield, rocketing him out of the saddle. He rolled in the dust, fighting for breath, but staggered to one knee to show he was unhurt and the crowd bellowed their approval.

Martin Browne wheeled his horse and accepted the salute of the man he had just beaten. His lance had splintered on impact and he rode to collect a second.

'Will you rest, Master Martin?' Hawtrey asked him, ever the caring steward as well as Master of the Lists today.

'Get me some wine, Hawtrey. No sense in wasting time. I'm on good form today. Who's next?'

Edward Chamberlain was next and Browne knew that this one would be more difficult. The man was older than he was, and he was a soldier, born and bred and of infinitely more experience. He adjusted his visor and waited. By the time a servant came scurrying out with a salver and wine, the trumpets had blared again and the fight was on. This time, neither lance struck home and, unsplintered, the combatants whirled back to try again. This time, Browne's strike was less true. His blunted lance bounced off Chamberlain's and it nearly threw him off balance, but Chamberlain had lost control of his horse and suffered the indignity of being thrown. His pride was hurt more than his body and he fumed inside his helmet at being bested by a boy.

Browne tilted the visor and took the wine. He thrilled to the roars and clapping of the crowd, saw the pride in his father's face and ordered up his third lance. Again, the double pass, the crack as the ash poles splintered and the thud and grunt as Browne's third opponent hit the ground. That was it, he was master of the field against all comers. Now was time for feasting and merriment. The crowd, still laughing and clapping, began to break up at the pavilion, and Lady Montague was leading her guests to their places at the tables.

A trumpet call stopped them and for several moments confusion reigned. Surely, there were no more bouts?

'Anthony,' Lady Montague shouted to him from the pavilion, 'what's going on? Isn't it all over?'

'Damned if I know, Mrs B.,' he said, frowning under his helmet. 'Looks like there's another challenger in the field.'

There was. He walked his grey towards the pavilions, lance already in his fist, pointing to the sky. There was something strange about him, unreal, as though a ghost were riding the lists that day. Montague, Hawtrey, Marlowe; none of the assembled lords, ladies and gentlemen had ever seen a man wearing armour like that. It was spiky and angular, with pointed sollerets and fluted tassets, as if the knight had ridden out of the past to joust on a day before he was even born. His face was hidden behind a German sallet and a high beaver. Only his eyes flashed clear as he wheeled the grey to face the pavilion.

He looked at the banners hanging there, the cloth fluttering on the breeze, the shields of Maskell, Lumley, Montague and the rest. His horse snorted, pawing the ground in its eagerness for battle. The knight jabbed his lance forward, ignoring all shields but Montague's and knocking it off its housing.

Montague himself cantered into the lists. 'Do you challenge me, sir?' he asked.

'Not you, old man,' the knight answered through the thickness of leather, mail and iron. 'That arrogant whelp of yours.'

Martin Browne had not dismounted yet and he trotted over, staring at the stranger in his obsolete armour. 'Do you mean me, sir?' he asked.

'Who are you, sir?' Hawtrey wanted to know. 'For the lists.'

'You'll know me soon enough,' the knight said and clawed a silver talisman from his belt. It was a wolf-dog, chained and with lolling tongue. 'In this sign, conquer,' he said.

'I'll take him, Father,' Martin said, 'and then he'll be only too glad to tell us his name.'

'I don't think . . .' Montague was saying, but his son was in no mood to back down. He rode closer and smashed the knight's plain shield with his gauntlet, accepting the challenge. Both men wheeled to their respective ends of the lists.

'Hawtrey,' Montague was frowning, uneasy about this turn of events. 'What's all this about? Did you know about this?'

'No, my lord, the knight is a stranger. I suppose there's no harm in it.'

'No harm?' Montague snapped. 'Look, the man has a sharpened lance.'

But there was no time to stop it now. Without a trumpet call or a lowered hand, both men were thundering towards each other, Browne the more heavily armed, his lance locked and level. The newcomer's grey was lighter and faster and he braced his back for the impact. Montague and Hawtrey could not look away from the deadly tip of the challenger's lance. Neither could Marlowe. With the Massacre at Paris still forming in his mind for Henslowe's Rose, he knew all too well that the chaos in France had been caused by the King of that benighted land going down in the lists in a 'friendly' bout, a lance tip where his brain used to be.

The clash of steel and the splinter of wood were eclipsed by the scream that rang from inside Martin Browne's helmet. The heir to Cowdray was catapulted from the saddle and bounced several times in the dust. He tried to rise, but collapsed as Montague and Hawtrey galloped to him, jumping from their saddles and cradling the stricken boy.

The strange knight, his unbroken lance red with blood, had already hooked its tip around the blue colours from his opponent's lance and trotted over to the pavilion, silent now. A hundred faces looked at him, horror-stricken as he pointed his lance towards Lady Montague. 'Your colours, my lady,' he said. 'Next time, give them to a worthier opponent.'

As if in a dream, her tears bubbling, her heart thumping, Lady Montague took the scarf and the stranger knight wheeled away, riding past young Georgie, who, with his new-found courage, considered trying to stop him. It was Marlowe's hand on his arm that checked him. 'Not this one, boy,' he said softly, watching the man go, his grey breaking into a canter as he left the lists. 'Not this time.'

'Kit!' A voice broke the new silence. 'Kit Marlowe!'

Two men were trotting up from the periphery of the arena. Tom Sledd was grinning from ear to ear and there seemed to be a giant riding with him. 'Bugger!' Tom said. 'A tournament! It's been years since I saw a good tournament. And I've missed it.'

Marlowe looked at the men clustering around Martin Browne, his body convulsing in the settling dust as they tried to loosen his armour without hurting him even more. 'A good tournament, Tom?' he murmured. 'There's no such thing.'

It occurred to Marlowe that virtually since he had first met her, Lady Montague's eyes had been filled with tears – overwhelmed by the honour of her Queen's imminent arrival; proud with the martial achievements of her younger boy; and now, fretting over the physical condition of her eldest. For that, at least, there was some reason. Martin Browne lay propped on his pillows, servants coming and going at the behest of the man's parents and the doctor, a cadaverous old boy who looked to be nearer the grave than any of them.

'Can *you* explain it, Marlowe?' Anthony Montague was pacing the floor of the solar, exactly as he had twenty years ago when little Martin came screaming and wriggling into the world. He wasn't screaming or wriggling today. His eyes were glazed, his skin pale, except the angry purple swelling around the wound in his chest where the lance tip had rammed home. 'Who *was* that knight? Hawtrey here knew nothing about him. He just came out of nowhere.'

'Forgive me for saying this, my lord.' Marlowe had not touched his claret. 'But a man like yourself must have enemies.'

'Of course I have,' Montague frowned. 'That goes with the territory. Masterless blackguards who envy my wealth. Established lords who see the Brownes as Johannes-come-latelys. Bible-thumping Puritans who don't like the way I celebrate Mass. But he didn't take *me* on, did he? He specifically challenged Martin.'

'So,' Marlowe reasoned, 'a man like Martin must also have enemies. Heir to Cowdray, as nouveau riche as you, my lord. And, I assume, of the same religious persuasion.'

Montague was unwilling to see the mote in his son's eye. 'I suppose so.'

'And women . . .' Marlowe suggested.

'Certainly not!' Montague erupted. 'I know what they say, but . . .'

'There *was* the Lady Angela, my lord.' Hawtrey had not been offered any claret. He was a steward; he knew his place.

'Lady Angela?' Marlowe echoed.

Montague grunted and swigged from his goblet. 'Old Beaumont's youngest. Slip of a thing who took a shine to my boy. Rumour has it in the area that Martin had his way with her and left her with child.'

Marlowe waited for more and when none was forthcoming, asked, 'And did he?'

'Could have been anybody,' the Lord of Cowdray grunted. 'The Beaumont girls rut for England, all four of them. Must be something in the water. Beaumont was perfectly good about it – he knows his own children. Anyway, that was two years ago. If this stranger knight was some sort of avenger, he took his time about it.' He walked over to the mantelpiece and slammed the goblet down on a projecting piece of heraldry, carved out of local stone. 'One thing's certain. The pointed lance – the bastard was trying to kill him.'

Marlowe shook his head. 'I don't think so, my lord,' he said. 'There was something about the man . . . I don't know . . . I can't explain it. But I think if he'd intended to kill your son, the boy would be dead now.'

Montague looked at him, with a hint of a tear in his eye. 'It may only be a matter of time,' he said. 'If only I'd ridden after the bastard, stopped him, ripped off his helmet . . .'

'My lord.' Hawtrey was ever the loyal servant. 'Don't reproach yourself. *I* should have done that.'

'Well,' Montague sighed, slapping the man's shoulder as he passed him, 'there it is. What can't be cured must be endured and other pointless aphorisms. Marlowe – how far along are your plans for the Queen?'

'The Queen will not be coming, my lord,' Marlowe told him.

Montague and Hawtrey looked up. 'What?' Montague growled. 'What the Devil do you mean? Mrs B. will go demented.'

'Her Majesty would not wish to impose, my lord,' he said, 'with Master Martin's life hanging in the balance. I shall recommend otherwise.'

'Otherwise be buggered,' Montague snapped. 'We'll be ready. This . . .' he waved vaguely to the air, 'this is nothing.'

Marlowe bowed and took his leave.

'Damnedest thing I ever saw.' Jack Norfolk stretched himself and quaffed his ale. 'Came out of the mist and challenged Montague in front of everybody.'

'But who *was* he?' Tom Sledd wanted to know. Ever since he and Leonard Lyttleburye had met Jack Norfolk, it was almost the only question he had asked. And he still had no answer that made any sense.

'Could be a ghost,' Lyttleburye muttered. The others looked at him.

'Come again?' Sledd blinked. He had ridden all the way from Tyburn with this man. The giant said little and what he did say was largely incomprehensible, usually relating to the last topic of conversation but one.

'Well, I'm just saying,' Lyttleburye expanded. 'He comes out of nowhere. He vanishes just as fast. That's a ghost, that is.'

'Know a lot about ghosts, do you, Leonard?' Norfolk asked.

The giant loomed forward out of his chair, wiping the ale-froth from his moustache, 'There are more things in Heaven and earth, Master Norfolk, than you and me have had hot dinners.'

'Very deep,' Sledd nodded. 'But not very helpful. Why the old armour, Jack?'

'Hmm?'

'You said this knight was wearing an obsolete harness. Leonard and I didn't actually see him.'

'Looked old to me,' Norfolk nodded. 'Before my time, certainly.'

The door swung wide and Kit Marlowe swept in, sealed letters in his hand. 'Gentlemen,' he nodded to them, 'Tom – a word.'

The playwright and his stage manager walked out along the landing and lodged themselves in the window seat, heads together, silhouetted against the last purple bars of the sunset sky to the west. 'I haven't exactly had a chance to talk to you. Tell me about Lyttleburye.'

'Vegetable,' Sledd said. 'Think of the simplest of the ground-lings. Then think of any of the things they throw. The dumbest one of those is Leonard. But for some reason, Sir Robert rates him. Wouldn't take no for an answer. I'll wager he'll be useful enough in a tavern punch-up, though.'

'Which is where Jack Norfolk came in.'

'Aha,' Sledd nodded. 'I was going to ask you about him. This is a sort of . . . you show me your man; I'll show you mine, is it?'

'Something like that,' Marlowe chuckled. 'Tell me, could you bear Norfolk's company for a few days?'

'If the choice is him or the genius of Tyburn, the answer is yes. God, yes, a thousand times.'

'All right,' Marlowe said, 'but don't thank me yet. I want you both to go to Petworth.'

'Isn't that . . .?'

'The home of the wizard earl, yes.'

'It'll be creepy to meet him again. What does the Queen want there?'

'Fireworks, apparently; squibs. His Lordship's particularly adept with the Devil's inventions if memory serves. Hold the fort there until I arrive. I'm sending Norfolk with you in case of any trouble. Trust me, he can handle himself.'

'Where will you be?'

'Staying here for a day or two. Seeing how Martin Browne's coming along.'

'And lugubrious Leonard?' Sledd asked.

'He's Cecil's man. He can go and see him, with this letter. What he does after that, no doubt the Spymaster will tell us.'

In his right hand, Sir Robert Cecil held a miniature portrait of Walter Raleigh. The great Lucifer twinkled at him from the painted oval, all ruff and swagger, feathers and pearls. In his left hand, Cecil held a similar portrait of Robert Devereux, the Earl of Essex, before he'd decided to disguise his ugly chin with a beard. The man was smiling slightly, pleased with himself and with the ridiculous embroidered coat he wore over his armour.

'Arseholes!' Cecil muttered and slammed both miniatures face down. It was cool in the oak-panelled office under the eaves at Whitehall, and above the rooftops he could see the stonework of the palace of the Archbishop of Canterbury at Lambeth. Around the curve of the river, the tall ships of the Queen's wharves rode at anchor, taking the woollens of the World and bringing back riches without end. Such was the economic theory of the country he was pledged to protect. Yet Robert Cecil was still merely a knight, for all he was old Burghley's son and the number of Privy Council meetings he had attended could still be counted on the fingers of one hand. He had yet to prove himself. And the Progress was the way to do it.

There was a sharp rap on the door and a guard stepped in, all scarlet and gold in the Queen's livery. 'Master Lyttleburye to see you, sir.'

'Send him in.' The Queen's imp sat back in his high chair and waited.

'Your servant, sir.' The giant marched in, his tread making the glassware tremble. He bowed low.

'You are indeed, Lyttleburye,' Cecil acknowledged. 'What news?'

The giant handed the Spymaster Marlowe's letter and he read it quickly. He looked under his eyebrows at the messenger, 'Did Marlowe confide these contents to you?' he asked.

'No, sir, merely that I was to reach you post-haste.'

'Hmm.' Cecil pointed to a chair and Lyttleburye sat on it, gingerly as was his habit, grateful to have his arse in something other than a saddle. The Spymaster's large eyes narrowed and he tapped the parchment. 'This strange knight,' he said. 'Tell me about him.'

'I didn't see him, sir. Sledd and I arrived moments after the bout. I'm not sure he was real.'

Cecil blinked at the man. 'Not real?' he said. 'How so?'

'Well, nobody knows who he was. Where he came from. Or where he went. Creepy, if you ask me. Er . . . and you did ask me, sir.'

'Yes,' Cecil sighed; that was probably his first mistake.

'Is there a message for Master Marlowe, sir?' Lyttleburye wanted to know.

'There is indeed. It tells me here he intends to wait a little while at Cowdray, then on to Petworth. Join him there. So far, so good.' And he smiled at Lyttleburye, who knew perfectly that a smile from Robert Cecil was like the silver plate on a coffin.

SEVEN

All day, Kit Marlowe had been uneasy. He had left the packhorse with Tom Sledd so all he carried today was his sword and a water bottle. The sun was bright by the time he reached Marley Common, the sheep grazing on the springy grass. Behind him, the high ground of Black Down lay bathed in sunlight. Twice he had halted in the forests of dappled oak and Scots pine, listening, watching. He could swear that there was someone behind him, but each time he turned, easing his legs, he could see no one. The very birds in the trees seemed complicit with his follower, if he actually had one. Every time he thought he heard a twig snap or a breath sigh, a blackbird would go into a frenzy of song, trilling up and down the scale, telling the world of the joy of early summer, unravelling pure music from its quivering throat. And when the blackbird stopped to think up his next stanza, a trio of wrens would start wrangling it out above his head. He had had quieter rides in the middle of Town.

A play was forging itself in his brain, hammering a refrain over the open fields of the south country as they once did in the choking, blood-cobbled streets of Paris. They were just words at the moment, tumbling out of the blue, echoing and re-echoing through his mind – 'But he that sits and rules above the clouds doth hear and see the prayers of the just and will revenge the blood of innocents'; yes, he'd better put that in somewhere – Henslowe's backers would expect it and it might soften the Puritan hysteria at *another* Devil-gotten play from that atheist Kit Marlowe. He looked up at the sky – 'If ever day were turned to ugly night and night made semblance of the hue of Hell . . .' The play was about murder, because murder had been done in Paris in the year of the Lord 1572 and there was no escaping that. Assassination. It was a soft word, spoken in sibilance, wafted in whispers. It was why he was on the road today – to stop it from happening to the

Queen. In his play, in the twisted politics of the French court, how could it be done? A musket? Messy. Loud. Dangerous, as he knew all too well. Poison? That was silent; that was deadly and on stage, the administering of it caused no problems at all. He could just imagine Ned Alleyn wringing every ounce of drama – the uncorking of the bottle, the drip, drip, drip of something noxious into an innocent drink; oh, yes, plenty of scope there.

'A groat for your thoughts,' he suddenly heard the words and reined in sharply. 'I doubt they're worth more than that.'

Ahead of him, a man sat on a bay horse pointing a wheel-lock at him.

'A pistol,' Marlowe said, his hands half-raised. 'I hadn't considered that.'

The wheel-lock's hammer clicked back and the gun slid into its saddle-holster. 'How've you been, Kit?'

Marlowe let his hands fall to the pommel again. 'Nicholas Faunt,' he said. 'The last I heard, you were dead.'

'That's the last I heard, too,' Faunt said, laughing. He slid out of the saddle and led his horse to a stand of trees by the roadside. 'Cider?' He was unbuckling a goatskin.

Marlowe dismounted too. 'You were following me,' he said, hitching his chestnut alongside Faunt's gelding.

'Was I? Going in the same direction, let's call it. Following is so . . . well, it makes me sound like a spy of some kind.' Faunt held out a gloved hand. 'It's good to see you, Kit.'

'And you, Nicholas.' Marlowe shook the man's hand and they sat together under the elms.

'On your travels, I gather.' Faunt produced bread and cheese to accompany the cider.

Marlowe looked at him. Nicholas Faunt had been Francis Walsingham's secretary, his right hand, a projectioner par excellence; no one sharper, no one faster, no one more deadly. 'Really? And from whom did you gather that?'

'Tom Sledd,' Faunt munched the loaf.

'I'll kill him,' Marlowe said simply, shaking his head.

'Ah, he means well enough, Kit; you know that. It's just that, in our business . . .'

'Are you still in "our business", Nicholas? I seem to

remember that you and Sir Robert parted as a little less than the best of friends.'

'Oh, yes, the little monstrosity is "Sir" now, isn't he? Well, it was inevitable, I suppose, his papa owning half England and having both ears of the Queen.'

Marlowe laughed. 'Shame on you, Nicholas Faunt,' he said. 'You're bitter.'

'Me?' Faunt widened his eyes and passed the bread to Marlowe. 'Heaven forfend. Odd business at Farnham, I understand.'

Marlowe frowned. 'Is there *nothing* Tom left out?' he asked.

'Perhaps,' Faunt nodded. 'And where is everybody's favourite stage manager exactly?'

'Oh, he pops up now and then,' Marlowe said. 'Like the creatures he creates from his trapdoor at the Rose.' He had no intention of sharing any more information with Nicholas Faunt than he had to. The man had been his master under Walsingham and, if truth be told, he had learned much from Secretary Faunt; but he would die rather than say so. 'But I'm more interested in why *you've* popped up.'

'I ran into Tom by chance the other day. I had some business along the Bank and there he was, coming from the Rose, stinking of glue and that moth-eaten old bear that Henslowe keeps.'

'And Tom just opened his mouth and it all came tumbling out.'

'Along with much else,' Faunt yawned. 'I know every twinge his wife is feeling with her near-confinement; exactly how he plans to stage your *Tragical History of Doctor Faustus* one day; oh, and that little piece that Philip Henslowe has found near the Bear Garden – the one *Mrs* Henslowe doesn't know about.'

'Really?' Marlowe hadn't known that either. '*Henslowe*? I thought he'd stopped . . . anyway, don't try and deflect me, Master Faunt. I know your tricks. None of this explains why you're here.'

'There's been a murder, Marlowe,' Faunt said, straight-faced, 'at Farnham.'

'Murder, was it?' Marlowe tried to play the innocent, but Faunt knew him too well for that to work.

'Suit yourself,' the former secretary shrugged, 'but as soon as Sledd coughed, I thought to myself – Kit's in trouble. He's one-handed, or near as dammit. And he's getting in too deep in troubled waters.'

The dramatist in Marlowe ignored the mixed metaphor and repetition of words. Nicholas Faunt was not known where poets gathered; even Will Shaxsper was better than he was. 'You know my task, then,' he asked Faunt, 'to prepare for the Queen's Progress?'

Faunt nodded. 'Farnham, I know about. Where else is she going?'

'Cowdray's next. I've just come from there.'

'And then?'

'Petworth. The wizard earl.'

'Ah.'

'They're Papists, Nicholas,' Marlowe said grimly, 'all of them. The Middlehams, the Brownes, the Percys. If Her Majesty had invited herself to the Vatican, she couldn't be in more danger.'

Faunt nodded. 'Peculiar,' he said. 'You've told Cecil?'

'Of course. I've yet to hear from him, but at this rate, Her Majesty will be progressing from her bedroom to her tiring room and back. At least we can keep her safe there.'

'I'm more concerned about keeping you safe,' Faunt told him.

Marlowe smiled. 'That's touching, Nicholas,' he said, 'but, really . . .'

Faunt closed to him. 'You've got one pair of eyes, Marlowe,' he told him, 'one pair of ears and one right hand. Your enemies, I fear, have more than that. And who knows, in a little room, perhaps, or . . .' he looked around him, '. . . in God's own garden; there will be a reckoning, one day. I'm here to see that doesn't happen. That's all.'

Tom Sledd was lost. He hadn't told the others yet, but he had no idea where he was going. He corrected himself in his silent colloquy – of course he knew where he was *going*. He even knew where he had been. It was joining up the two which was giving him a bit of trouble. He let his reins hang loose and the horse ambled along at its own pace, nibbling from the roadside green from time to time. The lane they were currently in was so narrow that Tom, leading his little caravan, was whipped gently with the soft fronds of lady's mantle and cow parsley. There was wild garlic in the mix as well; his horse would have breath fit to stop a clock in the morning.

'Master Sledd?' A low rumble like a distant earthquake alerted him to the fact that Leonard at the very least had begun to wonder where they were.

'Leonard?' Tom Sledd had learned a lot over the years from Philip Henslowe, and answering a question with a question was perhaps his most useful gambit.

'Are we there yet?'

'Nearly,' Sledd said, brightly. 'Just up this lane and we'll see Petworth, I'm sure.' He chose to ignore the gentle snort from Jack Norfolk.

'Only . . .'

'Only what, Leonard?' Tom Sledd had a toddler at home and he might as well have brought her with him.

'The horses need water,' the big man pointed out. 'Mine's eating ramsons and it'll be scouring like the Devil tomorrow if he eats many more.'

Sledd turned in the saddle. 'I didn't have you down for a country boy, Leonard,' he said.

'My old grandsire had a stables, Master Sledd. Lyttleburye's Livery, it was called. I used to work there, when I was a little 'un.'

'Useful skill,' Sledd muttered, privately doubting whether Leonard Lyttlebury had ever even been a little 'un. 'Let's keep their heads up, then, and get to the end of this lane.'

'And I'm a bit peckish myself.' A man of few words, Leonard Lyttleburye was hard to stop once he got going. 'Are you peckish, Jack?'

Jack Norfolk seemed to wake up for the first time. He was bringing up the rear and had not really got involved in the banalities of the conversation. He was enjoying the warm sun on his back, the birdsong, the smell of the sweet grass cropped

by the horses, overlaid with a smell of . . . could that be garlic?
'Sorry, Leonard,' he said with a smile which lit up his face.
'I wasn't listening. What did you say?'

'Are you peckish?'

'I could eat.'

'Well, I'm really hungry . . .'

Suddenly, Lyttleburye's horse reared, eyes rolling in his
head. It took all the ex-stable boy's skill to calm him and,
when he had, all three men saw the cause. A little nutbrown
creature was standing in the roadway, almost under the animal's
hoofs. It had a hand up to its toothless mouth and was snick-
ering behind it. It was hard to tell the sex as it was wearing
a shapeless garment made of sacking. It was hard to tell the
age; it was certainly no spring chicken, yet seemed limber
enough.

Jack Norfolk, furthest from the creature, was first to recover.
'Who in the name of God are you?' he snapped. 'You could
have been killed.'

'Not I,' it said with a mad giggle. 'I bin a-jumpin' out at
horses in this lane man and boy—' that sorted out one dilemma,
at least – 'since 'Arry were naught but a lad.' And there, in a
few more words, so was the other.

Tom Sledd wished with all his heart that Marlowe was with
them. He would talk to this mad thing and find out all sorts
of useful stuff, such as where in Hades was Petworth House.
And, if not that, he would have a fine fool to put in his next
play. He tried a Marlovian question, just to move the madness
along. 'That's what you do, is it? Jump out at horses?'

'I just said so, din' I?' The old man capered a little in the
road and Lyttleburye's horse, by now totally unnerved, jumped
backwards, bringing down clods of earth from the high bank.

'I mean . . .' Sledd was at a loss.

'I think what my friend here means,' Norfolk spoke from
the rear, 'is this; is jumping out at horses what you do for a
living?'

The old man looked blank.

'Do you, in some way, make money from jumping out at
horses?'

This earned him a withering look. 'Are you soft in the

head?' the creature grated. 'What money's to be made in jumping out at horses? No, I makes what money I make from cursin' people. It's not much, but it's a living. Jumping out at horses is what I does for a laugh. A jest. A joke.'

'I'm going to kill him,' Lyttlelburye rumbled. 'Just see if I don't.'

This made the little old man double up and slap his knees. He was laughing so much it looked as though Lyttleburye would be spared the effort; he had turned purple and was beginning to cough.

'Slap him on the back, someone,' Jack Norfolk urged. 'Not you, Leonard,' he said, hurriedly; the man looked all too keen to comply. 'Tom, slap him on the back.'

Tom Sledd looked at the back in question and decided not to – it was altogether too dirt encrusted to be at all a welcome thought. But it didn't matter; with a final ferocious hoick of phlegm into the hedgerow, the elderly prankster was himself again, wiping his eyes on a filthy sleeve.

'No, I tells you why I were laughing when I jumps out at yer. I heard him, the big 'un, say he was hungry. And this 'ere's, this 'ere's called Hungers Lane.' He presented the punchline as if it was the wittiest thing he had ever said, which might of course have been the case. 'Hungers Lane. He's hungry.'

In the silence, an early grasshopper chirped and one of the horses tore a mouthful of green from the verge with a noise like ripping silk.

'Yes.' Sledd was stuck for any other comment. 'I see. Can you tell us if we're near to Petworth, at all?'

The old man looked from face to face, still chuckling to himself, although he could now scarcely remember why. 'Ar. Up the lane, turns right. You'll sees it yonder.'

'Thank you.' Jack Norfolk clicked his tongue and his horse nudged Leonard's gelding in the quarter. 'Leonard, give the man something for his trouble.'

Lyttleburye clicked his tongue too and his horse moved off. 'You give him something for his trouble,' he growled. 'My purse is deep but I have short arms. And in any case, he makes his money from cursing, not jumping out at horses.'

'That's true, master, very true.' The ancient tugged on his

sparse forelock as they passed. 'Cursin's the game if you wants to make money.'

When Norfolk's horse had been swallowed up by the burgeoning green of the lane, a glint came into the old man's eye and he stood up rather straighter.

'But you won't need cursing by me, if it's Petworth House you seek. Oh, no, my masters. You'll be praying for a simple curse right enough, if you go there.'

The three horsemen broke from the clinging fronds of the narrow lane with relief and turned right. None of them expected to see Petworth House when they turned the first corner and yet, there it lay, cupped in a fold in the countryside as if it had grown there, surrounded by its wall, its paddocks, its stands of woodland. The house was clearly very old and had grown bit by bit, as the Percy coffers had waxed and waned, and now it looked like a child's toy, with turrets balanced on gatehouses, windows cut haphazardly in a gable end. And yet, it seemed to welcome them, to throw out its arms to offer them comfort and shelter from the growing heat of the day. Tom Sledd was humble in his acceptance of the congratulations of the other two, if 'congratulations' was the word.

'Well done, Tom,' Jack Norfolk said, slapping him on the back. 'I really thought we were lost for a moment there.'

'It's nothing,' Sledd said. 'I was brought up in a travelling show. My sense of direction is second to none, say it myself as perhaps shouldn't.'

Leonard Lyttleburye was less polite. 'Lucky,' he murmured as he urged his horse forward with his heels. 'There's a stream down there, let's get these horses down to it for a good long drink. Mine has been farting fit to beat the band since he ate those ramsons.'

Norfolk patted the stage manager's back again. 'Don't worry, Tom,' he said. 'I can tell he's impressed really. He just doesn't know how to show it.'

Sledd fell into line behind the other horses then hung back a little; Lyttleburye might be a man of few words, but he was dead right about his horse.

*   *   *

Petworth was a house to wander in, with passageways which went nowhere, stairs which suddenly took a person by surprise as they turned a corner. From every window, there was a view to tear a man's heart from his breast, of fields shimmering in the summer sun, of coney-cropped meadow reaching into the cool of the wood. In a courtyard, maids hung acres of snow-white linen from ropes slung from eave to eave, hauling them up high in the air with wooden pulleys, white with water and age. They sounded like the flock of starlings which wheeled and twittered over the wood, mysterious under its haze of heat and distance. Tom Sledd was entranced. The wizard earl had greeted this friend of Kit Marlowe as if he was his own oldest and dearest companion and had given him the freedom of the house to plan his revel.

Tom Sledd had no idea how lucky he was in his timing. Henry Percy was in love; nothing so very special, as he was always in love. But just now, he was in the happy reverie which all men must inhabit when the object of his love loves him back. Had the stage manager told him he must demolish the house and set fire to the ruins to please the Queen, it may well have been that the wizard earl would have simply nodded his agreement and wandered away, singing a happy tune.

Jack Norfolk and Leonard Lyttleburye were off on errands of their own. Tom Sledd was no drama snob – or, at least, no more a drama snob than any other stage manager of the best theatre in Town who had been charged with planning a revel for the Queen – but he was happier on his own. He didn't know what Jack Norfolk's views on the theatre were, but Leonard had shared his general thoughts already and he had made it clear that, should Hell freeze over, even then, he, Leonard Lancelot Lyttleburye would not be seen as a groundling or anything else within a theatre, unless it was as the man tasked with burning it down. After that, there seemed little left to say on the subject.

Around another corner, Sledd came upon the most beautiful room, with windows all along one side and an enormous fireplace, with the Percy arms bitten deep into the ancient stone. The windows had, here and there, fragments of a once-magnificent design, now reduced to the odd hand, foot,

halo and word in Latin, enigmatic in its single state.
'*Poenitet*', the panes exhorted. '*Pacem*'. And, the wizard
earl's current favourite, '*Adorant me*'. The windowsill was
low and worn at one end, the wood of the architrave made
smooth by the backs of many Percys, dreaming there as
their acres unrolled beneath them. The stage manager
couldn't help himself; he sat down, the sill almost moulding
itself to his rear. He leaned back and looked out at the scene.
There was Leonard, wandering through the herb garden,
trailing a hand across the lavender and rosemary. Sledd
couldn't help but chuckle; who would have thought that
Lyttleburye had a sensitive side? And there was Jack Norfolk,
sitting on the edge of a carp pond, further away from the
house, towards the road which led to the village. He was
staring into the water as into a scrying glass. The languid
air of Petworth and its love-struck lord seemed to have got
under everyone's skin this afternoon. A fly buzzed somewhere in the room, blundering every now and then against
the diamond panes. Then, it was further away, then further
still, and Tom Sledd slept in the sun, like a cat.

When Tom Sledd woke, the sun had moved round and he was
sitting in shadow, warm still with the memory of noon. The
house which had been so still was now a hive of industry,
with men carrying tables and maids strewing fresh rushes on
the floor. The stage manager stretched and got up from his
seat, hoping that by acting naturally he could just merge with
the background, his nap unnoticed.

'Sleep well, Master Sledd?' a soft voice asked.

He jumped a mile and spun round. A woman stood there,
Tom's age or perhaps a little less. She wasn't beautiful exactly,
but there was something about her face which made men want
to look at it and nothing else, preferably for the rest of their
lives. She smiled at him and he relaxed. 'I was . . . I was just
resting my eyes. It helps me think,' he said, trying to keep the
truculent whine from his voice.

'Of course. I knew that.' She stepped forward and linked
her arm through his. 'I am Barbara Gascoigne, Master Sledd.
More correctly *Lady* Barbara Gascoigne, but please, don't

trouble yourself over that. I want us to be friends. But more especially, Master Sledd, I want to be part of your revel.'

He looked down at her in consternation. He had heard, of course, that the ladies of the house often took part in revels for the Queen, but he would not presume to plan anything to involve them. If they insisted, of course, that was another thing. But old habits died hard. 'Lady Barbara,' he said, thinking on his feet, 'I'm not sure if . . .'

She stamped a perfectly shod foot and dropped his arm. 'If you are about to say, Master Sledd,' she said, with steel suddenly in her voice, 'that Henry won't allow it, then to that I say simply, fiddlesticks. I want to be in the revel, and you must write me a part.'

'I do no writing, Lady Barbara,' Sledd protested. 'Master Marlowe will be doing any writing that goes on. I make the sets, arrange for the costumes, the music, that kind of thing.'

'So . . .' her eyes flickered around the room, 'where is Master Marlowe? I must speak with him.'

'He will be here shortly, I believe,' Tom said. In fact, he had half expected to find him there when he had arrived; the master of fire and air often kept to a schedule that would tax Dr Dee himself. 'I'm sure he would be delighted to . . .'

Suddenly, a shadow, both real and metaphorical, filled the room. The wizard earl loomed at them through the gathering twilight and swept down the long space between them and the door with seven league strides. 'Barbara,' he said, his voice rather high and tight. 'I've been looking for you everywhere.'

With a bright smile, she moved away from Sledd and into the arms of her lover. Outside, in the world, in the court, they had to be careful, but here at Petworth there was no need for such caution. 'Henry,' she breathed, reaching up for a kiss. 'I have been looking for you too. Where *were* you? Not in your nasty laboratory, I hope. Nor with your silly books.' She tapped him on the chest with an ivory finger, no harder than the beat of a butterfly wing. 'You will wear out your brain with all this thinking. Look,' she said, and traced between his eyes with the forefinger of the other hand, so she had to turn to face him, pressing herself against him, 'you're getting lines on your Lovelly face.'

The couple were practically giving off steam and, although none of the staff seemed to notice, going about their business as they were, Tom Sledd felt very superfluous indeed and, sliding one careful foot behind him and then the other, made for the door and the peace and quiet of his room, where he could splash his face with cold water before going to find Norfolk and Lyttleburye.

Tom Sledd was secretly rather delighted to find himself elevated above the salt when the evening meal came around. Peering down the table in the gathering dusk not yet lit by the many candles spaced along the table, he could see Lyttleburye and Norfolk, flanked by assorted guests culled from the estate; no one important enough to be near to Henry Percy and his current lady, but deemed able to eat without spraying their neighbour with crumbs, intelligent enough to make conversation of a sort. Lyttleburye was looking down at his bread trencher with longing eyes. Norfolk was looking enigmatically at the goblet in front of him, but whether it was with longing or loathing, Sledd at this distance and in this lighting was unable to tell.

'So tell me, Master Sledd,' Henry Percy leaned over the table and pierced his man with his gaze. 'What plans have you for entertaining Gloriana, may she live forever?'

Sledd was startled. He wasn't used to holding the fort for quite this long; Kit had promised he would be with him long before now. 'Oh, ah, well, I am more in the way of being the man who does,' he said. 'Kit . . . er . . . Master Marlowe will *write* the masque, I will just . . .' he waved an arm in the air, 'make it all take place.'

Lady Barbara Gascoigne leaned forward too and Tom smelled a whiff of frangipane as she did so. 'But will there be a part for *me*, Master Sledd?' she asked. She knocked away Percy's restraining hand and then grabbed it, taking it down into her lap. 'I want to have Lovely clothes.' With her free hand, she sketched out sweeping skirts and a magnificent hat. 'I want to have a retinue of beautiful girls – not *too* beautiful, of course – cavorting in the trees.' She broke off and leaned in to whisper in Percy's ear and smiled, wriggling in her seat.

'Music, I shall need music . . . will anyone be composing a special piece, Henry?'

'I . . . I hadn't thought of that,' Percy said. 'I daresay I could do something about that, if that is what you want, my love.' He looked deep into her eyes. '*Is* that what you want? Or is *that* what you want?'

She gave a small cry, quickly suppressed. 'That is one of the things I want, Henry, yes.' Her eyes were half closed. 'But perhaps . . . later.' She snapped back into the moment and put her lord's hand firmly back on the table, with a tap. 'So, Master Sledd . . . where were we?'

'Music.' Tom Sledd spent his life among actors, possibly the most libidinous crowd to be found in a long day's march, and had learned over the years to never open a cupboard suddenly or walk into a room without knocking, but these two made Alleyn and Burbage look like amateurs. 'Specially composed music.'

'That's right,' she smiled lazily, a cat's smile, the smile of the one who had got the cream. 'And fireworks.'

'That goes without saying,' Sledd agreed. You couldn't beat a good firework, he always said. And he knew the wizard earl was not called that for nothing. He had the Devil's own fire in that inner sanctum of his.

'But . . .' Percy's brow darkened. 'Might the Queen be . . . jealous, if you appear in all your beauty, with your ladies, with music, fireworks and the rest? This is supposed to be *her* Progress, you know.'

Tom Sledd nodded. The man had a point.

Barbara Gascoigne stuck her bottom lip out and her brow darkened. 'I want to be in this masque,' she said, her voice low and quivering. 'I *want* it, Henry.'

No one at the table took any notice. If they had even the smallest coin of the realm for every time they had heard Barbara Gascoigne say that, they would all be rich.

'Can we talk about this later, dearest?' Henry Percy had more reason than most to know what it was like to face the wrath of the Queen. He had been reduced to living at Petworth rather than his estates in Northumberland because his father had upset the Queen. His father had been in the

Tower for what seemed like forever because he had upset the Queen; in fact, it had been forever. He had died there, shot through the heart in his quarters. The verdict of suicide had been passed unanimously, the lack of gun in the room being no bar to the wheels of justice. So Henry Percy, ninth of his line, did not intend to upset the Queen. But Barbara . . . It was a hard choice to make. He had spent much of the afternoon writing a sonnet to her and finding rhymes for Barbara had not been easy; he didn't want to waste all that work.

The woman got to her feet, a little too fast for the waiting lackey, who rushed to move her chair. 'You don't love me, Henry!' she shrieked.

'I do, I do, I do love you, Barbara!' he cried. 'With all my heart.'

'Here we go again,' muttered the man on Sledd's left. 'I'll tell you how this goes. She rushes out. He rushes out. We make our own entertainment, as will they when the tantrum passes. She comes in later with another jewel at her throat and he drinks for the rest of the evening. You see if I'm right.'

Tom Sledd turned to the man. 'So . . . this happens a lot?' He had rather thought it did.

'Most nights,' his neighbour nodded. 'We have got quite used to it. Once the meal is over . . . how is your pigeon, by the way? Mine's rather stringy.'

'Um . . . delicious.' He realized he had hardly tasted it in all the hullabaloo.

'We don't eat too much on a weekday. Just eight or nine courses as a rule. But when that's done, we'll gather round for some entertainment. Music, a bit of dancing perhaps.' He looked closer at Sledd. 'You're from London, aren't you? Are you Christopher Marlowe?'

'No . . . I . . .'

'That's a shame. He could have done a turn, you know, a recitation. Never mind. What do you do?'

'I build things.'

The man looked askance. 'That's a bit slow for an after-dinner turn, isn't it?'

'I'm not an entertainer, Master . . .'

'Gascoigne. Andrew Gascoigne. Barbara's brother, Heaven help me.'

'Oh. Pleased to make your acquaintance, Master Gascoigne.' Tom Sledd felt sure there was a title knocking about somewhere, but wisely stopped talking before he put his foot in it. 'Thomas Sledd. Stage manager, the Rose.'

'Oh. I see. The dreaded Progress.'

'Dreaded?'

'Well, isn't it? It costs a fortune; the whole place is turned upside down. The Queen turns up with an army of retainers, annoys the real servants of the house, stays a day or so and leaves financial ruin and chaos in her wake. And for what? It isn't as if Henry needs any more titles. And if anything goes wrong . . .' he made a chopping motion on the side of his neck, '. . . it's goodbye Henry. I said to Barbara the other day, best get him married, girl, or we'll be out on our ears when he gets the chop.'

'Isn't that a little cynical?'

'Cynical or realistic. You choose. What she needs is a belly full of the next line of Percys, that's what she needs, and the sooner the better. And a nice Protestant wife is what Percy needs, take the edge off, if you know what I mean.' Gascoigne slurped from his goblet and belched. '*In vino veritas*, old man, sorry about that. Perhaps best if you forget all I've said.'

'It's forgotten,' Sledd said, obligingly.

'What is?' Gascoigne looked down at his plate. 'That's not a pigeon,' he said, surprised. 'It looks like vomit.'

The lackey standing behind leaned forward. 'Frumenty, sir,' he said.

'Well, take it away; nursery slop. And fill this goblet while you're about it. What's the entertainment for tonight?'

'I believe that Sir Guiscard Percy, Sir Henry's uncle, will entertain tonight, sir,' the lackey said. 'Some family tales, as I understand it.'

Sledd's heart fell. That sounded pretty boring.

Gascoigne smiled and nudged Sledd in the ribs. 'That's good news,' he said. 'Old Guiscard's got a mine of stories. Depends on the company, but if there aren't too many ladies, he can tell some stories to put some wind in your whistle.'

He looked down the table, where candles now glowed to light the way. 'Oh, that's a shame. There is quite a bit of the old distaff side here tonight, so that means it will probably be ghost stories. They're good, but not like . . .' and he nudged Tom Sledd again in exactly the same spot, which was becoming rather sore. 'A bit of the other sort, if you get my drift, Master Sledd. My particular favourite's the one about the abbot and the duchess.' He looked into the man's face. 'You married?'

'Yes. I . . .'

'Pity. Pity, that. Never mind . . . ghost stories are good as well. You'll enjoy them.' He drained his goblet noisily and pushed back his chair. 'Must be away. Heard them all before, you see. I've got to go down to the village, see a woman about a coney.' This time he slapped his hand down on Sledd's shoulder. 'You'll get that, being a theatre man. Play on words, you see. Coney. Means . . .'

'Yes, thank you.' Tom Sledd also thought the frumenty looked like vomit, but he applied himself to it rather than talk more. What was the matter with the Gascoigne family? Could they talk of nothing else?

'Well . . .' Andrew Gascoigne wiped the fragments of pigeon and droplets of wine from his beard and twirled the ends of his moustache. 'I'll see you later, I feel sure, Master Sledd.' And with wandering step, he left the room.

EIGHT

There had been dancing and music, after a sort. Jack Norfolk remarked in an undertone to Tom Sledd that he had heard better played by the town drunk blowing across the top of a bottle, but everyone had clapped politely and the company had meandered out into the courtyard, where a fire was burning brightly in an enormous wrought-iron brazier and cushions and rugs were ready for anyone who wished to join Sir Guiscard Percy for some of his celebrated stories. Pokers were heating in the heart of the fire to warm up the toddies and when everyone was seated and wrapped against the scarcely perceptible chill of the moonless night, Sir Guiscard cleared his throat and began.

Tom Sledd was sharing a blanket with Jack Norfolk and Leonard Lyttleburye. He had shared a blanket with worse; sitting in the lee of Lyttleburye was like being sheltered by a wall, and Norfolk had his back half turned and was keeping his bony knees to himself. Sledd loved a good ghost story. He had scared himself witless on many a night at the Rose when, last man out as he was always first man in, he had run the gauntlet from the highest eave to the wicket gate in total blackness, the shades of the dead characters of every play snapping at his heels. He would reach the street with heart pounding and sweat running into a freezing pool in the small of his back but he wouldn't miss it for the world. In fact, sitting there with the shapes of those in front of him black against the glow of the fire and Lyttleburye's bulk to his right, he felt very nostalgic for the Rose, for the walking gentlemen, Philip Henslowe and yes, even the actors. Even Will Shaxsper; that's when he knew for sure how bad his theatre sickness was. And Meg. What of Meg? Had she given birth? Was he now the father of two? And what was it? A feeling of panic filled his heart and a tear sprang to his eye. He must get back . . . He gave himself a shake. Petworth was not the end of the world. It was a mere two days' ride from the doorway of the Rose and, if he were to be needed, he would be fetched. He took a shuddering breath and calmed himself down.

'Welcome, welcome all.' Guiscard Percy raised his voice and the hum of conversation ceased. 'Welcome, old friends and new. It is a while since we met here at Petworth and a fine night for a tale it is; dark, yet not too dark. Chill, but not too chill. But before I end my tale, I can promise you, my golden lads and girls, you will be shaking in your shoes.' The old man looked around the company. He lived a comfortable life at Petworth, mostly in the library, where he spent his days looking up his ancestry. It wasn't hard to do; the Percys went back to the harrying of the north and before, well documented with every rung of the ladder they climbed. They hadn't always backed the right horse – Richard II was a period the family glossed over – but by and large, when men were rising, the Percys rose with them. When they fell, even when they lost their crowns, somehow, the Percys were elsewhere until the dust settled; even his brother, though he lost his life, passed on the title to his son. So, when it came to telling tales of ghosts and ghouls, knights and damsels, kings and queens, Guiscard Percy was always the man to the fore.

In this audience, he could see a few who were cream-faced already; they were the ones who had been before. He remembered one in particular, who had made the night hideous with eldritch shrieks and groans, right on cue. Of course, the bishop had claimed later it was a bad oyster, but it had made the experience for many that night; shame it couldn't be relied upon. He saw a hulking shape towards the back and, alongside it, a huddled form with bright eyes. Yes; that would be the face he would speak to tonight; an old actor friend had taught him that, one night on the town chasing through the Winchester Geese like two foxes on the loose. Don't talk to the crowd, the man had said. Talk to just one man. So, fixing his eyes on Tom Sledd's, he began.

'To those who know Petworth and those who don't, it must be clear that it is full of the ghosts, spirits, shades – call them what you will – of all those who have lived and loved and, yes, died, within these walls. The rumour goes that the first ghost ever seen here at Petworth was many hundreds of years ago, when the first additions were made to the long house, which makes up the very heart of the house. As you ate your repast tonight, beneath your very feet was the room that once housed the Percy forebears, their servants and their livestock. If they could cast up their cold, dead eyes now, they would see a ceiling where once there were smoke-blackened rafters, and beyond that, unimaginable comfort to those who lived in what we would call squalor.'

The company snuggled down further into their blankets. Against the fire, servants moved as if in a dream, thrusting red-hot pokers into red wine and old brandy, making a steam rise that was fit for the gods. The goblets were handed around, and the old man went on.

'Ghosts from those days walk these halls, of course they do. It doesn't need a violent death to make the dead want to walk the haunts of the living. Petworth puts its hold on all who come here and it is no surprise, then, that people have seen the ghostly servant girl in her drab sacking, the old cook in his white apron.'

Drab sacking! Tom Sledd's eyes were wide. But . . . that had been no serving girl, surely? But had any of them touched the crazy old thing back there in Hungers Lane? He couldn't remember and now it was too late to ask.

'But it is not of ancient ghosts I tell tonight, no. Nor even of a ghost of a man who died within these walls. Petworth can call back its dead, no matter where they meet their end.'

Heads nodded in the crowd and not a few felt the uneasy stirrings of fear in their gut. The old man could only be talking about his brother, surely, dead these six years and more, by his own hand, or so they said. A suicide; could there be a ghost more vengeful?

The old storyteller chuckled to himself and stroked his beard thoughtfully. 'I see that many of you already know some of what is to come. Do not be disappointed, you will still have a tale to chill the blood. To those of you who do not know, I say, *beware!*' He raised his voice and looked to the sky as he said the last word and at least one woman screamed. '*Beware!*' He had rather enjoyed the effect, so did it again. 'My brother

Henry died on Midsummer Day, six years ago; his anniversary is near. Very near. And since his death, it has been said, in the weeks that lead up to the longest day, the eighth earl walks his home, looking for someone to destroy, to release the anger that builds up in his poor dry bones, buried so far from his beloved home, under St Peter in Chains. He, sad shade, can shed the chains of his sin and walk where'er he will, for one month and one month only, in every twelve. It is said,' and the spinner of stories dropped his voice so that everyone had to crane closer, 'that when he walks, there is not another sound to be heard. The small sounds of the night all cease, all save his footsteps, pacing, pacing, pacing down stair and through hall, looking for a way to slake his lust for blood.'

Leonard Lyttleburye's arm, little by little, stole around Tom Sledd's shoulder and Tom Sledd let it lie there, dead weight though it was. Jack Norfolk had slunk from under the blanket and was just a dark shape on the ground, curled in on himself, fast asleep. The whole crowd held their collective breath but they had nothing to fear – the fire crackled and the goatsuckers churred the night away; the earl was clearly not of the company. Yet.

The flames flew up higher in a maze of sparks, burning blue and hot, and a log burst scattering hot embers over the flagstones with a crack like that of doom, making everyone jump. 'They say, the men who know, that when the earl finds another soul passing over as he walks by, he can steal its path to glory and leave this earthly plane, this vale of tears. But it must be someone meeting death by violence. Since my brother started his walks, three people to my certain knowledge have dropped dead with fear just to see his cadaverous face – for, my friends, I am afraid to say that though his mortal soul is frozen here on earth, his body has rotted as nature intends. Worms writhe in and out of his eye sockets, rats nest in his chest, their naked babies looking out through the hole wrought by the pistol ball which tore away his beating heart. The sight of him alone is enough to bring death to anyone not of the strongest disposition. But it is not one of those souls he seeks, oh, no. As he paces, paces along the corridors he loves in boots eaten away by vermin, with hair dropping from his head in hanks, what he seeks is someone who is meeting a grisly end, an end as grisly as his own. So, my lords and ladies, friends old and new, when you go to bed tonight, search your bedfellows to the skin.'

A nervous laugh was quickly smothered.

'Search every inch of every one, and if there is a knife, a wheel-lock, even a grain of poppy that should not be there, scream the house down. Raise the alarum. And if you do, then perhaps the earl will not get what he came for this night.'

The fire, after its burst of sparks, had collapsed in on itself and the brazier, once red hot, was now almost black. The logs had stopped crackling, even the nightjars had moved away to better hunting. The people hanging on every word now hung on the silence instead. The old man sat still, his head bowed, so no one could see the smile. For a ghost story he had just made up out of his own head on the spur of the moment, it had not gone at all badly. He counted slowly to ten in silence and then straightened up. 'Ladies and gentlemen . . .' he began, and then stopped as though shot as a door was flung open and light from a hundred candles flooded the courtyard.

Henry Percy, ninth Earl of Northumberland stood there, in dark silhouette, the silk nightgown fluttering in the speed of his flight. 'Murder!' he screamed. 'For the love of God, murder!'

Every head turned and, for a perceptible moment, no one moved.

'Murder, I say!'

Then everything seemed to happen at once. The men, those not encumbered by a screaming woman, all ran towards the earl, who still stood as a man turned to stone. Leonard Lyttleburye, a well-trained man of Robert Cecil, despite his lumbering body and ham-like face, was the first there, having flung his blanket and Tom Sledd with it aside in one deft movement. Jack Norfolk appeared almost instantly at his side. Only Tom Sledd stayed where he was, held back by a hand on each shoulder. Glancing to his right, he saw the face he had wanted to see all day; Kit Marlowe, in the flesh. To his left, Nicholas Faunt, not so welcome but still a good man to have by you in a crisis.

'Stay here, Tom,' whispered the playwright. 'Tell me what's

going on. Who are all these people? And why are they wrapped
in blankets? Has there been a fire? Flood?'

'Or murder,' muttered Faunt. 'But if murder, why are they
all out here when the earl – it is the earl?' Sledd nodded.
'When the earl is still standing there, shouting it at the top of
his lungs?'

'We were . . . well, we were listening to a ghost story,'
Sledd explained. 'The earl's uncle . . .'

'Guiscard?' Faunt knew everyone.

'Yes.'

'Mad as a house. They all are, the Percys. But some are
madder than most. And Guiscard is the maddest of the lot, by
a fair margin. What was the story?'

'He . . . he said his brother walked the house, looking for
a soul which had met its end by violence. And then . . .' Sledd
could hardly believe what he was saying, even as the words
tumbled out, '. . . and then, the earl ran out, shouting Murder.'
He glanced across and then goggled. 'Is that *blood* on his
nightgown?'

Faunt and Marlowe didn't need to get closer to know blood-
stains when they saw them and the earl's nightshirt had a large
patch just at chest level. Yet, he was clearly uninjured, judging
by the way he had run out into the courtyard and the volume
of his cries.

'Something for you, Nicholas,' Marlowe said. 'I need to
talk to Tom.'

Faunt let go of the stage manager's shoulder with a valedic-
tory pat. Raising his voice, he walked towards the house. 'Make
way, step aside. Thank you, everyone, back away, give the man
some room. Nothing to see here.'

Nicholas Faunt was in his Heaven. And if all was not quite
right with the world, it soon would be.

Tom Sledd was surprised at himself. He had always thought
that he was immune to the smoke and mirrors of a theatrical
performance and yet Guiscard Percy had taken him in, hook,
line and sinker. He could remember little of the gathering
outside around the brazier; apart from Leonard Lyttleburye,
who had had his arm over his shoulders, he had no idea where

anyone was, whether anyone had left, moved or spoken. All he could remember were flames and the voice, telling of unimaginable horrors.

Marlowe was disappointed but not surprised. Leonard Lyttleburye was no better, and here the playwright was surprised as well as disappointed; this man was supposed to be trained by Cecil himself, but he had been, if anything, rather more terrified than Sledd, though he refused to concede the arm over the shoulders. Jack Norfolk had not believed a word of it; ghost stories were for children in hanging sleeves, for fools who swore they saw three suns in the sky at once; if he recalled, he had curled up in his blanket and caught a few well-earned minutes of sleep.

Marlowe followed in Faunt's footsteps, and by asking here and there amongst the muttering knots of retainers who clotted the hallway, found his way to the chamber where the murder was said to have taken place. The door was half open, its lock hanging off and the wood around splintered and raw. Through the gap, he saw three men clustered round a still form on the bed. The candlelight made a nimbus around each head and they looked like angels bending there, winging the soul to Heaven or to Hell.

Then, the spell was broken. Faunt turned to see Marlowe in the doorway and beckoned him in.

'Christopher Marlowe,' he said, extending a hand to the man opposite him across the bed. 'Doctor Windham has looked at the victim and pronounced life extinct. Sir Henry, my lord . . .'

'I know Master Marlowe,' the wizard earl said, shortly. 'And I hope he knows that I do not need a doctor to tell me when life is extinct. Especially when it is the life of my beloved Barbara, the love of my life, my own dear one, my . . .' His voice trailed away and there were tears in his eyes.

'Yes, yes.' Faunt knew the stories about Percy and his women. It was a dramatic end to this particular romance; as a rule, things were thrown, hearts but no bones were broken, and soon the earl would move on to his next one and only love. But murder . . . this was an altogether different thing. He couldn't overlook the bloodstain on Percy's nightgown, but that could be – and had been – explained by his clasping of his beloved to his breast when he found her. There was no sign of a wheel-lock and it was doubtful that Percy could have hidden it very carefully and still got to the courtyard to scream his loss to the sky in the time available. The blood was still wet and the body warm; this had happened in the last half an hour at the very most.

'Who is the lady?' Marlowe was trying to garner at least a few facts if any were available.

'Lady Barbara Gascoigne,' Percy replied, drawing himself up and calming down as best he could. 'My own, my darling . . .'

'Yes, yes, indeed. She looks a very Lovelly person,' Faunt said. 'A guest here, I assume?'

'*My* guest, yes,' Percy said. 'I . . . we had had words, over the evening repast. Just before the pigeon, if memory serves. She . . . well, perfection though she was, sometimes she could be a little volatile. She wanted to take part in the revel, but . . . let's just excuse her by saying she was young and didn't know the Queen.'

The doctor, who had been near enough at the table to hear the argument, raised a wry eyebrow. He had brought the wizard earl kicking and screaming into the world. He had put up with his eccentricities ever since.

'But apart from that, you were getting on well?' Marlowe had to ask, but the fact that the earl was in the woman's bedroom dressed in just a nightgown probably answered that question.

'She was my own. My darling.' But the earl sounded a little less convinced than he had earlier. 'My one true love.'

'Did you shoot Lady Barbara, my lord?' Faunt asked. 'Sorry to be so blunt, but if I don't ask you, the coroner will.'

'The coroner?' The wizard earl was aghast. 'What does the coroner have to do with it?'

The doctor pointed to the body. 'This woman has been shot in the heart, my lord,' he said, in reasonable tones. His bedside manner was known to have no equal and he was employing it now to the hilt. 'I am a generous man, I hope I may say, and I will always find a natural cause for a death when I can, but a gaping wound in a person's chest does not really give me that option. There must be an inquest into this death.'

'But Barbara . . . well, she would have hated the fuss.'

The door crashed back and the men turned. The man standing there was clearly deep in drink but his wandering eyes focused on the figure on the bed.

'Is that . . . is that *Barbara*?' he wailed.

Percy stepped forward, forgetting the bloodstain on his nightshirt.

The newcomer stepped back, his finger pointing, trembling, at the wizard earl. 'What bloody man is this?' he screamed. 'You've killed my Barbara!' He lurched forward and threw himself across the foot of the bed, weeping.

Marlowe and Faunt looked a question at the doctor. Percy was trying to pull the man off the feet of the love of his life. 'Andrew, for the love of God . . .'

'His sister,' Windham mouthed.

'Ah.' Marlowe was disappointed in a way. Had this been a rival for her affections, at least the case might have been clearer.

'I believe he has been on an . . . assignation . . . in the village.' The doctor's ears were keen and he had overheard that conversation over the frumenty as well.

Faunt looked around. The candles were beginning to gutter and the corpse was not going to tell them anything more. 'I think if we all go somewhere else,' he said, 'it might be as well, my lord, if you take Master Gascoigne to his chamber and call his man if he has one, I would be grateful. And if you would join us in the solar when you have changed out of . . .' he gestured to his own chest and the earl looked down and seemed to see the bloodstain for the first time.

'Who are you, to order me about in my own house, under my own roof?' the earl sputtered.

'I am Nicholas Faunt, late secretary to Sir Francis Walsingham, may he rest in peace. But now, I work for the Queen. So I can order you about whenever and wherever I choose, my lord. Please get dressed and join us in the solar, as soon as is convenient.'

Percy looked at him and flared his nostrils. Did this man

not know that he had lost the only love of his life? But the
Queen's man . . . that made it difficult. He couldn't see the revel
happening now, anyway; Gloriana wasn't prone to visiting houses
where murder might be part of the playing. Even so, it didn't
do to annoy her more than necessary, so he retired, dragging
the weeping Gascoigne with him, with as much dignity as a
man in a bloodstained nightgown could muster.

Tom Sledd joined the little group in the solar and, before the
earl appeared, told them a shortened version of the ghost story.
Faunt nodded throughout – the facts themselves were true
enough, up to the point of the ghost wandering around looking
for a soul to borrow for its broken journey to Heaven. Faunt
and Marlowe had seen all things in Heaven and earth and
some that belonged in between, but the story of the earl's
father's ghost did not ring true. And, even if it did – ghosts
did not kill people with wheel-locks. People killed people with
wheel-locks. The earl seemed to be the most likely candidate,
but Tom and the doctor both swore that he was deeply in love
with Barbara, though Windham conceded this was by no means
rare. Her brother would only lose at her death – he was enjoying
all that Petworth could offer by way of a very pleasant life,
with the obvious addition of the run of the village maidens,
though he made sure swiftly that they were not maidens for
long. Besides, as Marlowe pointed out, he seemed to have a
very strong alibi for the time of the death. Lady Barbara
Gascoigne was an exacting mistress but her little lady's maid
was still prostrate with weeping at her loss; of her place, if
not of her employer, and besides, she would not have been
able to manage a firearm to inflict such a neat and tidy wound.
In short, someone had killed Lady Barbara, and for all they
had been able to find out, they might as well say it was the
shade of the eighth earl and be done. For all the death had
taken place in the house of a peer of the realm, there were
standards. The Lord Lieutenant would call in the coroner who
spoke for Her Majesty, and sixteen of the great and good of
the shire would view the body, decide the deodand and give
their verdict – murder by person or persons unknown.
       All that was by the way, the due process of law that the

state demanded. But it was not enough for Kit Marlowe. Few of the Percy household slept that night and the rumours flew with the pipistrelles from their roosts in the barns and yews. It was the ghost of the dead earl, wandering the lonely night in search of a soul. He, men said, had died by gunshot. How fitting, then, that Lady Barbara should go the same way.

A numb and uncomprehending Andrew Gascoigne sent his man galloping north to tell the family of the tragedy. He watched the horse clatter out into the first breaking of dawn's rays. Birdsong swirled in the wake of the galloping hoofs and he wanted to silence them all – how dare they sing, when Barbara lay dead? He wanted to go back to his sister's chamber, to the girl he had known all his life, to see her sit up, laughing, and tell him it was all a jest. But he could not bear it. It was just a shell that lay on that bed; life, breath and love had flown. There was nothing for Andrew Gascoigne there.

There was everything for Kit Marlowe. He sent away Percy's women, who wanted to strip the girl's body, wash it and prepare it for the grave. Working by candlelight, he paced the room. To his left, near the bed, an oak panel in the wall stood half open. Through it, Marlowe could see the earl's chamber, the tester unslept in, the curtains thrown back. The Queen's man went in, taking stock of what he saw. More shirts and venetians in the presses than Marlowe could wear in a year, the doublets heavy with damasked silk and rich brocade. Books of heavy, polished leather lined the shelves, their contents, in Greek, Latin and Hebrew, arcane and mysterious. Men didn't call this man the wizard earl for nothing. Marlowe smiled; in one corner, he recognized one of the many tomes of his old friend Dr Dee, the Queen's magus. On the table, half finished in the earl's own hand, the semblance of a poem; a sonnet, certainly, but without the greatness that marked Marlowe. He read the words silently at first, and then out loud, the only way to make a poem sing.

> 'The love that loves the light of day alone,
> The eyes that shine and sparkle in the sun,
> If you can break my heart and yet atone,
> Then you will be my soul, my love, my one.'

It needed work. But could there be a clue here? When had Percy written that, and was it about Barbara at all? If so, had she broken the earl's heart and not atoned? Had she rebuffed him, turned him down, and had he killed her in jealous rage? And if the 'eyes' of the sonnet were not Barbara's, but another's, had she discovered the earl's duplicity and did a row between them lead to murder?

Marlowe returned to the scene of the crime. The earl's chamber connected with Barbara's via the secret panel in the wall. Most country houses had such hidden ways, gifts for the Jesuits who prayed privately with Papist families unwilling to break, as their country had long ago, with Rome. He looked at the dead woman's face. It was peaceful, the eyes closed, the lips pursed just a little, as though to deliver a kiss. Hating the moment, he lifted Barbara's shift. There was a bloody hole just below the left breast that would have smashed the lung and heart below it. The blood, congealed now and turning black in the candlelight, had sprayed outward and upward. Gently, he turned her over. There was no wound to her back; the ball was still inside her.

'Anything?' Nicholas Faunt's voice made Marlowe turn and he laid the corpse back in its position.

'Tell me about the lock,' Marlowe said, nodding in the direction of the door. 'You got here first.'

'I did,' Faunt nodded. 'That *was* curious. The door was locked.'

'You broke it?'

Faunt drew his dagger and tossed it in the air. 'Needs must,' he said.

'So, only Percy had access,' Marlowe reasoned, 'through the panel. There's no other way in.'

'Not that I can see.' Faunt was routinely tapping the oak-panelled walls. Nothing gave under his fingers, nothing sounded hollow. The few candles in the room burned straight and true; no draught gave away a hidden room. He shrugged and turned back to Marlowe. 'Looks bad for His Grace.'

'Looks too bad,' Marlowe nodded. 'What do you make of this?' He passed Faunt a miniature portrait which had lain on the cabinet beside the bed.

'Percy,' Faunt squinted at in in the candle flame, carrying

it across to the window to see if the burgeoning dawn could give him a better light. 'It looks like one of Hilliard's.'

'Not one of his best,' Marlowe said. Even men of Hilliard's undoubted talents were presumably allowed the occasional off-day. The wizard earl lay on his side in the painting's foreground, his head supported by the right arm, the left hand holding a lace handkerchief. His gloves lay nearby, together with a book. Behind him, dwarfing the earl, tall trees rose to the sky out of a walled garden and a curious globe hung like a balance from the branches, counter-weighted with a single word.

'Tanti,' Faunt read it, translating in his head. 'So great, so little.'

'Applies to us all, doesn't it,' Marlowe said, half to himself, 'in the scheme of things?'

'No time to get philosophical, Kit,' Faunt said. 'A woman is dead. That intrigued me, though.' He was pointing to a divan in the corner and to a large tabby cat curled up on it, fast asleep.

'Did it?' Marlowe asked. 'Why?'

'The animal was here when we broke in. It hasn't moved.'

Marlowe knew cats. Nine lives they may have, but they were infinitely more magical than that. Many had been the hours he had spent poring over Aristotle at Corpus Christi with Tiberius, the college cat, snoring contentedly in his lap. He crossed to this one and ruffled its fur. The cat lifted its head and yawned at him, whiskers pointing forward and teeth bared momentarily in the candle flame. It extended its front feet and spread its toes, showing its claws as a reminder to touch not the cat. Marlowe stroked its fur back into position and gave it a final pat, at which it tucked its nose back under its flank and went back to sleep.

'The curious case of the cat in the night-time,' Marlowe murmured.

'Does that tell us anything?' Faunt asked. He was a dog man, through and through.

'Of course not,' Marlowe said. 'The animal's probably deaf. The only one who can tell us anything is the heir of the Percys. Shall we?'

NINE

For the umpteenth time, as the great house came to life all around them and the gossip started again, Marlowe told the Earl of Northumberland to focus on what had happened. One of the men in that book-encrusted study was a peer of the realm; the other, a shoemaker's son. But murder had made them equals. Murder was like that.

On their way to talk to Percy, Faunt and Marlowe had visited the earl's armoury. He owned four wheel-locks and none of them had been fired recently. There was no powder residue, no smell of sulphur. If the wizard earl had killed his light o' love, he had either not used one of these guns or he was a wizard indeed. Faunt had stayed behind to make sure. Petworth was, after all, a house of hidden passageways and hollow walls.

'Once more, my lord,' Marlowe said, plumbing depths of patience he hadn't known he had, 'for the record.'

Percy sighed, shuddered and closed his eyes with the effort. All in all, it had been a truly shocking night and no one had slept. 'We had had words, Barbara and I,' he said, looking at the floor, 'and I felt guilty about it. We left the meal early; she did that when . . .' he looked down at his clenched fists in his lap for a moment and a tear splashed onto his cuff. Then, he continued, '. . . when she was in a temper. And she did have a temper, my Barbara, but it was usually over like a summer shower. I left her for a while and when Guiscard was holding forth with his rubbish, I went to her.'

'Via your room?'

'Of course. I always used that door. It saved . . . well, it saved talk.'

Marlowe doubted that the servants had missed much, but this was not the time to say so. 'And you didn't notice whether her door was locked?'

'No. Why should I?'

'Was Lady Barbara in the habit of locking her door?' Marlowe asked.

Percy looked at him. 'As I told you, Master Marlowe, she had a temper. Flounce is what she did. She was furious with me. I'd told her she couldn't take part in the revels for the Queen.'

'There'll be no revels now,' Marlowe assured him. 'It wouldn't be safe.'

'You know it's a conspiracy, don't you?' Percy said. For the first time since he had burst out onto the terrace crying Murder, his face showed some animation.

'What is?'

'Barbara's death, of course. It's six years, almost to the day, since my father was found dead in his cell in the Tower.'

'Uncle Guiscard's ghost story.' Marlowe knew the gist.

Percy could just about manage a smile. 'Not still coming out with that old rubbish, is he?'

'You don't believe it?'

'I believe my father was murdered,' Percy told him. 'Do you know the Tower, Master Marlowe?'

'Parts of it,' the Queen's man said.

'My father was in the Wakefield Tower. Days before his death, Sir Christopher Hatton – may he rot in Hell – appointed a new gaoler, a knave called Bailiff. I am certain that this pizzle killed him, with a lead ball through his heart. Sound familiar? Hatton gave it out as a suicide, though no pistol was found near the body. There was a tract published in Cologne – I have it somewhere – that accused Bailiff and Hatton of the crime.'

'And the Queen?' Marlowe asked.

Percy nodded, looking at the man full in the face for once. 'Of course, the Queen. I am under no illusions, Master Marlowe. When my father was sent to the Tower, it was for the third time. He had been loyal to Her Majesty, but not, I have to admit, consistently.' He got up and crossed to the latticed window, gazing out to the deer herd grazing in the summer morning. 'Our roots are in the north. Berwick, Tynemouth, the Border lands, we controlled the Scots Marches for generations . . . Ever since Hotspur, we have rattled the chains of government, defied kings to their faces. I would beg you to believe that I have no interest in those things. Give me my books, my laboratory, a poet's pen . . .' his voice faltered, '. . . and the woman I love, and I am content.'

Marlowe crossed the room to join him. It was easy to be content in a house like Petworth, with your own land stretching to every horizon, but he forbore to remind the man of that. 'But you don't have the woman you love now, do you? Is that Gloriana's fault too?'

Percy glowered at him. 'You're a cold-hearted bastard, Kit Marlowe,' he growled.

'Somebody has to be, my lord,' he said. 'As the Queen's representative, I will stay until the coroner arrives. Expect more questions from him. Expect another bastard, more cold-hearted than I will ever be this side of the grave. If you'll take my advice, you'll tell him nothing.'

Percy nodded, turning back to the window.

Marlowe half bowed and made for the door. 'One final thing,' he said. 'Who has keys to Lady Barbara's room, my lord?'

Percy spread his arms without turning around. 'No one,' he said. 'Everyone.'

Marlowe waited. Hoy-day, a riddle – that was all he needed.

'All the keys to the house are kept by my steward, Critchley. And all the spares are hanging in the kitchen.'

Steward Critchley was loyalty itself. No, he assured Faunt, no key had ever left his possession. And yes, anyone had access to the spares. The Percys, after all, had nothing to hide; that remark alone made Faunt raise an eyebrow.

'That means,' Faunt told Marlowe, as they put their heads together before the arrival of the coroner, 'that it must be one of the servants. No stranger would know which key was which.'

'All right,' Marlowe said. 'You find me such a servant. According to Tom, she was not an easy lady, except where Sir Henry was concerned, in which case she could make a whore blush. The servants seemed to take it all in their stride, but perhaps one of the more straitlaced ones might have taken offence; but it doesn't seem a shooting offence, even so. And that offended person would need to have a wheel-lock and the skill to load and fire it. They would need to time it perfectly, so no one heard the shot. If you can find me that servant, Nicholas, we can all sleep peacefully in our beds. As it is, we must leave this crime reeking to Heaven for the moment. We have other places to be.'

The meadows lay dumb in the heat as Marlowe's little band saw the spire of Chichester Cathedral. It pointed to Heaven like a finger, the only one of God's houses visible to those in peril on the sea.

Tom Sledd was rather more concerned with those in peril on the land as they rounded a bend in the road and were faced with a huge flock of sheep. The animals just stood there, chewing the grass by the roadside and raising their heads occasionally to stare with vacant, glassy eyes. Sheep didn't bother the Londoner at all. They grazed at will on the Bishop of Winchester's land south of the river and it was almost a daily progress that saw the bell-carrying drovers prodding them over the bridge on their way to slaughter at Smithfield.

No, what bothered Tom Sledd was the rough-looking gang of shepherds forming into what looked suspiciously like a phalanx ahead of their beasts. They bristled with weapons; pitchforks, scythes, sickles and clubs. And one of them had a vicious-looking dog on a tight leash. It was like no sheepdog any of the riders had ever seen; a smooth-coated, liver-coloured, wall-eyed beast with a huge head and jaws, its ears battered and chewed, its tongue lolling – a fighting dog, if ever there was one. The horsemen reined in.

'What's this, then?' Sledd murmured to Marlowe out of the corner of his mouth. 'Welcome to Chichester?'

One of the shepherds almost answered his question. 'Bound for the city, masters?' he asked.

Marlowe and Faunt read the same message into that. The man was proud of his probable birthplace, referring to Chichester as a city, and he knew his place, recognizing good clothes and horses when he saw them. It was the tone of the word 'masters' that caused the pair to exchange glances.

'What's that to you?' Sledd called back. Didn't the oaf

know who he was, that a knighthood hovered in the wings and that Kit Marlowe – yes, *the* Kit Marlowe – carried the Queen's cypher?

'We have business with His Grace the Bishop,' Marlowe glared at his stage manager, who refused to be cowed.

'So, you see,' Sledd went on, 'that means it's no business of yours.'

'That's where you're wrong, pretty boy,' the shepherd growled. 'You're from Lunnon, ain't you, by your accent?'

'What if I am?' It had never occurred to Tom Sledd that he had an accent, having lost it so frequently playing various heroines of the stage.

'We don't like folk from Lunnon.' The shepherd was cradling a pitchfork as if he longed for a chance to use it.

'Show him the cypher, Kit,' Faunt muttered, 'or we'll be here all day.'

'We are here on the Queen's business,' Marlowe said and produced the silver dragon from his purse.

'We know that,' another shepherd shouted. 'And we've seen that gewgaw before. What do you say, Wat, five more for the pig trough?'

There were guffaws and mutterings among the shepherds. Wat summed up the situation. The odd cleric on a donkey, a couple of merchants travelling in ladies' shifts, even two or three of the bishop's lads. But there were five of these travellers, all full grown, three of them certainly armed, the others probably, and the one with the full beard was built like a Sussex shithouse.

'Give us the gewgaw,' a third, younger or more stupid than the rest piped up, 'and we'll let you pass.'

Marlowe urged his horse forward and leaned down to the boy as a few of the sheep began to scatter. 'I *could* give you this,' he said over the saddlebow, 'but since this is the Queen's cypher, I would have committed an act of treason. By accepting it, so would you.' He sat upright again, letting the dragon flash in the sun. 'What does Master Topcliffe do with those who defile the image of the Queen, Nicholas?'

Faunt played along, shaking his head at the contemplation of it. 'Hanging's the kindest part,' he said, smiling at the boy, 'but of course, that's just the beginning. Richard's a master of his art, of course, so he times it all to perfection. Well,' he chuckled, 'you know Topcliffe, Kit, always one to please the crowd. He'll wait until you've turned blue, lad, and the veins are standing out on your neck. Then, he'll cut you down.'

'That's when the fun really begins,' Marlowe took up the tale. 'They'll strap you down to a table and show you the instruments they're about to use.'

An unaccustomed smile broke across the face of Leonard Lyttleburye. 'That's my favourite part,' he rumbled.

'Make *your* weapons look like playthings,' Faunt nodded. 'Having feasted your already bulging eyes on razor-sharp glaives and hooks, old Richard will go to work on your joints. You'd be used to that, though, being shepherds and all. Just four little cuts, one for each limb and there you are, ready for the next bit.'

'But Nicholas,' Marlowe tutted, grinning like a death's head at the nearest shepherd. 'You've missed out the best part of all.'

Faunt slapped his forehead. 'If this wasn't screwed on,' he said. 'Of course, between the hanging and the dismemberment, there's the drawing.'

'That's what we scholars call a euphemism,' Marlowe beamed. He wasn't one to pull rank, but the Chichester welcoming committee had annoyed him. 'Actually, it's disembowelling. Master Topcliffe will use his favourite hook to slice your abdomen and haul out your entrails . . .'

'To be fair, Master Marlowe,' Norfolk chimed in from the rear of the little column, 'I have heard that most people have passed out or died of the pain by then.' He rubbed his chin in thought. 'Though, thinking about it, how do we know? Nobody's ever lived to tell the tale, after all.'

'Good point well made, Master Norfolk,' Faunt said. 'A very good point.' He added his lupine smile to the rest and the shepherd phalanx rocked on its collective heels.

The youngest shepherd had been turning slowly ever greener as the men from London held forth, and he suddenly jack-knifed sideways and vomited all over a sheep. There were growls and groans of disgust.

'So you see,' Marlowe said, 'I'm afraid I cannot let you have this. Of course,' he drew his sword ostentatiously, 'if you'd care to try to take it . . .'

Faunt drew his rapier too. Jack Norfolk slid the schiavona into his fist and watched Leonard Lyttleburye unhook the studded club he carried tied to his saddle. Faced with an array like that, Tom Sledd's solitary knife would have looked rather puny, so he didn't draw it, merely looked daggers at the shepherds.

Marlowe nudged his chestnut with his spurs and all five of them rode on, shepherds and sheep dispersing as they rode.

'Friendly lot,' Sledd muttered to Marlowe. 'What did they mean, they knew we were here on the Queen's business? How come people of the clay like that know Her Majesty's itinerary?'

'We'll have to ask His Grace the Bishop,' Marlowe said. 'I'm sure he'll enlighten us.'

His Grace the Bishop had been enlightening people for years. His Christianity was muscular, especially when he had been Warden of Merton College, Oxford, and many were the young churchmen who still carried the weals on their arses from the powerful right hand – and leather-thonged cat – of Thomas Brickley.

Marlowe's party was ensconced in the Almoner's House, an ancient adjunct to the great cathedral, and their horses were tethered in the stables in the Pallant nearby. It was rather cramped, since Marlowe's stout lad had now become four and Norfolk, Lyttleburye and the less-than-enchanted Tom Sledd all bickered over the single bed under the eaves. Only Marlowe and Faunt had a bed each, as befitted their status as *generosi*.

'*Generosi*, my arse!' Sledd muttered when Marlowe was out of his hearing. 'His old man is a cobbler in Canterbury. If that makes him a gentleman, I'll grow a pair of tits and play the women for real.'

'Now, now,' Jack Norfolk scolded, smilingly, trying to find somewhere to hang his doublet. 'From what I've seen and heard of you two, you'd follow that man through Hellfire.'

Tom Sledd grunted, annoyed all over again because Jack

Norfolk was right. It didn't help that Marlowe had just told
him that the Queen expected no revels in Chichester, merely
a service in the cathedral. Tom could sit this one out.

'When you say "merely a service" . . .' Bishop Brickley
did not care for Kit Marlowe's choice of words. The man was
a scribbler, a writer of plays, an abomination in the eyes of
the Lord. Surely, Her Majesty could do better than *this* to
arrange her Progress?

'Forgive me, Your Grace.' Marlowe half bowed. 'I meant
no disrespect. I was a chorister myself.'

'Were you, indeed?' Brickley narrowed his eyes. He found
it hard to believe that the roisterer before him, all velvet and
lace, had ever attended a service, much less sung in one.
'Where?'

'Canterbury,' Marlowe said. 'In the days of Archbishop
Parker.'

Brickley's eyes narrowed still further. 'Who was Master
of the Music?'

'Master Bull.' Marlowe's eyes glinted with the memory of
the merry dance he and his fellows had led that well-meaning
man.

'Tell me, Master Marlowe,' the bishop circled his man in
the room over the chapterhouse, 'can you still carry a tune
in a bucket?'

Marlowe looked up at the saint in the window, who looked
enigmatically back. It was hard to think of anything that
sounded right without a few trebles and a rumbling bass.
Catches would work, but he didn't think this was the right
setting. In the end, he decided and cleared his throat, then
sang, 'My soul doth magnify the Lord, and my spirit hath
rejoiced in God my Saviour. For He hath regarded, the lowli-
ness of His handmaiden.' As the golden notes of Byrd and
Tallis rolled out, he tried to keep his mind off the constant
conundrum with which the choristers had badgered Thomas
Bull; why were they singing a song a lady is singing to God?
If they could sing this song, Master Bull, why can't they have
girls in the choir? This could bring the organ master to his
knees in frustration and Marlowe's voice had a smile in it as
he brought the music to a gentle close.

For a moment, there appeared to be a tear in the old man's eye, but he sniffed and brushed it away. 'Very well,' he said, a little converted by Marlowe's performance. 'Very well.'

'Tell me,' Marlowe crossed the room to him, 'about the shepherds.'

'Shepherds?' Brickley repeated.

'We met some on our way into the town . . . er . . . city.'

'From the north?' Brickley gripped the man's sleeve. He suddenly looked greyer. And older. He was already a shadow of the warden of Merton.

'The north-west, yes.'

'Damn!' The bishop hissed, slamming down a prayer book so that the dust jumped on his sideboard. 'So we're surrounded.'

'Surrounded?' Marlowe echoed. Sheep could give that impression sometimes, probably because they were so notoriously hard to count, but it seemed a little extreme a reaction.

'Tell me, these men,' the bishop closed to him again and grabbed a handful of velvet. 'Did you catch a name at all? What did they say?'

'One was called Wat,' Marlowe remembered, gently disengaging the bishop's clutching hand. 'He appeared to be their leader.'

'Ah, that's just a front.' The bishop was clearly agitated, pacing the floor, his skirts flying. 'The man's a vegetable. No, Simeon's behind this – you mark my words.'

'Your Grace . . .' Marlowe frowned. One moment he had been talking about a service for the Queen in the cathedral and now he was whispering like a conspirator with a frightened old man.

'You haven't told me what they said,' Brickley interrupted him.

'They seemed to know we were coming.'

'Really? What makes you think that?'

'I showed them the Queen's cypher and they said they'd seen that before.'

Brickley was nodding slowly. 'So they have,' he muttered, 'so they have.' He turned suddenly and poured himself a large claret. 'Drink?' he offered.

Marlowe shook his head. 'What's going on?' he asked. 'In the interests of the Queen's safety . . .'

'Yes, yes, of course.' The churchman looked at Marlowe and then into the middle distance above his head. The same impassive saint met his gaze. 'You know, Master Marlowe, I had dreams of the See of Canterbury, once. Thomas Cantuar . . . still sounds good.' He suddenly frowned. 'Perhaps not, though, in the case of Becket.' He crossed to the latticed window, cradling his cup of wine as he went. 'Look out here,' he said. 'What do you see?'

Marlowe joined him at the window. It was well and truly dark by now, a series of torches flickering in the night breeze around the buttercross. 'The heart of Chichester,' the playwright encapsulated it.

'Unbeliever!' Brickley hissed, speaking, all unaware, nothing but the truth. '*This* is the heart of Chichester.' He flung his arms around so that some of the claret spattered over the wall. '*I* am the heart of Chichester.' He looked out of the window again. 'What you see there is the centre of the cross, its four arms opening to the four quarters of the world.'

Marlowe rather liked that. Perhaps he could squeeze it into *The Massacre at Paris*, still reeling in his brain.

'Look again,' Brickley told him, 'at the foot of the buttercross.'

'Two men,' Marlowe murmured. 'Sitting.'

'Waiting,' Brickley nodded, standing alongside him.

'For what?' Marlowe asked. 'Surely, the buttercross is where you could meet all of Christendom if you waited long enough.'

Brickley looked at him. 'Doomsday,' he said solemnly.

'Aren't we all?' Marlowe smiled.

'I'm not talking figuratively,' Brickley said. 'In this world, not in preparation for the next. Though it might add up to the same thing.'

'You've lost me,' Marlowe said.

'Doomsday is what Simeon calls it,' the bishop told him. 'A day of rage, a day of revenge. Those two out there are spies.'

Marlowe knew a thing or two about spying and couldn't help wondering how Sir Francis Walsingham would have dealt with two of his men who carried out their work by sitting on the steps of the buttercross in the middle of the market place. 'Really?' He raised an eyebrow. 'Everywhere, aren't they?'

'They are,' Brickley growled. 'And all because they cannot accept change. It's for the best. Believe me, in the long term, it's for the best. Look, there, now.'

Marlowe followed the man's pointing finger. The two men who had been sitting, heads together, at the buttercross got up, one moving north along one street, the other south. Two other men, halberds at the slope, were strolling towards them, swinging a horn lantern.

'That's the Watch. They've orders to move them on. Anybody suspicious. But as soon as they've turned their backs, the bastards are back again. You'll see. There'll be another at the campanile and at least one more at each of the gates.'

'Waiting for Doomsday?' Marlowe pitched his voice low and calm; he knew paranoia when he saw it.

'Those oafs who stopped you on the road. Did they ask you where you were from?'

'They didn't have to. My man, Tom Sledd, has a London accent. They picked that up straight away.'

'Simeon's taught them well,' Brickley murmured, his eyes wild and bulging. 'I tell you, it's terrifying.'

'I will say again, Your Grace,' Marlowe rounded on the man, 'in the interests of the Queen's safety, I need to know what you are talking about. Insinuations and hints are not enough.'

Thomas Brickley looked from right to left. They were alone. Or they *appeared* to be alone. He crossed the room suddenly and hauled open the studded door. He put out his head and looked down the passageway in both directions. There was no one there. He closed the door again and went back to Marlowe. 'Enclosures,' he whispered.

'Enclosures?' Marlowe wasn't afraid of the word and said it out loud.

'Ssh! Good God, man,' Brickley hissed. 'Why not shout it from the rooftops?' He did his best to calm himself. 'You will not be surprised to know that, as bishop, I own a considerable parcel of land in these parts.'

Marlowe was not surprised. After the Queen, the Church of England owned most land in the country. 'I'm having it enclosed, turned to crop-growing. It will provide food for my flock . . .'

Marlowe understood at once. 'But it will deprive the shepherds of their flock,' he pointed out.

'Precisely.' The bishop seemed unrepentant. 'There's no reasoning with them, of course. They cannot, it seems, understand that arable farming is the way ahead. Good God, Marlowe, we've found a New World; we've even mapped the heavens, if that is not too much of a heresy. These morons are still drowning in the medieval shit their grandfathers wallowed in. Enclosure will increase their food, their health, their strength . . .'

Marlowe could not help himself. 'Your wealth,' he added.

Brickley stopped in mid-sentence. 'Yes, well, there it is. You're a perceptive little sub-Master of the Revels, aren't you? For a playwright, I mean.'

Marlowe had known some pretty unpleasant churchmen in his time – more unpleasant than otherwise, if truth be told and the accounting was accurate. But this man really did take the cake.

'I won't deny that the revenue from my new fields will increase. But I have to bear the costs, damn it – the commissioners, with their chains and rods, the court fees . . . Do you know how much it costs to push through an Act of Parliament?'

Marlowe smiled. 'So that's how they thought they knew us,' he said. 'Men from London carrying the Queen's cypher. They thought we were commissioners, come to rob them of their livelihood.'

'Precisely.' The bishop was glad he was finally understood.

'Can't the mayor do something?' Marlowe asked. 'Other than endlessly moving on undesirables after dark?'

'Caldecote? The man's a mouse. And an imbecile one at that. It's too big for him.'

'The Lord Lieutenant, then? The Queen's man?'

'Sackville? The last comment he was heard to make about me was that if I was afire, he wouldn't piss on me to put it out. I'm not holding my breath.'

'But if it's a matter of the Queen's peace,' Marlowe said, 'personal differences must surely be set aside.' Anyone listening to the projectioner would think that he had never stepped from the primrose path in his life.

Brickley scoffed. 'In a perfect world,' he said, 'but Simeon is too clever for Sackville, Earl of Dorset or not. The man's a lawyer.'

'A lawyer?'

'Gray's Inn. Some well-meaning member of my flock went to London to petition him. And if I ever find out who it was . . .' The bishop suddenly seemed to realize how he must sound. '. . . I will of course take him gently aside and explain to him, in God's name, the error of his ways. But it is a fact, Marlowe, that Simeon is not normal. He's as oily as a snake and is quite prepared to use violence.'

'First, kill all the lawyers,' Marlowe murmured, 'before they kill you.'

'What?'

'Just a line all we playwrights use eventually,' he said with a smile. 'So, Simeon plans what . . . a rebellion?'

Brickley nodded, watching as the two shadowy figures crept back to the buttercross, looking up at him in his window before disappearing into the pool of inky black at its foot. 'Doomsday,' he whispered, 'and I don't know when that is.'

TEN

'A rebellion?' Jack Norfolk had only become one of Marlowe's little band by default, but keeping things from him proved impossible. After all, Tom Sledd was of the company. Faunt and Marlowe were trained in the world of silence; it fitted them both like a glove. Leonard Lyttleburye said virtually nothing about anything, so all was well there. But Tom Sledd never met a secret he didn't want to roar from the rooftops, together with clarions and drums as though announcing a play. He called that 'telling no one'.

'Tom mentioned it,' Norfolk said by way of explanation to Marlowe's enquiring look.

'We've had them before.' Faunt was helping himself to a pancake and honey in the bishop's buttery. Clerks came and went with boxes of parchment, builders clattered past with ladders and buckets. There was always work to do in a cathedral like Chichester; after all, the thing had been there since the days of the Conqueror and it was looking a little work-worn in places.

'Not round here, they haven't.' Marlowe buttered his bread; there was nothing quite like a manchet loaf, still warm in the crust, to start the day. 'Not in our lifetime, at any rate. Brickley's panicking. He's already shipped Mrs Brickley out – visiting relatives in the country, if anybody asks.'

'Any ideas, Kit?' Faunt popped the last of his pancake into his mouth and paused to wait for the answer before embarking on the ale.

Marlowe closed to him. Clerks and builders might not be all they seemed. 'I'd like you to see a man called Caldecote,' he murmured in Faunt's ear. 'He's the mayor. Not very effectual, according to the bishop, but perhaps when he's reminded who's coming to town in a few weeks, he'll grow himself a spine.'

Faunt nodded. He'd put the fear of God into minor officials before. 'And you?'

'I'm going to have a word with this Beelzebub lawyer who has Brickley quaking in his cassock.'

'Not a place to go alone, Kit,' Faunt advised. 'Take Lyttleburye.'

All eyes swivelled to the man obliviously cramming his mouth with pancakes and bread.

'No,' Marlowe said. 'Jack, fancy a stroll?'

Norfolk smiled. 'Seen one rebel, seen them all,' he shrugged.

It was already hot in the large house along the Priory Lane, mangy dogs trying to find somewhere to lie in the shade. A little clerk, scratching himself through his fustian, was trying to make his quill work on the sluggish parchment. The ink had gone thick and sludgy and in that respect was almost an equal for his brain. A drowsy fly ricocheted from the window-pane to the fireplace and back again. The whole house seemed half asleep and happy to be so.

'Master Simeon's residence?' Marlowe swept in, the hem of his swirling Colleyweston cloak knocking over the clerk's inkwell.

'You can't just barge in,' the clerk blurted out, jumping to his feet and trying to stem the glutinous tide of ink over his papers.

'Yes, I can.' Marlowe called back to him.

'Do you have an appointment?' the little man shrilled.

'No,' Norfolk told him flatly, and followed Marlowe into the inner sanctum.

John Simeon wore the unfashionable haircut of the Lower Rhine, a fringe of dark hair above his eyebrows. His doublet alone could have fed a shepherd and his family for a year.

'Oh dear,' he frowned at the pair. 'You've upset William as well as his ink. The poor lamb won't be fit to live with all day.'

'Not our concern, I'm afraid,' Marlowe said.

'What is?' Simeon put down his quill and rested with both hands on the table.

'Enclosures,' Marlowe told him. 'Specifically, the bishop's.'

'Ah, yes,' Simeon smiled. Brickley had been right about

him. Oily indeed. Then the smile turned to a frown. 'I know you, don't I?' he asked. 'Aren't you Christopher Marlowe?'

'I am,' the playwright admitted.

'Yes. Yes. Machiavel.'

'Some men call me that,' Marlowe nodded.

'I saw you at the Rose . . . God, it must be two years ago. Your *Tamburlaine*. Masterly. Masterly.' Simeon got up. 'Allow me to shake your hand, sir.'

Marlowe kept his hands at his side. 'Flattered though I am, Master Simeon, this is not a social call.'

'No.' The lawyer's smile vanished, as if snuffed out. 'No, I don't suppose it is. Old Brickley been bending your ear, has he?' He gestured to the seats and Norfolk was about to accept when Marlowe cut him short.

'Thank you,' he said. 'We would rather stand.'

Simeon thought for a moment. 'Tell me,' he said, 'what a playwright is doing interceding for a bishop. A playwright who, if the gossip is to be believed, has about as much in common with the Church of England as white knight to black pawn.'

'You shouldn't believe gossip, Master Simeon,' Marlowe said, folding his arms. 'The gossip around Chichester, for instance, is that you intend to lead a rebellion against the bishop.'

'I do?' Simeon raised an eyebrow.

'And a rebellion against the bishop is a rebellion against the Queen, whose man, like it or not, Thomas Brickley is. That's where I come in.'

'You do?'

'I do. I am here from the office of the Master of the Revels to arrange the Queen's Progress. And I appear to have stumbled into a war.'

'Oh, I think war is too strong a word,' the lawyer smiled.

'I can fence all day with you, sir,' Marlowe told him. 'We both of us use words as playthings in our different ways. But this is not the wooden O. Nor is it the court of chancery. Time for plain speaking.'

'Very well.' Simeon leaned back in his chair, rocking back and forth on the back legs which cracked in protest. 'You first.'

Marlowe lifted a heavy purse from his belt and dropped it onto Simeon's table.

The lawyer didn't move, but liked the sound of the thud. 'Weighty.'

'We both know that every man has his price,' Marlowe said. 'What's yours?'

'Well, now,' Simeon smiled and let the front legs of his chair crash back to the floor. He reached forward and pulled the purse towards him, slowly undoing the straps and revealing the silver coins inside. 'I'll need to have William work on my expenses. I doubt His Grace could afford me and this,' he pushed the purse back towards Marlowe, 'would barely cover the cost of my clerk's ink.'

'You don't come cheap.' Jack Norfolk spoke for the first time.

'That's right,' Simeon nodded. 'I don't.'

There was a silence.

'You've spoken plainly,' the lawyer said. 'There's an eloquence about money that appeals to me. Let me answer you with a riddle. "When Adam delved and Eve span, who was then the gentleman?"'

'John Ball's sermon,' Marlowe said. 'The Peasants' Revolt.'

'You know it,' Simeon laughed. 'I am impressed, Master Marlowe, even for the author of *Tamburlaine*. Would you like to explain it, for the benefit of your man here?'

Marlowe looked at Norfolk. He knew nothing of the man's background, but he had brought him into this and it was as well that he knew all the facts. 'John Ball,' he began, 'was a leader of the Peasants' Revolt.'

'They marched from Blackheath,' Norfolk chimed in, with a straight face, 'on London, complaining about the cost of foreign wars, the Statute of Labourers. When was that? Over a century ago.'

The lawyer nodded his respect to Norfolk, who didn't meet his eye. Marlowe was neither impressed nor surprised; for all he knew, Norfolk could be Master of a University somewhere, travelling incognito. Had he had to put coin on the table to support his thoughts, it would have gone on the section that said 'brought up quite genteelly in straitened circumstances and thrown on the world when grown enough to fend for himself.' And just knowing a little history didn't change that view.

'Ball's message was simple,' Simeon said. 'In the days of the Creation, there were no lords and masters, no serfs and slaves.'

'Look around you, lawyer,' Marlowe said. 'There are no serfs or slaves now, either. Ball was a madman, but his wishes have come to pass.'

'Spare me the civics lesson,' Simeon sneered. 'We have lords and masters aplenty, children who die in rat-infested hovels while the bishop and his ilk dine on roast swan and pick their teeth with pure gold.'

'So what do you intend to do?' Marlowe asked.

'Right a wrong,' Simeon said. 'Strike a blow for justice. Today, the bishop's enclosures in Chichester. Tomorrow . . . who knows?'

'Ball's rebellion failed,' Norfolk said, 'if memory serves. His rabble pulled down the palace of the Savoy and then ran into the immoveable wall that was the government of England.'

'Well, well,' Simeon smiled, 'you *do* know your history. John Ball's rebellion failed because he was a dreamer, with visions of the Second Coming and help from the Lord.'

'And that's not you at all, is it, Master Simeon?' Marlowe said.

'No, it's not; any more than it is you, Master Machiavel. "Moses was but a conjuror – and Christ and John the Baptist were bedfellows." Sound familiar?'

Marlowe's face showed no emotion at all. 'You can quote *Tamburlaine* all you like,' he said, 'and Barabas too. Even Dr Faustus, if you find a theatre troupe brave enough to put it on. But don't *mis*quote me, Master Simeon, I beg of you.'

'You didn't say those things?'

'Never.'

'But you believe them.' Simeon would not let it go. 'You and I, Master Marlowe, we're men of the world. I've called what's coming to Chichester Doomsday because of the superstitious simplicity of the oafs for whom I speak. We know there's no such thing, no God to wreak his vengeance. Only man. Weak, corrupt, vengeful.' He stood up. 'The bishop's days are numbered,' he said, and he threw the purse at Marlowe who caught it expertly. 'Now, get out.'

The question was – who to send? Neither Tom Sledd nor Jack Norfolk had the necessary gravitas to make enquiries in the Inns of Court – they wouldn't get past the gates. Nicholas Faunt was his own man and went his own way; Marlowe couldn't send him. Neither could he go himself, with the Queen's cypher as his passport. That left Leonard Lyttleburye. True, he was an oaf, given to strange non-sequiturs in his speech and his reason; but he *was* Robert Cecil's man and that would have to be enough. Accordingly, he trotted out later that day, bound for London with instructions to find whatever dirt he could on John Simeon.

'Pickering,' the bishop said after a moment's reflection. 'Hugh Pickering.'

'Who's he?'

'The man who would have engaged Simeon,' Brickley threw his arms wide. 'Wasn't that what you asked?'

'I mean, what is the man's status, Your Grace,' Marlowe said.

'Oh, I see, well, he's the foremost landowner around here, after me, of course. We've never seen eye to eye. He had his own creature lined up for my job before I got it. That put his nose out of joint and it's been downhill ever since then. Why?'

Marlowe thought for a moment. 'John Simeon is the means to an end,' he said. 'He knows he can't beat you legally over enclosures, so he's resorted to threats. I couldn't buy him off this morning.'

'So, what do you propose?'

'We buy the man who bought him,' Marlowe said, getting up and crossing to the door. 'Where can I find Hugh Pickering?'

The geese honked at him as he cantered over the salt marshes, his horse's hoofs splashing and spraying as he rode. To his left, the sea glittered in the morning sun and the fishing boats bobbed at anchor. The gulls wheeled in the cloudless blue and

Marlowe told his horse, the birds and the sky, 'It's a glorious day. Watch Hugh Pickering spoil it.'

The manor of Rymans lay squat and low on the edge of the harbour, its outer walls crumbled now from the days of the Roses when Squire Ryman had fortified the place against the Yorkists. Sir Hugh Pickering, its current owner, clearly had no interest in old wars – perhaps he just enjoyed creating new ones. He sat on the edge of the knot garden watching a group of children letting loose their goose-feathered arrows into straw targets.

'Good shot, Peter!' he shouted, passing Marlowe a goblet of excellent claret.

The little boy in his velvet turned and half bowed. 'Thank you, Grandfather,' he called.

'Peter,' Pickering smiled at Marlowe. 'My eldest grandson. Do you have children, Master Marlowe?'

'No, Sir Hugh, except those that tumble from my quill.'

'Ah, the theatre, yes. It's all the craze now in London, I hear. Don't get there much myself. Perhaps, one day, we'll have a theatre of our own, right here in Chichester, eh? What do you think?'

'I'd be proud to write for it,' Marlowe smiled.

'Yes, yes. Full back, Peter, right back to your ear – that's a good lad.' Hugh Pickering was greying now but his eyes were bright and his senses sharp. 'But you didn't come to talk about drama. Or to watch my grandchildren going through their paces.'

'John Simeon,' Marlowe said. The name fell like lead through the golden air and Pickering took a while to answer.

'Ah,' he said at last and put his goblet down. It was warm and mellow in the knot garden and the scent of lavender wafted in the air. 'Not a social call, then?'

'I carry the Queen's writ, Sir Hugh,' Marlowe explained. 'It is not for me to take sides, but I have to consider the safety of Her Majesty.'

'Look there,' Pickering pointed to the children. Little Peter was all of seven and, if truth be told, the bow was too big for him; but he refused to be beaten and braced his back anew as the gut slapped his arm and the shaft hissed through

the air. There was a thud as the straw bounced. 'There goes
another of the Queen's enemies,' the old man said. 'In this
corner of England, Marlowe, we follow the Queen's edict.
My grandchildren practise daily with their bows, as my
children did before them. Look yonder,' he pointed out across
the low levels of the marshes to where the sea rippled and
swayed. 'Spain? France? God knows who can mount an
armada against us, and Rymans will be the first place they'll
come. I don't know how long we can hold them, but no one
can say the Pickerings won't be ready; that the Pickerings
aren't loyal.'

'Forgive me, Sir Hugh,' Marlowe said. 'From the look of
the manor house, I would have said that yours was an abode
of peace, not war.'

'Lady Pickering,' Pickering muttered. 'Agnes won't have a
weapon in the house. She tolerates the butts because she sees
archery as a sport.' He leaned in to Marlowe, whispering. 'Agnes
is of the Puritan persuasion,' he hissed. 'I have to tread
carefully.'

'I see,' Marlowe nodded. A man prepared to mount a
rebellion who was afraid of his wife? It didn't make sense.
'But the enclosure issue . . .'

'Ah, that's the shepherds,' Pickering assured him.

'The shepherds?' Marlowe smiled wryly. 'In my experience,
they are the mildest of men, despite a handful I met on the road
the other day. Give a shepherd fat lambs and good pasture, clear
water and a lockram shirt and he's content.'

'And if he hasn't got those things?'

'Loses his land, you mean?'

Pickering nodded. 'Loses his land, his livelihood. What if the
clear water isn't his own? What if the good pasture becomes
the bishop's? What price his fat lambs then? They'll belong to
Thomas Brickley, may he rot in Hell.'

'His Grace intends to build enclosures for arable land,
Sir Hugh,' Marlowe told him, 'for the benefit of all.'

'Master Marlowe,' Pickering laughed aloud. 'What court
did you say you were from? His Grace will take the shepherds'
lands because they cannot prove, legally, that it is theirs.
Arable land, my arse! He won't plant a pea or bean. The

money's in wool and the bishop knows it. Take my word for it, that man gives Christianity a bad name.'

'So you sent for Simeon?'

'I?'

'There's bad blood between you and the bishop, Sir Hugh. Will you deny it?'

'Not at all.' Pickering poured more wine for them both as the arrows flew and laughter trilled from the field. 'Now, Peter, your sister's not as big as you. Play the gentleman, sir, and help her.'

'Yes, Grandfather,' the boy called back, shaking his head at the girl's incompetence.

'Brickley and I go back a long way,' Pickering said. 'I knew what he was up to and I was all for going to law to stop him. Before I could, however, John Simeon turned up; like manna from Heaven, really.'

'To take the matter before the courts?'

'That was my intention, yes. But he, I believe, had other ideas.'

'Rebellion,' Marlowe said flatly.

'Oh, come now, Marlowe,' Pickering chuckled, his little eyes dancing in the sun. 'An exaggeration, surely?'

But Marlowe wasn't chuckling. He wasn't even smiling. 'I wish it were, sir,' he said. He was about to get round to that most ticklish of subjects, a bribe, when there were shouts and the thud of horses' hoofs from the gateway that led to the sea, and all eyes turned that way. Tom Sledd was galloping Hell for leather up from the marshes, his horse flecked with foam.

'Kit! Kit!' he was shouting. 'It's started. You'd better come.'

It was noon as Marlowe and Sledd clattered into the Pallant; the cathedral bells were calling, angry and wild, as panicky ringers hauled at the ropes, watching their backs as they did so. At the south gate, the pair had cantered through a cordon of armed men, scattering them with the speed and momentum of their ride. Curses and spit had followed them, but their backs were broad and they'd both known worse at the Rose any afternoon of the week.

Nicholas Faunt was standing with the bishop on the leads

of the cathedral roof, looking down at the circus below. The buttercross was surrounded by a mob of lockram-smocked shepherds, scythes and billhooks flashing in the sun.

'We've locked the doors, Marlowe,' Brickley said. 'I don't know what else to do.'

Marlowe looked at the man, a jabbering wreck now that his flock had come to him in such numbers. Had the cathedral *ever* been that full? 'You could give them their land back,' the Queen's man said, 'in the interests of Christian charity. In the interests of staying alive.'

'I haven't taken their land,' Brickley assured him. 'Not yet.'

'Then tear up your petition,' Marlowe said. 'Do it here. Now. As Pontius Pilate washed his hands of Christ's blood, you must do the same with your pilfering parchment.'

'Pilfering?' Brickley snapped at him. 'You've changed your tune. I am a bishop of the Church of England.'

Marlowe faced him squarely. 'If you don't use your sense, Your Grace, you will be a *late* bishop of the Church of England. Nicholas, how goes it?'

'They started massing soon after dawn,' Faunt told him. 'I sent Norfolk to check the town's defences. All the gates are sealed, except . . .'

'The one Tom and I rode through, yes. And I suspect there was method in that little piece of madness. They could have stopped us. How many, would you say?'

'I counted above two hundred in the centre here. More on the town walls and gates.'

'My God, my God,' Brickley muttered, crossing himself distractedly when he wasn't wringing his hands. 'What can we do?'

'Without the Earl of Dorset and his trained bands,' Faunt shrugged, 'not a lot, Your Grace. There's one good thing.'

'There is?' Tom Sledd couldn't see it.

'They've got no artillery.'

Will Shaxsper couldn't have written a worse line for one of his efforts at the Rose. Nor could his timing have been as bad. As if on cue, there was a guttural roar from the mob and men were hauling a cannon into position, surging through the throng below the cathedral.

Brickley had gone white.

'That's a culverin,' Faunt told him casually. 'It weighs four thousand five hundred pounds and has a bore of five inches. It fires a seventeen-pound ball, Your Grace, and it will make matchwood of your doors here below. It won't do your masonry much good either.'

'Where, in the name of God, did they get that?'

'The Greenwich arsenal, originally,' Faunt told him. 'That's where they make them. Since then, only God knows.'

'Brickley!' A voice rang out from the shouting, shifting mob. 'Thomas Brickley!'

All four men on the leads leaned over and looked down. John Simeon, in his crimson velvet, stood foursquare, facing the great doors, the cannon's mouth beside him and dangerous-looking armed men at his back.

'What do you want, Simeon?' Marlowe threw back.

'That snivelling wretch hiding at your elbow,' the lawyer called back.

'I think he must mean you, Your Grace,' Faunt smiled and he hauled the bishop front and centre.

'This is an outrage,' Brickley found his voice, a hundred feet above his murderous flock. 'You are desecrating God's house!'

'Drop your petition, Bishop,' Simeon called. It seemed an eminently sensible solution to all of the men jostling on the ground and most of them on the cathedral roof.

'And if I do?' Brickley asked.

'Then we'll walk away,' Simeon said. 'Having lightened your load of the cathedral plate, of course.'

There were roars of approval and much hilarity among the mob.

Brickley spun to Marlowe and Faunt. 'This is intolerable,' he spat. 'The enclosures are one thing, but stealing God's artefacts . . .'

'It's the way of rebels, Master Bishop,' Faunt said. The 'Your Grace' status seemed to have slipped.

'Wat Tyler, Thomas Wyatt,' Marlowe listed just two of them and then added a third. 'The revolt of the North; however noble the cause, there'll be those who are only there for the loot and the beer.'

Brickley hesitated. His life was flashing before him and suddenly a few thousand sheep didn't seem all that important.

'If I relent on the enclosures,' he shouted, 'will you disperse and leave the cathedral alone?'

'Gottlieb,' Simeon shouted to a man with a linstock in his hand. The gunner had lit the fuse and two others were ramming a cannonball into the culverin's mouth.

'Ears!' Simeon roared and the gunner touched his flame to the powder. There were sparks and a hiss and those nearest the gun scattered, their hands over their heads. There was a plopping sound, barely audible beyond the buttercross, as a handful of earth landed on the cannon's touchhole and the flame died.

Marlowe saw him first. Jack Norfolk had come out of nowhere, in the rough lockram of a shepherd, and a fistful of soil deftly dropped had stifled the gun. At a signal from Simeon, calloused hands grabbed him and hauled him to the ground. He disappeared under their kicks and curses.

On the roof, Bishop Brickley felt Marlowe's dagger blade nick his throat. 'Simeon!' the playwright bellowed. 'Call your dogs off.'

The lawyer snapped his fingers and the crowd pulled back, a dishevelled Norfolk lying battered and dusty on the ground. Marlowe raised his hand an inch or two and the bishop's head rested at an impossible angle. 'Now, Your Grace. You have a choice. Either you tear up the enclosure petition now or Faunt and I will throw you to them – give them someone worthier to tear apart.'

'Or kick to death,' Faunt murmured, 'whichever you prefer.'

For an instant, Brickley's jaw flexed and his eyelids flickered, then he nodded and Marlowe let the blade drop.

'I renounce my claim,' the bishop shouted so that all around the buttercross could hear him. 'I will not petition parliament for your lands. The lands will be yours . . .' he glanced at Marlowe, who nodded, 'and your heirs, in all perpetuity.'

The blade came level again. 'So help me God,' Marlowe growled.

'So help me God!' Brickley almost screamed.

There were roars of delight from the mob. They hugged

each other, laughing and crying, dancing around the buttercross as the ale flowed and monsters became men again, as monsters will, given the right circumstances.

'Tell him,' Marlowe muttered. 'Tell Simeon he can have his silver too, but he must come to the Lady Chapel, alone, to get it.'

'Never!' Brickley felt braver now that the cannon was being hauled away. He felt the ground disappear beneath his feet as Marlowe and Faunt took an arm each and hoisted him onto the wall. He was screaming hysterically. 'The silver,' he yelled, feeling the breeze of one hundred feet and more whistle around his knees. 'You can have the plate, too.'

The crowd roared again, some of them turning to march on the cathedral, but Simeon held them back. 'We've got what we came for, lads,' he said. 'Mustn't be greedy.' He looked up at the turrets overhead and doffed an imaginary cap. 'Master Marlowe.' He bowed. 'It's been a pleasure working with you.'

'If I see you again, Simeon,' Marlowe called, 'the pleasure will be all mine.'

The bishop, still pale, still quaking, gripped the stonework as if it would crumble any instant. 'Damn you, Marlowe,' he muttered, his face a livid mask of anger.

'I've been damned by the Church before,' Marlowe said. 'Now get below and sort out the enclosure paperwork. I'll be checking it later. Tom,' he motioned Sledd to his side, 'see that the bishop finds his own chapterhouse, will you, then get Jack Norfolk in. He'll probably need an apothecary.' He glanced down to where the hero of the hour – once again – was limping his way towards the cathedral, jostled by the peasants he passed.

'Did you catch that gunner's name?' Faunt murmured to Marlowe when they'd gone.

'Gottlieb,' Marlowe nodded. 'German.'

'So was the gun. It no more came from Greenwich than you do. Now, tell me, Kit Marlowe, how a handful of shepherds have access to foreign ordnance and professionals to fire it.'

'That all depends,' Marlowe said, only now sheathing his dagger, 'on who John Simeon is *really* working for.'

*   *   *

For a man who had looked death in the face, Jack Norfolk had come through miraculously unscathed. He had a split lip and a bruised temple and, in the scuffle, he had twisted his ankle. Other than that, he seemed well. Even so he was more than ready for his bed in the almoner's house that night, wedged next to Tom Sledd though he was. The mayor's Watch patrolled the buttercross, their torches flickering in the darkness. But there was no one to move on. The shadowy figures who had been drifting through Chichester's streets for weeks now were in their hovels in the countryside, nestling with their wives and soothing their fractious babies. Some slept with their flocks, having long ago given up the notion the Bible had given them, that one night, they might catch a glimpse of an angel of the Lord, clothed in glory.

So Jack Norfolk did not hear Leonard Lyttleburye's horse clatter over the ancient flagstones not long after cockshut. He didn't hear him climb the creaking stairs to Marlowe's apartments and he certainly didn't hear the brief, whispered conversation that followed.

'Waste of time, Master Marlowe,' the giant straightened until he felt his back click after so long in the saddle. 'I checked every Inn of Court, under Sir Robert's sign, of course. The odd thing is that nobody has ever heard of anyone called John Simeon. Many people called John, but none with a name even close to Simeon; the closest match was John Salmon, but he's dead. There was a Simeon Levelle and a Simon Smythe . . .'

Marlowe was shaking his head. 'You did well, Leonard,' he said. 'It isn't odd that he isn't on the lists. No, it isn't odd at all.'

ELEVEN

The travellers slept late the following morning; in one way or another, they had all had an eventful night. Norfolk, black and blue, lay as still as possible for as long as possible once he awoke, trying each limb separately, to see if any of them might still be in working order. Lyttleburye, the stable lad still there beneath the many extra pounds of flesh, had not suffered unduly from his ride, although he would prefer not to be in the saddle for a day or so, given his own choice in the matter. Tom Sledd had slept the sleep of a stage manager without a bad deed on his conscience. Marlowe and Faunt had both lain awake, plotting their plots and hoping they would see the morning at least one step ahead of any miscreant; and indeed, of each other.

Leonard Lyttleburye was out of luck. With the breakfast platters came a message, sent by galloper from London. Sir Robert Cecil would be pleased to see Christopher Marlowe in his office at his earliest convenience. The final words were struck through with an angry quill. Sir Robert Cecil would in fact be pleased to see Christopher Marlowe in his office as fast as a fast horse could carry him; and if this did not happen, Sir Robert Cecil would not be pleased at all. This was also struck through and at the bottom of the by now rather ravaged looking parchment, was the legend, 'Marlowe. Get here now. C.'

Marlowe read his missive with surprising calm. Most people, summoned by Robert Cecil, were on a horse and down the road while the dropped paper was still twirling in the air, but Marlowe was made of sterner stuff. He carefully buttered his bread and added honey, not too much, so it all ran off, not too little so that it disappeared, but just the right amount; he would be needing his strength. He finished his ale, and only when he had finished did he lean back and address his little band.

'I have had a request . . .' he glanced again at the piece of
parchment folded neatly beside his plate, '. . . a summons, I
suppose I should more rightly call it, from Sir Robert. It may
be that he wants to congratulate me on a job well done.'

He looked around the table and noticed that everyone was
smiling except Leonard Lyttleburye, who had more reason
than most to beware of the wrath of Robert Cecil. His knee
sometimes still gave him gyp in cold weather.

'But whatever the reason, I need to go back to London and
I suggest you all do as well.' He looked at Norfolk. 'Sorry,
Jack, that was thoughtless – I know you are not a city boy. I
meant, go wherever you call home. Shall we agree to meet
in . . .' he looked from face to face, '. . . four days, in the
Slaughtered Lamb, at eight of the clock? If anyone doesn't
turn up . . . well, if *I* don't turn up, you can draw your own
conclusions. If one of you doesn't, I will just assume you have
other fish to fry. Does that suit everyone? Nicholas?'

Faunt inclined his head and slid out of his seat, hefting his
bag in one easy movement. 'Home for me, Kit,' he said, settling
his hat rakishly over one eye. 'See if Mistress Faunt and all
the little Faunts remember who I am.' With a nod to all around
the table, he left, flinging a coin to a serving wench who
watched him go with calf eyes.

When the door had swung to behind him, Tom asked, 'Is
there a Mistress Faunt and all the little Faunts?'

Marlowe shrugged. 'Who knows? I think that Master Faunt
has more lives than a cat and he lives them all at one and the
same time. But he'll be there, in the Slaughtered Lamb. He
won't be able to keep away.'

'I'll be away too, Master Marlowe, if you don't mind.'
Norfolk got up less easily than Faunt, his joints clearly giving
him some pain. His thick lip was now looking very painful
and his black eye belied its name, being every colour of the
rainbow. 'My family will be glad to see me, even looking
like this.' He made for the stairs to fetch his bag and left
the three Londoners alone at the table.

'Does four days give you enough time, Tom?' Marlowe
asked. 'I know you'll need to go and check on Meg and the
little one.'

'Or ones,' Sledd added.

'Or ones. Indeed. Or ones. If you don't want to meet us at the inn, I can always come and find you. You'll be at home or at the Rose?'

'Same thing, really,' Sledd said, pulling a face, but there was no concealing his delight. He had found on unpacking his bag the night before that it no longer gave off the smell of hoof glue and powder that had tied him to home. He needed to get back in the wooden O for a while. 'If I'm not there, it isn't because I have changed my mind, so don't worry. You can always find me at the Rose.'

Lyttleburye was looking a little bereft. He enjoyed working with Cecil, even though it was like putting your hand inside a wasps' nest every day and hoping to get away unstung. It was a living; the trick was to keep on living and not join the pile of unnamed corpses in the Hounds Ditch. But he had no home but nowhere and everywhere; he knew that Cecil would expect him to arrive before Marlowe did, that went with the job at hand. But just for once . . . he looked beseechingly at Marlowe. 'Could you . . .' he could hardly believe he was going to ask someone to lie to Robert Cecil, but if anyone could, Kit Marlowe was that man. 'Could you tell Sir Robert that you had already sent me on an errand?' he asked. 'I haven't had a day off since . . .' he cast his eyes up and muttered, counting on invisible hordes of fingers '. . . since I don't know when. I would just like to wander for a while.'

Marlowe felt for the man. He knew what it was like to be in thrall to the Spymaster, even though it wasn't this particular one; Sir Robert Cecil made Sir Francis Walsingham look as undemanding as a pet rock. 'I can do that for you, Leonard, yes. Everyone deserves a rest from time to time. Will you go to friends? Family?' He held up his hand. 'I don't mean to pry; I just need to know where to find you.'

Lyttleburye shrugged. 'I don't have any friends, or family,' he said, with no trace of self-pity. 'But I promise I'll be at the inn in four days' time, at eight of the clock.'

Tom put his hand on the man's enormous forearm. 'Why don't you come home with me?' he asked. 'See Meg and the children.' He had decided by now that his second child had arrived and was lusty and strong; it was no good worrying with just hours to go before he found out for sure. 'I can show you around the Rose. Have you ever seen behind the scenes in a theatre?'

Lyttleburye's face broke into a grimace of horror. 'I've never been in a theatre at all,' he confessed, 'They're the Devil's outhouses.'

Marlowe and Tom Sledd looked into each other's eyes for a moment. It was indeed true, the look said; they walk among us. They both took a deep breath, but Sledd got in first. 'No, they're not, Leonard. They're places of laughter and magic – and love, of a sort. Will you let me show you?'

He pulled Lyttleburye to his feet – no mean task – and propelled him to the stairs to gather his things. He was prattling about flats, aprons and other arcane theatrical phrases before they reached the turn of the stairs and Marlowe watched them go with an almost paternal look. That was all his children settled in their journeys; now, he just needed to go and face the rough music doled out by Robert Cecil.

The palace of Whitehall lay wreathed in the river mist that night. The guard saluted Marlowe as he flashed the Queen's cypher at them and made for the back stairs. Lights blinked at the windows overhead and he heard the swallows settling in their nests under the eaves as they quietened their fractious, greedy young for the night to come. No one checked him beyond the courtyard. Kit Marlowe was expected.

'Ah, Marlowe.' Robert Cecil was sitting at his desk, as he usually was, his ruff laid aside, his shirt undone. 'Good of you to call.'

'Sir Robert.' Marlowe half bowed. There were the remains of a meal on a plate next to a pile of correspondence and a bottle of claret glowing in the candlelight.

'You know my cousin, Francis Bacon?'

'By reputation,' Marlowe said. 'Sir Francis.'

'Christopher Marlowe, by God,' Bacon said. 'Your reputation far exceeds mine, sir. It's an honour.' The men shook hands. Marlowe knew that this man had a fearsome reputation as a scholar and a lawyer of some eminence. He worked from

Gray's Inn and was a Member of Parliament for Liverpool, a scruffy little port somewhere in the north-west. Modest man though Bacon was, he let everybody know that his aims in life were to uncover the truth, to serve his country and to serve his church. For the life of him, Marlowe could not see how the first and third of those aims were compatible with each other. But then, he was only a Master of Arts from Cambridge University and the foremost playwright in England; what did he know?

'It's not going well, Marlowe, is it?' Cecil tapped the pile of correspondence.

'Well, I'll leave you both to it, shall I?' Bacon got up and was making for the door.

'No, cousin. We all serve the same Queen here. Master Marlowe won't be with us long.'

'Do you drink smoke, Master Marlowe?' Bacon was wrestling with a pipe and a tobacco purse.

'I doubt I'll be here long enough,' Marlowe smiled.

'I won't beat about the bush,' Cecil would not be deflected. 'Tell me about Fareham. The Middlehams.'

Marlowe had not been invited to sit, so he stood, arms folded, eyes fixed on the Queen's imp with that imperturbable stare. 'A man died,' he said. 'The grandfather of the family, Sir Walter Middleham.' He knew that Cecil knew all this already but the imp just wanted to hear him say it.

'When you say "died" . . .?' Cecil wanted more.

Marlowe decided to be obtuse. 'I'm sorry, Sir Robert, Sir Francis,' he said, nodding to each man. 'Was that too blunt? Would you prefer me to say "passed away"?'

Cecil's eyebrow and sneer said it for him.

'Well, not that then. How about "murdered"?'

'Person or persons unknown?' the Spymaster nodded.

'Ah, those words,' Bacon breathed, his face lost in a cloud of smoke. 'Frustrating, aren't they? One day, we'll be able to find a murderer without resorting to corpses that bleed in their presence. One day . . . one day . . .'

'I look forward to it,' Marlowe said. 'But until then—'

'Until then,' Cecil finished the sentence for him, 'your report said that someone threw him off his own battlements.'

'It certainly looked that way,' Marlowe nodded.

'Then came Cowdray,' Cecil sighed. 'The Montagues.'

'The knight of ancient armour,' Marlowe remembered all too clearly.

'Ancient armour?' Bacon echoed, reaching for his goblet.

'Gothic, I'd say,' Marlowe said. 'Augsburg, unless I miss my guess.'

'What happened?' Bacon asked.

'He came out of nowhere,' Marlowe told him. 'A knight incognito, with no device on his shield and no tabard. He challenged the heir of the Montagues.'

'And?'

'Nearly killed him.'

'My God!' Bacon was aghast. 'Not a blunted lance, then?'

'Sharp as a witchfinder's bodkin, Sir Francis.'

'One murder,' Cecil recapped. 'One attempted murder. Petworth – what happened there, Marlowe?'

'Another murder, Sir Robert,' the projectioner told him. 'No doubt this time. No tragic accident, no wandering soldier of fortune seeking the bubble reputation. Just a pistol at point-blank range.'

'But,' and Cecil's smile was a basilisk's, 'at Chichester, merely a rebellion.'

'Merely,' Marlowe agreed.

'In which the bishop of the benighted place could have been torn limb from limb. Do you see a pattern here, Marlowe?'

'I do, Sir Robert,' the playwright told him, 'but it's more intricate than a knot garden. Some sort of maze.'

'None of which bodes well for the Queen's Progress,' Cecil snapped. 'You've failed, Marlowe.'

'Sir Robert,' the playwright could see the end of his tether getting too close for comfort. 'Are you aware that in every place except Chichester, there is a strong Catholic tendency? The Middlehams, the Browns, the Earl of Northumberland, they're all Papists.'

'Of course they are,' Cecil roared. 'I didn't get where I am today by not knowing which way my God's wind blows. Why do you think I sent you?'

'I have no idea,' Marlowe snapped back, 'but it would

have been useful to know that before I put foot to stirrup, wouldn't it?'

Cecil was suddenly on his feet, for all the difference that made, and instantly sat down again, regretting the move. 'We've vetted these families for years, my father and I,' he said, staring Marlowe down. 'We know exactly how far to trust them. There's something else. Some other threat to Her Majesty that I expected you to uncover. And you haven't. These . . .' he snatched up the sheaf of letters on his table, 'are from all those up whose nostrils you have so assiduously climbed over the last few weeks. Blanche Middleham and her brothers,' he glanced down at the first one, '"Heartbroken that Her Majesty will not be coming" . . . Anthony Browne, "The incident at the mock tournament can have no bearing on the Queen's visit" . . . Henry Percy, "I can assure Her Majesty of my undying loyalty" . . . the Bishop of Chichester, "All is well and we look forward to receiving Her Majesty to pray under God's roof after all" . . .' Cecil threw the letters down and they skidded this way and that on the polished table. 'A lot of disappointed people, Marlowe,' he hissed. 'And all of them, *all* of them, speak of the high-handed arbitrary decision by the visiting Master of Revels to cancel the Queen. These were sent to Edmund Tilney, of course, but I had them intercepted.' He shrugged one shoulder and glanced at his cousin. 'I have everything intercepted, naturally.'

'Naturally,' Bacon replied, with a nod.

Marlowe stepped forward. 'When it comes to the Queen's safety, Sir Robert, surely, I can be as high-handed as it takes?'

'No, Marlowe!' Cecil was shrieking now, his face purple, his large eyes watering. 'No, you can't. I'm taking it out of your hands. But not until,' he threw his hand across the letters, 'you have personally made amends to these good people. They are *our* people, Marlowe, at least Francis's and mine. *How* you make amends is your problem; but it had better work and it had better cost Her Majesty's government nothing. Do I make myself clear?'

'Perfectly, Sir Robert,' Marlowe said, hoping as he spoke that he sounded like a man who knew exactly what his next move would be.

'I will let you keep Lyttleburye for one more week; I am not an unreasonable man, I hope.' Again, he looked to his cousin for affirmation and got a nod and a smile. 'Now, get out. And, before you go,' Cecil paused for maximum affect, 'you will leave Her Majesty's cypher on this table. Now.'

Marlowe ferreted in his purse and threw the silver dragon onto the oak.

Francis Bacon was on his feet. 'Master Marlowe,' he smiled, 'I'll see you to the courtyard. I have a question about Tamburlaine.'

Marlowe half bowed to Cecil and spun on his heel, the man's cousin in his wake. 'Tamburlaine,' he said, trying to keep his temper as they marched along the passageway.

'Tamburlaine be buggered,' Bacon murmured. 'In here,' and he slipped through a door into a tiny anteroom. 'You'll have to forgive Robyn. He's new to the job. A bit on his dignity. And when every other street urchin is taller than you, well, it's a bit of a shit, I suppose.'

'We all have our problems, Sir Francis,' Marlowe was in no mood to see the other man's point of view.

'Yes, and yours is a knight in ancient armour.'

Marlowe looked at him. 'Do you know anything about that?'

Bacon had brought his pipe with him and he tapped out the ash onto the floor. 'As a matter of fact . . . But, no, it's just a coincidence.'

'What is?' Marlowe waited.

'No,' Bacon said, reaching for the latch. 'Forget it.'

'Sir Francis,' Marlowe blocked the man's exit. 'I am currently chasing two murderers, perhaps a third. The Queen's life is at stake, for all your cousin believes that not offending people takes precedence over that.'

'Very well,' Bacon relented. 'It's just that I can't see any actual connection. It's something I was reading the other day. Thomas More.'

'Tut, tut, Sir Francis,' Marlowe shook his head, '*Catholic* literature?' He raised an eyebrow.

'I know, I know,' Bacon was flustered. 'But you and I, Marlowe, are men of the world. You know your Machiavelli, banned by both our universities though he is. It's my guess you've read Giordano Bruno and many other political texts of a heretical nature. We both know that not *everything* that is printed in the English College is nonsense.'

Marlowe had been to the English College, the Scorpion's nest as the Puritans called it. He knew that Bacon was right. 'So?' he said.

'Thomas More writes of a disaffected lord, back in the days of the wars of York and Lancaster, a man who was badly wounded at the battle of Stoke.'

'And?'

'He was buried in his armour, sitting at his table as though waiting for news when he would be needed again; when the Yorkist cause would have need of him. His tomb, they say, is in a vault in his castle. And I happen to know that that vault was broken into recently and the tomb disturbed.'

'I don't see . . .' Marlowe frowned.

'Neither do I,' Bacon shrugged. 'But, apparently, only one item was taken – the Lord's family crest, a silver wolf-dog.'

'A silver . . .' The hairs on the back of Marlowe's neck began to crawl. 'Who was this disaffected lord?'

'Oh, didn't I tell you?' Bacon asked. 'My namesake, Francis. Francis, Viscount Lovell.'

Tom Sledd prided himself on being a down-to-earth sort of man, not a flibbertigibbet like all the theatre crowd; even the most humble of the walking gentlemen had a tendency to speak louder than the typical man along Bankside, would throw his arms about and be extravagantly excited about the least thing. But not Tom Sledd; oh no, not the stage manager of the Rose. Leonard Lyttleburye considered Sledd to be as fey as it was possible to be and not actually fly away on gossamer wings; but Leonard Lyttleburye was made of the clay of England, he didn't believe in extravagant gestures. He hardly recognized a muttered civility. And the dour Puritanism of Geneva was in his blood.

So they were both overcome by the emotion that swept over them when they walked into the little scullery at the back of the house that Tom and Meg Sledd called home. The hot summer's day had precluded the need for a fire, so all the

cooking was being done outside in the washhouse and Meg
had ensconced herself in the oak settle beside the empty grate.
At her feet, a flaxen-haired child still in hanging sleeves was
amusing itself by gently teasing the cat. On her lap, wrapped
in old lace handed down by her family for generations, lay a
baby, so new that it was still damp, with skin like a rose petal
that has unfurled itself into the morning dew just seconds
before. Its eyes were closed and its nose was snub, its cheeks
tempted the stroking finger as they framed its rosebud lips,
making soft sucking motions with just the hint of a questing
tongue showing between. The men stopped dead in the
doorway. Meg looked up and smiled hello; she didn't have
the strength to do much more. Then, when the silence went
on, she raised the baby up to its father.

'Meet your son, Master Sledd,' she said, grinning. 'And
introduce him to your friend, do.'

'I . . . My son?'

'Yes!' And this time, she had a laugh in her throat. 'Yes,
he arrived this morning. At cockcrow. A fine boy. Here. Take
him.'

Sledd wiped his hands on the sides of his coat and stepped
across the uneven flags of the floor. The little one at her
mother's feet left the cat and toddled over to grasp her father's
leg. He took his son gently, cradling his head as he had learned
when his daughter had burst into his life to change everything.
With one hand on her curly head, and his other arm about his
new child, he bent his head and cried.

Leonard Lyttleburye, forgotten for a moment in the doorway,
did the same; sometimes, an extravagant gesture was the only
one. With luck, no one would notice, but at that moment, he
hardly cared.

The Rose slumbered in the noon heat like an enormous beast,
crouching at the top of the lane, ready to pounce on the unwary
and drag them in to the magic that lay within. It didn't matter
to Tom Sledd how many times he walked up the slope to the
wicket door; it didn't matter how late it was, or early, he still
felt the tremor of excitement under his ribcage. He could
already smell the smell, hear the noises of a large building

full of people intent on their jobs. He turned to Lyttleburye, lumbering at his side.

'And you really, truly have never been to the theatre?' It sounded as foolish in his ears as asking someone had they ever eaten bread, drunk ale.

'No. My old grandame, she didn't hold with theatricals. And of course, the Brethren rail against it . . .'

Sledd flapped a dismissive hand. 'It's all different now,' he said. 'You wait and see.'

'She said how theatricals were wicked people, who were no better than they should be. She said how the men would dress as women and make up to the men. That's wrong, that is. The Brethren think so, too.'

'Well . . .' there was no way to deny that and still tell the truth. 'Only when the play needs it. They don't *mean* it.'

'So, they're lying, then.' To Lyttleburye, it sounded an accurate enough summing up.

'Not *lying*, no. Pretending.'

'Pretending is lying, though. You shouldn't pretend.' The ghost of Goodwife Lyttleburye spoke from beyond the grave. Not to mention the Brethren, clustered on Leonard Lyttleburye's ample shoulder.

Sledd had an epiphany. 'You work for Sir Robert Cecil, don't you?'

'Yes.' This smelled like a trap, but Lyttleburye couldn't see the trick.

'And he is the Queen's Spymaster?'

'Yes . . .?' The giant didn't like the way this was going. 'How do you know that?'

'Well . . . everybody knows, don't they?' It had always seemed to Tom Sledd that it was the worst-kept secret in town. 'So . . . you pretend for a living. You don't go into a room and tell everyone who you work for, do you?' Sledd was pleased with himself; this was logic chopping to match Kit Marlowe himself.

'Nobody asks me, as a rule,' Lyttleburye pointed out. 'They just think I'm . . . oh, I don't know, it depends where I am; a carter, something like that.'

'But you don't put them right?'

The big man shrugged. 'Why would I?'

'Ex *actly*!' Sledd poked him in the ribs and nearly broke his finger. 'Well, that's the same in the theatre. Everybody just assumes the people on the stage are who they pretend to be; nobody asks; nobody tells. Ergo,' Latin as well! Sledd almost burst with pride. 'Ergo, it isn't lying.'

They were almost there and suddenly, Lyttleburye swung his head, sniffing the air. 'Can I smell . . . can I smell a *bear*?' he said, incredulous.

Master Sackerson was so much part of Tom's world that he hardly noticed him any more. 'Yes,' he said, with pride of almost ownership. 'Over here, look, over the wall.'

'A *bear*?' Lyttleburye's eyes lit up. 'I remember the bears dancing when I was a little 'un. Can I see him?'

'Of course,' Sledd said, piloting him over as a pinnace would move a warship. 'There he is.'

And there indeed he was; moth-eaten, toothless, but undoubtedly all bear, sprawled out on a rock warmed by the sun, Master Sackerson looked up with his little glittering bear eyes and met the astonished gaze of Leonard Lyttleburye.

'Is he here every day?' he breathed, almost silenced by awe.

'Um . . . yes. He lives here. He belongs to Philip Henslowe, owner of the Rose, among other things.' Sledd was waiting to hear what the Brethren thought of bears, but it was not forthcoming.

'So . . . when you're not out and about with Master Marlowe, you see him *every day*?'

'Yes.' Sledd felt he should be honest. 'He doesn't do much. He isn't very exciting.'

Lyttleburye turned on him, eyes flashing. 'He's a bear!' he announced. 'One of God's creatures. And he's here, for you to see every day, and you say that isn't *exciting*? That is almost blasphemy, Master Sledd.' Ah, so *that* was what the Brethren thought!

Tom took a step back. There was just too much of Leonard Lyttleburye to risk annoying him; no one had seen what he could do, but surely he could snap a man like a twig, if he had a mind. 'Perhaps I've just got used to him.' He looked over the wall, holding his breath automatically; Master

Sackerson was probably many things, but fragrant was not one of them. He tried to see the animal through fresh eyes and actually, yes; it was a miracle that he could be looking at one of God's creatures, laid out before him in all his somewhat faded glory, for him to admire. He looked round at his companion, leaning over the wall, rapt. He let him stare in wonder for a few more minutes, then patted him on a substantial bicep. 'Come along, Master Lyttleburye,' he said. 'Time to introduce you to the Rose.'

It had been a bit of a day, one way and another, for Leonard Lyttleburye. Almost as dawn was breaking, after a long ride, he had seen a new baby up close and personal for the very first time in his life. He had even held him for a while, with the new father trying not to hover. He had never seen something so tiny, so perfect, and he had cradled him as though he were made of glass. When the boy had opened one eye and looked at him with the piercing gaze of the newborn, he had nearly died from sheer pleasure and happiness. And now, a bear, a bear of all creatures. His life had not been an easy one. He had never been aware of much love coming his way. But he did remember, just once, seeing a dancing bear in the street, and he had been hoisted up onto his grandfather's shoulder, so he could get a better view. He could still remember the warmth of the old man's hand on his back, supporting him; feel the rough cloth of his collar, slick with the grease that comes from sweat and toil. He could smell the aroma of horse, singeing hoof and warm, unwashed skin that came from him. So it was perhaps unwise of Tom Sledd to introduce into this soup of emotion, the Rose. And yet, he did it, and Leonard Lyttleburye's life would never be the same.

The first thing that struck Lyttleburye was that the whole place must have just caught fire. Although there were no obvious flames, it was as hot as Hell and everyone was milling around like a poked anthill, so surely, there must be a disaster somewhere in the building. Then his eyes got used to the general gloom, pierced with a shaft of sunlight coming through the open roof, filled with motes made up of kicked-up straw, powder, dust from costumes long stored in trunks and attics and the breath and skin of what seemed like a hundred people.

Out of the corner of his eye, he saw people coming up to
Tom Sledd. The men were clapping him on the back. The
women, dowdy little creatures with pins in their sleeves and
swatches of bright fabric in their hands, kissed him on the cheek;
news of the newest Sledd had travelled fast. On the stage, in
the middle of the puddle of sun, two people stood. One was a
man, very slim, straight and tall, standing with one leg out to
the side. Lyttleburye's newly awakened heart went out to him;
he must be deformed, poor man, but he seemed to be making
the best of it. The other seemed to be a woman, a girl, really;
slight and demure, with flaxen hair over one shoulder and
downcast eyes. Lyttleburye knew that this was a boy; a woman
on the stage would be an abomination, after all. But they
looked . . . they looked like the embodiment of adoration as
they stood together.

Suddenly, there was a shout from the shadows and a man
stormed out into the patch of sun.

'Never! Never, never, never, never! Ned, how often do I
have to tell you, this isn't some tart from a corner somewhere.
It's the love of your life. You would die for this woman. In
fact, you *will* die for this woman, in Act Four. So can you
look as though you mean it? Hmm?'

Alleyn took off his hat and threw it to the floor and stamped
on it. 'It's all very well for you, Shaxsper, standing there in
the wings. You can't smell this oaf. His breath is enough to
fell a horse and if he's farted once since we started this scene,
he's done it a thousand times.'

Will Shaxsper stepped forward and looked sternly at the
lad. 'Is this true?' he said, then reeled back, a hand over his
nose. 'For the love of God! What have you been eating?'

The boy hung his head and muttered, tracing a random
pattern in the dust of the stage with his toe.

'What? Onions? That's never onions?'

The lad muttered again.

'Raw?' Shaxsper spread his arms and spun round, looking
for support. 'Why? Why would you do that?'

'Like 'em,' the love of Edward Alleyn's life said, truculently.
'He's no prize, neither. He likes this kissing a bit too much for
my liking. Dick Burbage, he just pretends, but this one . . .'

With a roar, Alleyn reached for the boy's throat and the lad took to his heels. Around them, the business of the Rose went on, regardless.

Tom Sledd turned to Lyttleburye to apologize for the behaviour of his colleagues. But it wasn't necessary – Leonard Lyttleburye was more than stage struck; he was in love.

TWELVE

Nicholas Faunt sat with his back to the wall in the Slaughtered Lamb in Knightrider Street. It was cool and dark in here after the glare of Smithfield, where the drovers and their animals vied with each other to see who gave off the worst smell. But Nicholas Faunt knew all too well that Smithfield had known worse smells – the roasting flesh of first the Puritans, then the Catholics who had annoyed the royal sisters Mary and Elizabeth. The stakes were still there and the stakes were high.

He watched the door carefully, every man who wandered in, every drunk who staggered out. His host was a man often on the wrong side of bars at the Compter or the Marshalsea and he owed Nicholas Faunt a few favours. One of them was that Nicholas Faunt had never bought a round at the Lamb in his life. Today would be no different.

He saw Marlowe before Marlowe saw him, which is how it should be with projectioners, and he raised a careless glove.

'What'll it be, Kit?' he asked as the man joined his table.

'Do they do a claret here?' Marlowe asked. His haunts were further east, beyond Paul's and Spital Fields.

'They *do*,' Faunt smiled, 'but I'd advise against it.' He clicked his fingers and a blowsy strumpet came waddling. She had to be all of fifteen. 'A tankard of ale for my friend,' he said to her.

'Is he payin' for it?' she asked.

Faunt fetched her a swift slap around the backside as she scuttled off, chuckling.

Marlowe tutted and shook his head. 'There's sore decline in pot boys these days,' he said.

Faunt looked at him. 'How old are you, Marlowe?'

'I'm twenty-seven,' Marlowe told him. 'Why do you ask?'

Faunt laughed. 'Too young to miss the good old days,' he said. Then he closed to his man. 'How did it go with Cecil?'

'Much as it went with you some months ago,' Marlowe said. 'He sacked me.'

'Ha!' Faunt leaned back. 'Small man, small mind. His loss, Kit. Your back is broad.'

'That's not the point, though thank you for more clichés than I would generally meet in a long day's ride.' Marlowe leaned back too and watched the pipe smoke wreath the space between him and the open door, giving the street outside an unearthly look. 'There's a job unfinished. Two murders I haven't got to the bottom of; three, but for the grace of what most would call God. And,' he looked Faunt straight in the eye, 'nobody – nobody – hands me my quill and says "Run". The imp also expects me to make amends for upsetting the Queen's would-be hosts. How I am supposed to do that, I have no idea.'

'Assuming you still had the job,' Faunt said after a while, 'where would the Queen have been going next?'

'Titchfield,' Marlowe said. 'The Earl of Southampton.'

'Southampton,' Faunt said loudly as the pot girl came back with Marlowe's tankard. 'Know it well. Harry the Fifth sailed from there for the Agincourt campaign. I was saying to Michael Drayton, the poet, you know, only the other day . . . ah, thank you my dear.' Faunt winked at her. 'Now, don't you go talking to any strange men, will you?' He nodded in Marlowe's direction. When she'd gone, Faunt dropped his voice again. 'So, what will you do?'

Marlowe sipped the ale. It wasn't bad, all things considered, reminding him of the hoplands of his home county. 'Something has occurred to me, Nicholas,' he said, wiping his moustache.

'Oh?'

'Who knows about the Progress?'

'Er . . . sorry,' Faunt said. 'You've lost me.'

'Who chooses the itinerary?'

'That's Burley's job, as her chief adviser and Privy Councillor. What with his *little* boy coming of age now, of course, it may well be that Cecil does the actual donkey-work. Submits the list to the Queen for her approval. It's a chance for her to see her loyal subjects, receive petitions, makes her feel good about herself.'

Marlowe chuckled. 'Do I detect a hint of cynicism there, Master Faunt?' he asked.

'That's what you get working for Walsingham as long as I did,' Faunt smiled.

'Who else knows?'

'Well.' Faunt had to think. 'Tilney usually, as Master of the Revels – except, until yesterday, that was you, of course, for this Progress only. The Privy Council generally – they'd have to fund it.'

'I thought the hosts covered the costs.'

'Not all of them. It would be prohibitive. Northumberland can afford it. So can Southampton. But the Montagues and the Middlehams – new money. It doesn't grow on trees. And anyway, when Gloriana is between hosts, who pays for that? The one before, or the one to come? So the Treasury has to fund those costs. Who else? Well, the Lord Lieutenants of the counties – Hampshire and Sussex in this instance – they'd need to know in case of trouble.'

'Not much use at Chichester, were they?' Marlowe grunted, taking another pull at his ale.

'Well, there's no accounting for personal animosities. Look, Kit, where's all this going?'

Marlowe looked at Faunt. The older man had been his mentor in the spying game under Walsingham for nearly seven years – an apprenticeship served in Hell. You never knew *quite* where you were with Nicholas Faunt, but in a world full of uncertainties, his was, essentially, a face to trust. 'Think back. What happened at Farnham?'

'Before my time,' Faunt shrugged, 'but a man died.'

'The lord of the manor,' Marlowe nodded. 'So I decided the Queen couldn't go there.'

'Right.'

'The Montagues at Cowdray?'

'A jousting accident that wasn't an accident. The run of the ancient knight.'

'So I came to the conclusion that the Queen couldn't go there either. Then came Petworth.'

'The shooting of Lady Barbara Gascoigne.' Faunt was filling in the missing details.

'Another bloody place it was unwise for Her Majesty to set foot. Chichester?'

'A small war,' Faunt said. 'Peasants up in arms against the local church. All rather nasty but, to be honest, it could have been worse.'

'But even so, not a fit place for the royal Progress.'

'Your point?'

'We're being manipulated, Nicholas, you and I – and, more importantly, Her Majesty. We're being steered away from these places – is it a grudge? And if so, who would have a grudge against such different people? Apart from their religion – and even then, you have to discount Chichester – they have nothing at all in common. So, it must be . . .'

Faunt leaned forward with a finger in the air. 'It must be that we are being steered *towards* somewhere else!'

Marlowe nodded. 'It could be all a coincidence,' he said. 'A man falls from a wall. Another is hurt in the lists. A woman is shot. The many-headed monster goes on the rampage . . .'

'But you don't believe in coincidence,' Faunt smiled.

'Do you?' Marlowe asked him.

'No.' Faunt was suddenly serious. 'No, I don't.'

'Unfortunately,' Marlowe said, 'There's damn all I can do about it. If we're being steered towards Titchfield, for whatever reason, I won't be there.'

'Yes, you will,' Faunt said, clicking his fingers for the ale to be topped up.

'I will?'

'Are you prepared to defy the Spymaster? Risk the imp's wrath?'

'In the batting of an eyelid,' Marlowe told him.

'There you have it, then. Cecil may have dispensed with you, Christopher Marlowe, but the Queen has not dispensed with me.' Faunt slid his hand into his purse and fished out a silver dragon and greyhound, the Queen's cypher. I fear I haven't been quite straight with you,' he said.

Marlowe sat back in mock amazement, arms spread. 'Tell me it isn't so, Nicholas,' he said, wide-eyed.

'The Queen sent for me, weeks ago. She's spent her entire reign under the watchful eye of Burghley, but his little boy?

Well, he's untried; hasn't finished shitting yellow. The imp appointed you – good move; sacked you – bad move. Perhaps Her Majesty guessed that something like this would happen. That's where I came in.'

'So you didn't just bump into Tom Sledd on Bankside that day?'

'No more than Moses was out for a casual stroll when the Lord gave him the commandments, no.'

'Moses was but a conjuror,' Marlowe remembered Simeon saying that *he* had said that.

'What?'

'Nothing. So, what now?'

'Saddle your horse, Kit. We have a journey to undertake. Titchfield. Business as usual.'

Marlowe smiled. 'In that case,' he said, Machiavellian to the last, 'I have an idea.'

'Out with it.'

'No,' Marlowe said, 'not yet. It needs to digest a while longer yet. I'll share another drink with you, Nicholas, and wait for our lads to join us, then I'm off to Paternoster Row, to the stationer's. There's a book there that I should have read a long time ago.'

Marlowe went nowhere without paper and ink; who knew when inspiration might strike? When he had first taken to the life of a playwright and poet, he had often written stanzas on shirtsleeves, odes on table tops, but that could become awkward and the laundresses began to complain. Quills he could fashion anywhere, but in his saddlebags he always had a roll of parchment and a sealed bottle of the best ink. A dab of wax when he had finished and he was good until the next lightning strike. Now, he flattened out four sheets of parchment and penned his missives to the disgruntled lords of Farnham, Cowdray and Petworth and the Bishop of Chichester. It almost gave him physical pain to write such simple words, but he refused to sugar this pill. He wrote the same to everyone – he was so sorry that for reasons of security it would not be possible to allow the Queen to visit anywhere that had been the scene of a crime, but he and the Queen would be more than delighted if – and here he changed the details to include siblings, wives, children and sundry hangers-on according to the recipient – would care to join the celebrations at Titchfield. Obviously, all accommodation would be under the roof of the Earl of Southampton and their servants would be given somewhere to sleep on the estate. He was their obedient servant, extremely faithfully, C. Marlowe, Esq.

Faunt looked over his shoulder as he sanded the final sheet. 'Who's C. Marley when he's at home?' he asked. 'Are you using a pseudonym?'

Marlowe looked closer. 'That is obviously Marlowe,' he said, testily. 'My writing is particularly clear.'

Tom Sledd piped up. 'You know that's not true, Kit. How many times do the copyists have to check with you what a word is?'

'My writing is clearer than Shaxsper's,' he pointed out, making ad hoc adjustments to the final signature. It did look a little like 'Marley', now he looked again.

'Everyone's writing is clearer than Shaxsper's.' Sledd wasn't letting it go. 'Being clearer than him is nothing to be proud of.'

Marlowe folded each letter and sealed and addressed them, glancing first to make sure the right person would get the right one. Then, he handed two to Lyttleburye and two to Norfolk.

'No need to make a meal of either of these,' he told them both. 'Just deliver and come home. Or don't come home, if you have anything else to do – as long as you are in Titchfield for the Progress, that's all I ask.'

'Meg has invited me for whenever I want,' Lyttleburye said, with something like awe in his voice. He had never had an invitation before – or, at least, not one that didn't include pain and suffering for someone.

'I'll be there,' Norfolk said, noncommittal as always. 'Wouldn't miss it for the world.'

When they had left, Tom turned to Marlowe. 'Where does he go, do you think?' he asked.

'I suppose he has a wife and a couple of screaming children somewhere out in the country,' Faunt said. Marlowe and Sledd gave him sideways looks; if anyone knew about clandestine families out in the country, it was Nicholas Faunt.

'And what about me?' Tom asked. 'Back to the Rose?' He sounded torn between disappointment and relief.

Faunt and Marlowe exchanged a glance, then Marlowe smiled. 'As it happens, Tom, that is what we had in mind. Sit down a minute; we need to talk.'

Leonard Lyttleburye was confused. It was not an unusual state of affairs for him, if truth be told. As Intelligencers go, he was on the lowest rung of the ladder placed against the wall of subterfuge by Robert Cecil. Yet, here he was, at Master Marlowe's behest, wandering a house that seemed deserted. Was this what a country estate was like when the Queen's Progress had been cancelled? He had ridden along the Hog's Back in the heat of the day, the fields of the south-lands spread on either side of him like a hazy patchwork quilt. Stooks had started appearing in a few places, but mainly the fields stood in blocks of dusty gold, waiting for the scythesman. At Farnham, he had expected woodsmen, shep-herds, labourers on their baulks and washerwomen spreading linen on the tenter-grounds. Yet, here was nothing. Farnham Hall was locked and barred, its shutters closed against the sun.

'Who are you and what do you want?' a voice called from the battlements of the old keep, rising in front of him. Lyttleburye shielded his eyes from the sun and saw a young gentleman in plumed pickadil and cloak leaning over the merlon and frowning down at him.

'Leonard Lyttleburye,' he answered, 'on the Queen's business.'

The young man turned to talk to someone behind him on the ramparts. Lyttleburye heard a woman's voice, soft, quizzical.

'You'd better come up,' the young man said.

Lyttleburye did, taking the tight spiral of the worn steps in his huge stride; for such a big man, he was light and graceful on his feet and the climb meant nothing to him. At the top, a doorway opened to the bright sun and two people stood there, a man and a woman. Cecil's man doffed his cap. 'I'm looking for Mistress Blanche Middleham,' he said.

'You've found her.' Blanche took half a step forward, but the young man stopped her.

'What business do you have?' he wanted to know.

Lyttleburye looked him up and down. 'None with you, sir,' he said.

'You untutored oaf!' the young man screamed. 'Know your betters, sirrah!'

A glove snaked out towards Lyttlebury's face but the giant was too fast. He grabbed the glove and the hand that held it, swinging the young man round and pinning him by the throat. He lifted him bodily off the ground and held him at arm's length with a powerful right hand, dangling him dangerously over the battlements.

'No!' the woman screamed, then softer, 'Sir,' she said, 'I beg you not to hurt him. I am Blanche Middleham. The gentleman in your grasp is my brother, James.'

Lyttleburye didn't move. He just stood there, looking at the woman.

'Stop struggling, James!' Blanche hissed.

'That's good advice, young master,' Lyttleburye said. With his spare hand, he pulled Marlowe's letter from inside his doublet. 'That's for you, that is,' he said. 'From Master Christopher Marlowe of the Office of the Queen's Revels. He's sorry for any misunderstanding. And can you . . .' he glanced at James for the first time. The boy had gone deathly pale, feeling nothing below his feet but the air of a forty-foot drop. '. . . and yours attend Her Majesty's Progress at Titchfield Abbey on the fourteenth inst.?'

Blanche blinked. Both the invitation and the messenger had unnerved her, to say the least. 'We'd be delighted,' she recovered herself with a tight smile, 'wouldn't we, James?'

A strangled squeak was all the boy could manage. Lyttleburye moved his arm as though the insufferable shit he carried was made of finest Cathay. He put him down on his feet again and the lad half collapsed against the stonework, clutching his throat and trying to catch his breath.

'Thank you,' Blanche held out her hand for Lyttlebury to

kiss, a completely wasted gesture as it turned out. 'Tell Master Marlowe the Middlehams would be honoured for a chance to meet Her Majesty.'

The wizard earl wore deepest black. He was still in mourning for his lost love, the Lady Barbara, and had ridden back only the day before from her funeral in the little church at Ashbery where she had been laid to rest among the Gascoignes and the lilies. Mourning became the Earl of Northumberland. His sad eyes looked dully at Jack Norfolk, standing before him in the entrance hall at Petworth. If truth be told, Norfolk had better things to do with his time than play postman to Kit Marlowe, but Kit Marlowe's coin was as silver as the next man's, and needs must when the Devil drives.

'I don't think so,' Henry Percy was shaking his head at Marlowe's letter, as though at the man himself. 'I'm not sure the Queen deserves company such as mine at the moment. There would be no mirth in it.' He walked over to the window and leaned on the sill, looking out into the park, seeing nothing. 'There's no sunshine when she's gone,' he said, turning to Norfolk with brimming eyes. 'Only darkness, every day.'

Norfolk looked at the broken man before him, but it was pointless wasting sympathy on him; he knew a man wallowing in it when he saw one. 'I'm not sure it is a request, my lord,' he said. 'I think it's more in the way of being a royal command.'

Percy looked at the man for almost the first time. 'This letter is from Marlowe,' he pointed out, quite reasonably. 'Look.' He held it out to Norfolk.

'I know, my lord,' the messenger said patiently, 'but, like all of us, he is a servant of the Queen. It is her bidding we do, ultimately.'

Percy sighed and nodded. 'So be it,' he said. 'Tell Marlowe I'll be there, but I won't be bringing any fireworks, that's for sure.'

'Oh,' Norfolk smiled. 'I'm sure there'll be plenty of those, my lord,' he said.

The bunting still fluttered on the tilt yard at Cowdray as Leonard Lyttleburye cantered over it. In the knot garden, he saw the man he sought, Sir Anthony Browne, Lord Montague to the life, standing with two young men, one walking stiffly with a bandage visible under his shirt. Cecil's man dismounted and handed the reins to a lackey, bowing to Montague.

Montague broke the seal and read it. 'Titchfield?' he growled. 'I wouldn't soil my boots on Southampton's ground. The man's a child, with unnatural inclinations, if rumour is to be believed.'

'What is it, Anthony?' Lady Montague bustled out from the house, recognizing Lyttleburye as one of the servants of the Master of the Revels, that Lovelly Christopher Marlowe.

'Nothing, Mrs B.,' Montague said, looking round for his jug of claret. 'Nothing at all.'

Lady Montague snatched the paper and read it. 'The Progress, Anthony!' she trilled, clapping her hands, letter and all. 'We'll see the Queen.'

'Not the same as having her here, though.'

'Well, no,' Lady Montague agreed, 'but think of the boys.' She grabbed an arm of each of her children and Martin yelped. 'Forgive me, my precious,' she said, automatically, her mind on other things. 'Her Majesty can lay her sword on their shoulders at Titchfield as well as she could here at Cowdray.'

That thought hadn't occurred to the senior Montague and his face lifted. 'By God, you're right.' He squeezed his tiny wife to his side and pulled his sons to him in a hug. '*Sir* Martin, *Sir* George, thank this gentleman for his kind invitation. Tell Master Marlowe we'll all be there. Me and my two sons.'

Lady Montague ducked under his arm, oozing between her husband and her younger son. 'And your wife, Anthony,' she said.

'Oh, of course, Mrs B. And my wife.'

Lyttleburye bowed and made for his horse.

'And tell Southampton from me,' Montague called to him. 'No forty-eight-yard-long tables. That's *my* idea!'

There was a faint and distant twitter.

'*Our* idea. Tell him.'

But Leonard Lyttleburye had stopped listening and was soon cantering back on the road to London, and to the smell of the greasepaint which wouldn't leave his nostrils.

*   *   *

Jack Norfolk's horse clattered into the Pallant a little after midday. Chichester was drowsing in June's stifling heat and Norfolk was one of the few going about his business. It was cool in the chapterhouse of the cathedral and Marlowe's man was glad of that. The sweat had soaked through his shirt and doublet and his buskins were hot to the touch.

'How are you now?' the bishop asked him, with Marlowe's letter in his hand. 'After that unfortunate business at the buttercross. We've been praying for you, you know.'

'It was nothing, Your Grace,' Norfolk said. 'And I thank you for your prayers; someone was already watching over me that night.'

'Amen to that,' the bishop said.

'And how are things here?' Norfolk asked. 'The shepherds?'

'Back with their flocks, where they belong. All a storm in a goblet, really.'

'But . . . your word still stands?' Norfolk thought he had better check; bishop or no bishop, men went back on their words more often than not. 'The enclosures?'

Brickley nodded. 'Yes, yes,' he said. 'My word stands, grate though it does. I can never be *quite* sure whether Simeon will be back one day.'

'He's gone?' Norfolk asked.

'Vanished like mist in the morning,' the bishop said. 'He and that snivel-faced clerk of his. The day after the trouble – the day after you left, in fact – I sent one of my people to see him. I wanted to be sure of his intentions, as well as showing him the enclosure paperwork. He wasn't there. There was no one there. The house on Priory Lane was locked and barred, as though he'd never been. Tell me,' Brickley's eyes brightened, 'there's no chance of a service at Titchfield, is there? I mean, as bishop . . .'

Norfolk smiled. 'I'm sure all things are possible in Her Majesty's presence, Your Grace.'

THIRTEEN

Nicholas Faunt was not comfortable with actors. Despite having spent most of his adult years working with people who wouldn't recognize the truth if it got up and bit them on the leg, he couldn't work out the extravagant speech, the fake bonhomie and, most especially, the sheer duplicity of almost everyone inside the Rose. Of all of its denizens, Philip Henslowe was perhaps the most confusing; to the outward eye, a man of business, pure and simple, concerned with the bottom line on a page of calculations; someone who could look at a sheet of crabbed figures and immediately tell if it was in credit or debit before anyone else could even bring their eyes into focus. He was rarely more than a groat or two out; he often said to Mistress Henslowe, on the day he couldn't calculate a bottom line to within a gnat's eyelash, that would be the day he retired. Or slashed his throat; it could be either.

But, underneath, Philip Henslowe was a man seething with repressed passions. He could work off quite a few of them with the little piece near the Bear Garden, but there were others that simmered and bubbled whenever he let them rise to the surface. He was indulging in one of his favourites now. His eyrie above the Rose was hot as Hell and he had opened the little dormer window and was hanging out of it, trying to catch what breeze there might be at this height. The smells of the river and its people were far below him and, up here, he was alone with the seagulls, which swung just past his head, their razor bills open with harsh cries. He closed his eyes and lifted his chin. Surely, it couldn't be that hard; one day, one day soon, he hoped, man would be able to fly. But in his more down-to-earth dreams, he didn't need flight; just the gentle touch of royal steel on his shoulder. He could almost hear the words, spoken in the soft voice he knew his Queen must possess. 'Arise, Sir Philip, knighted for services to the theatre but most of all, for saving my life when—'

'Master Henslowe?'

'No,' the theatre owner murmured, 'Sir Philip—'

'Master *Henslowe*!'

He jumped, banging his head on the window frame. Spinning round, he snapped at the clerk standing in the doorway. 'What?'

'Master Henslowe,' the man cowered, 'a Master Faunt to see you.'

Henslowe didn't know Faunt well, but he knew that a visit from him would not be merely to tell him how much he had enjoyed the show. He sighed, straightened his hair and tweaked his ruff into position. This hot weather played merry Hell with box-office receipts and now, Nicholas Faunt. And the day had started so well – waking up next to the cool back of his little piece near the Bear Garden; a brief interlude – necessarily brief, what with his age and the heat – and then on to the real love of his life, the Rose. Then, when he had arrived, what had met him? The distressingly low takings; someone had put their foot through Tamburlaine's chariot and one of the carpenters had nailed through his apprentice's hand, some were saying not wholly by accident. And now – Nicholas Faunt. Please, God, he said in his head, enough now, please don't test me any more.

'Master Faunt!' He stepped forward, hand outstretched. 'What a delightful surprise. Er . . .' he glanced at the clerk, 'I wasn't expecting you, was I?' Over Faunt's shoulder, the clerk shook his head.

'Not at all, Master Henslowe,' Faunt could gush for England if he had to. 'I called in on what you might almost call a whim, in fact. You see, I have a problem which I believe you can solve for me.'

Philip Henslowe could scarcely forbear from laughing in the man's face. He could hardly keep abreast of his own problems, let alone solve someone else's. But he had heard things about Nicholas Faunt, so he said, 'If I can, Master Faunt. If I can.'

'You may know about Master Marlowe and Master Sledd helping facilitate the Queen's latest Progress?'

Was this a trap? Was he supposed to know? Was it treason if he knew? Henslowe's eyes went from side to side like rats in a trap. This was Cecil's England as much as Gloriana's; you couldn't be too careful.

Faunt waited for an answer and when none was forthcoming, he continued. 'They have been planning masques, things of that nature. However, the Fates have not smiled on them in their endeavours. There have been . . . incidents . . . and so we have reason to fear for the Queen's safety.'

This struck a chord with Henslowe and his eyes both faced forward and focused on Faunt. 'The Queen? In danger?' This needed to be stopped; if his dreams of knighthood under Elizabeth were far-flown, he knew he stood no chance under that little Scottish gowk that most men said would surely follow. 'You have my attention, Master Faunt. How may I help you?'

Marlowe and the stage manager received their usual welcome as they penetrated into the rooms behind the stage; they were completely ignored by all present, both great and small. Most of the people milling around pretended they had never been away. The remainder didn't know they had been away, as they were part of the constantly replaced servants at the very lowest edge of humanity who were there to pick up thrown vegetables and whatever else the groundlings saw fit to leave behind when they exited the pit. The job was well paid as such jobs went – and it needed to be; most of those employed in it lasted on average three days before revulsion sent them screaming.

'How are you going to do this?' Sledd asked Marlowe. 'Surely, we're not going to ask them all one by one? It will take days.'

'No, no, Tom; you can't have forgotten already. If you offer any role to one person, you will be beaten down by the rush of all the others who know they can do it better. Watch.'

He grabbed a passing walking gentleman by the sleeve and pulled him closer, whispering in his ear. Before he had finished, there were five more clustering round, so he spoke a little louder for the benefit of all. His voice would still not have carried more than two feet if it fell on normal ears, but these were not normal ears; these were the ears of men who would kill their grandmothers for a speaking part.

'Gentlemen,' he murmured, 'I am here with an opportunity . . .'

The crowd grew to ten.

'. . . for anyone interested in taking part in . . .'

Twenty.

'. . . a Progress of the Queen. Not a masque, but to be part of her train.'

And there it was – Burbage and Alleyn were elbowing their way to the front and the task was complete.

Tom Sledd swept off his hat and made an elaborate bow to Marlowe, who accepted it with a raised eyebrow and an ironic smile.

'If you would like to make an orderly line – yes, that's right, out into the pit if you have to. Watch where you step.' He raised his voice a notch. 'This is for everyone. Pickers up as well; we need as many people as we can muster.'

When the line was complete, with Burbage and Alleyn still nudging each other to try and keep an inch ahead in the pecking order, Marlowe hopped up onto a table and clapped his hands. Now his voice was at full volume and he looked down to the human snake at his feet and smiled. 'Thank you everyone. Let's have some quiet now, please.' He waited until the two gossiping seamstresses almost at the back realized they were the only two talking and shut up. 'Thank you. Now, listen, because I won't be repeating this bit, and if you get it wrong, you won't be taking part and you won't be getting your fee.'

A murmur broke out at the mention of money; almost all of them would have done it for nothing.

'The job at hand is for people to take part in the Queen's entry into Titchfield, for her to stay with the Earl of Southampton as part of her Progress. Costumes will be provided . . .'

The seamstresses at the back raised their eyebrows at each other and shrugged. He was hopeful, their gestures seemed to say.

'. . . as will transport. When at Titchfield, you will have accommodation within the grounds with all found. And of course, a guinea for your trouble.'

Alleyn rolled his eyes and sneered. A guinea? He didn't get out of bed for that kind of pittance. Although – the Queen did rather change the tilting ground; he might well make an exception in this case. He took a deep breath and glanced sideways at Burbage. Damn! It looked as if he would be happy to settle too.

'What about Henslowe, though?' someone called from the back. 'He won't let us all bugger off for days on end. We don't want to be out of a place when we get back.'

'Master Henslowe has agreed to it,' Marlowe reassured the man, hoping that was true. 'He, of course, as a loyal Englishman and true, will do anything to help the Queen and guarantee her safety.'

'You want me to do *what*?' Henslowe roared at Faunt. The man had gone too far.

'I believe the phrase is "go dark",' Faunt said. His contempt for theatrical jargon knew no bounds.

'For how long?' Henslowe asked the question, as though the length of time had any bearing.

'Oh, I don't know precisely. Three days? Four? It all depends.'

'Four *days*? Are you mad? What do you think happens to a theatre if it has no plays for four days?'

Faunt shrugged, and it was not a rhetorical shrug either. He quite honestly had no idea.

'The audience forgets it, that's what. The plague. The Puritan complaints. It doesn't take much. They find somewhere else to go. They . . .' he stopped in mid-sentence, horror etched on his face. 'They might even go to the Curtain!' He flung up his arms. 'I don't know why I'm wasting my breath. It isn't going to be happening, Master Faunt. I am an Englishman, bred in the bone, but I will not allow you to ruin my business. I just won't.'

Faunt sank his chin on his chest. Marlowe had said this might be how the interview would go. He played his trump card. 'I am very disappointed, Master Henslowe,' he said. 'We had rather hoped you might take the part of . . . but, no, as you say, let's not waste our breath.'

Henslowe was, as all people who work within the theatre secretly are, an actor manqué. No one had ever even mentioned him and a part in the same breath before and he couldn't help himself. 'Part of . . .?' he let the sentence hang.

'No, please, we were unreasonable to ask it of you,' Faunt said, still hanging his head. 'I'm sure Lord Strange will be able to help us out.' He doffed his hat. 'Good morning to you, Master Henslowe. I'll see myself out.'

Henslowe scurried round from behind his desk. 'Part of?' he said, blocking the other man's exit. 'Part of . . . whom?'

Faunt raised his head and his smile was that of a stoat that knew he had mesmerized a nice fat rabbit. 'Sir Christopher Hatton,' he said, dismissively. 'But I see now that . . .'

Henslowe preened. He grew several inches and pointed what he hoped might be taken for a lissom toe. 'Sir Christopher Hatton? Me? But surely . . .'

'You seemed the obvious choice,' Faunt said. 'A certain feline grace, gravitas, intelligence. The foremost jouster and dancer in England. And of course, we mustn't forget, a favourite of the Queen. You would ride with her on her litter, I wouldn't be at all surprised.'

'But won't he *mind*?' Henslowe said, common sense beginning to surface. 'Sir Christopher, I mean.'

'I hardly think so!' Faunt was appalled. 'This is for the safety of the Queen's life, don't forget.' He closed to Henslowe and lowered his voice. 'Someone in the Queen's entourage wishes her ill. The only way we can ensure her safety is to replace every man jack of them.'

Henslowe nodded slowly and assumed a man-of-the-world expression. 'I *see*,' he said, though he wasn't really sure that he did. 'So . . . she doesn't mind? The Queen, I mean.'

'She will be given the details later,' Faunt hedged, 'but she would do anything to go ahead with this Progress and this is the only way. To see the people who love her and to assure them of her love for them.'

'I see . . .' Henslowe seemed to be stuck on the one safe phrase he could come up with. 'But . . . the theatre. Mistress Henslowe is already far from happy about the falling revenues . . .'

Faunt caught him a glancing blow on the shoulder with a glove. 'Mistress Henslowe can take part too, of course she can. We need as many beautiful women as we can muster. The Queen's ladies; gorgeous dresses, that sort of thing. Send a messenger, get her down here.' Faunt stepped back and smiled. He could read Henslowe's mind; could he squeeze in his little piece from near the Bear Garden, or would that be taking a risk too far? 'If you have any other . . . friends, they would be more than welcome.' The stoat's eyes narrowed and the rabbit walked right in.

'I'll send a clerk,' Henslowe said, and the deed was done.

'And everyone gets a guinea?'

'Everyone. And if you have wives, daughters, sons at home that can join you, they all get a guinea as well.'

The line murmured. The walking gentleman with six daughters and four sons almost fainted with sheer delight. The seamstresses looked at each other, this time in frank alarm.

'Master Marlowe,' the bolder of them said. 'Do they *all* get costumes? Only, there's only the two of us and—'

'We'll get help,' Marlowe said. 'Don't worry about that, Prudence; you and Alys won't have to make them all. Perhaps just a few alterations.'

The seamstresses didn't hear much more; Christopher Marlowe knew their names. And they were getting a golden guinea each. Could any day ever be better?

'Is that a guinea a day?' one of the walking gentlemen wanted to know.

Marlowe narrowed his eyes. 'Don't push your luck, Frizer,' he said. 'A guinea for the whole Progress.'

The man shrugged. There was no harm in asking, after all.

'What I would like you to do,' Marlowe continued, 'is to make two lines here, one in front of me and one in front of Tom. You could stand behind Master Alleyn and Master Burbage, couldn't you, to start things off?'

Alleyn and Burbage bridled but at least stopped nudging each other. And they were, after all, at the respective heads of the two columns.

'You will be given an idea of what kind of person you will be playing, but all you strong young lads,' he waved his arm generally over the crowd who were already beginning to muster into the two lines, 'will be given pikes, halberds, armour to make you into the Queen's bodyguard. You will also be given some training . . . is Will Shaxsper here?' He scanned the crowd; that giant shiny forehead was usually easy to spot.

'He's not here today,' someone volunteered. 'He's . . .' the speaker descended into giggles.

'Not another strumpet, surely?' Alleyn said languidly. If a pot had ever called a kettle black, then this was that occasion.

'He says he's in love,' a voice from the crowd shouted out, and the laughter nearly raised the roof. Marlowe hoped the man did turn up before everything was arranged; not only did he want him to drill the Guard, he must meet the Earl of Northumberland – two buttocks of one bum, if he was any judge.

'If someone could find him, I would be grateful,' Marlowe said. 'He can drill the troop. But that's enough from me,' he said, jumping down off the table. 'Don't push and shove, we'll get to you all eventually.' He sat behind the table and Tom Sledd took up his position next to him. 'Now, who's first? Ned; what about you? Any idea who you would like to play?'

Alleyn looked down his nose at Marlowe, who smiled back calmly. He had mentally allotted more time with Alleyn and Burbage than with all the rest put together. 'Well, Kit, I would have thought it was obvious.' He raised his chin and struck a pose. 'Hatton, obviously.'

'Hmmm . . . isn't he a bit . . . old, for you, Ned? I had in mind someone a bit nearer your own age. You do have to keep up the deception for four days, you know. It would not be easy.'

'Easy?' hissed Alleyn. '*Easy?* Do you imply that I need my roles to be *easy*? I can play any age you wish and you know it.'

'Even so,' Marlowe said, dipping his quill into the inkpot and taking the opportunity to move it further from Alleyn's flailing arms, 'I rather thought that Drake was the man for you to play. Handsome. Dashing. Hero of the Armada.'

Alleyn nodded. All that went without saying.

'Flamboyant. *Highly* intelligent and, of course, very much in the Queen's favour at the moment. You would almost certainly be riding on her litter.'

'*Really?*' Alleyn's eyes opened wide. 'Well.' He thumbed his chin, riffling the hairs of his trim little beard. 'Drake, you say . . . all right, Kit. Drake it is. But . . .' he leaned closer, 'what's my motivation?'

Marlowe's smile was bleak. 'I'm sure you will find that as you get into the part, Ned. Sign here.' He proffered the quill. 'Thank you. Next!'

Meanwhile, things were not going so smoothly between Burbage and Tom Sledd. Burbage had had no real preference until he heard Alleyn being given Drake.

'Any idea who you would like to play?' the stage manager asked.

'Sir Francis Drake,' Burbage said promptly.

'Ah. I rather think that Ned will . . .'

'Alleyn? Why? Drake is handsome, flamboyant, dashing, a hero of the Armada; all the things I am and he is not. I was born to play Drake.'

'Yes, but,' Sledd gestured to his right, 'I believe Ned has just signed on Drake. Can I offer you the Earl of Essex? Queen's favourite, you know. You'd be bound to be riding on her litter.'

'Essex. Hmm. I *could* do Essex. Tell me, is he wearing that stupid beard at the moment?'

'I believe he is,' Tom said, making it up as he went along. 'I'll check. But if he is, we can sort you out with a fake.' It was a well-known jest at the Rose that Burbage couldn't grow a beard if his life depended on it.

'Well . . . I would have been better as Drake, but Essex it is, then.' Burbage scribbled his signature and went off, stroking his chin and trying to look aristocratic.

The rest of the line took no time at all to sign up, the lusty lads being sent off to wait the arrival of Shaxsper, the less lusty ones being set aside for wigs and prosthetic breasts. Wives, daughters and the occasional little piece from near the Bear Garden notwithstanding, women were a little thin on the ground, and Gloriana went nowhere without her retinue of Lovellies, for preference not so Lovely that they made her look like the tired old woman she was inevitably becoming.

Eventually, with quills worn to stubs and throats aching

from so much talking, Marlowe and Sledd leaned back in their chairs and stretched. 'How many do you make it?' Marlowe asked, totting up his column. 'I have seventy-four, counting wives and others who will be joining us. And I haven't included the musicians.' That would not have surprised them at all; since when had anybody listened to the band? 'But we need them to play the Queen in to Titchfield but also to generally announce our Progress along the road, once we're all in character.'

Tom Sledd held up a finger. He was counting. 'One hundred and . . .' he muttered under his breath, 'seven. So, that's one hundred and eighty-one. Is that enough?'

'No. We're not far short, though.'

'How many more do we need?' Sledd was sure he could muster a few more.

'About two thousand. But, Tom, we are the theatre folk. We can use smoke. We can use mirrors. We can easily look like a retinue of two thousand, if we put our minds to it.'

Sledd was unconvinced. 'I know we can do miracles on the stage, Kit, but this is real life. You can't manipulate real life.'

Marlowe turned to his friend and clapped both hands on his shoulders. 'Do you really think that, Tom?' he asked. 'Just watch me.'

'There aren't enough, Nicholas,' Marlowe said. 'And we can't manage any more, even if they were available. As it is, we're going to have to commandeer every cart for miles around, just to get them within walking distance of Titchfield. And the Queen's litter has to be fairly sturdy – at the last count, at least four other people are expecting to be riding with her and they're just the ones I know about.'

'That's an easy one to solve,' Faunt said. 'We just make her litter fit for one and the others can carry her. Just as much honour, fewer problems all round.'

'Can Henslowe carry it the distance?' Marlowe said. 'He isn't as young as he was.'

'We'll let him try,' Faunt said. 'If he can't, we can pull in some lad from the crowd; they like that, don't they?'

'They?'

'The people. The populace. The subjects. You know – them. The reason that the Queen insists on these blasted Progresses in the first place.'

'True, that might be quite a winner. I'll mention that to Henslowe – he might like having a few lines.'

'Lines? We can't have every word written out, Kit. This isn't a play, you know. This is . . . well, in actual fact, I don't know what this is, except a quick way for an appointment with Richard Topcliffe if we fail.'

'I'm not writing lines as such, just giving everyone an idea of who they are, how to behave. You can't expect a picker up of thrown vegetables to know how to even walk like a gentleman, let alone eat like one, speak like one – they need help.'

'I see. Speaking of which, how is the Guard shaping up?'

'Shaxsper is in charge of them. He turned up late, so he hasn't got a main part, but he is really good at directing actors – if he sticks to that instead of scribbling and womanizing, he might get somewhere. He has them going through their paces as we speak, in the pit at the Rose, where no one can see.'

Faunt leaned back and looked at Marlowe. This was a mad-brained trick, but it might, it just might just work.

It had taken some doing. It had taken a lot of grovelling. It had taken the calling in of many favours everyone thought had been long forgotten. But in almost less time than it took to tell, the people of the Rose were assembled ready to mount their various carriages, carts and nags to begin their epic journey. They were not yet in full costume, though the basics were there; the boys who were wearing dresses and kirtles resented it most, but it would have been impossible to travel wearing ordinary clothes and with the costumes carried as baggage – finding transport had been difficult enough as it was. They compromised by not wearing their breasts – they could always find something to stuff down their fronts nearer the time. They sat on the folded tents in lieu of seats, everyone was handed a packet of food for the journey; the rest was stashed under the baggage, to be cooked on campfires when they halted on the road. To prevent them looking too much

like a ragtag army on the move, their departures were staggered. Each carter was given his itinerary, using as many
different ways as possible, and every set of carts left in waves
an hour apart. This meant that the first to arrive at their first
stop would put up the tents, but the last would have the job
of striking camp in the morning. All would be fair and equal
in Gloriana's train.

Marlowe balanced on the wall of the Bear Pit, leaning on
Leonard Lyttleburye's shoulder for support. Master Sackerson
might be toothless, but no one had tested his claws for quite
a while and Marlowe had no intention of doing it now.
Lyttleburye had gone hotfoot to the Rose as soon as he had
delivered his message at Cowdray. He was not playing anyone
specific – who in the Queen's retinue was as huge as he? – but
he knew he would cut a dash carrying the royal standard at
the front of the procession, so he was happy. He leaned his
weight on the wall to give the playwright stability and closed
his eyes; for possibly the first time in his life, Leonard
Lyttleburye was content.

'If I could just have your attention for a moment, everyone?'
Marlowe shouted and the rabble's murmur died away. 'I won't
go into every detail about what we're about to achieve, except
to say, it will very likely save the Queen's life and the life we
all lead under her. I can't stress too much that you need to
curb gossip and make sure you stay in character if anyone not
of the company is nearby. Some of you have specific tasks;
you know who you are. I just need to check that some key
players are here. Please raise your hand.' He looked down at
a parchment in his hand, but didn't need to refer to it; he had
the list off by heart. 'Ned Alleyn.'

The actor raised a languid hand. He was standing near to
one of the more comfortable carriages, draped in two inconsolable Winchester geese; they would miss the income over
the next week or so.

'Richard Burbage.'

'Here.' The actor was almost under his feet and it was credit
to Marlowe's nerve that he didn't fall back into the Bear Pit
with shock.

'Band leader.'

No response.

'Band leader? Do we have . . .?'

'He's not coming,' a voice called from the back. 'His wife says he can't come. The hautbois is taking over instead.'

'I don't really mind,' Marlowe said, making a note on the parchment. 'As long as you can make plenty of noise. Umm . . . Prudence and Alys I've already seen.' He looked up. 'Frizer? Skeres?' Two hands went up. 'You've had a word with Master Faunt?' The hands waved assent. 'Good. Well, if Tom Sledd is on the leading cart . . .' a hand waved, 'then off you go and I look forward to seeing your arrival at Titchfield with Gloriana in all her splendour. Break a leg, people. And thank you.'

Marlowe jumped down from the wall and turned to Lyttleburye. 'You have everything in place, Leonard, for . . .?'

'Sshh,' the big man admonished him. 'Careless talk costs lives, don't forget, Master Marlowe.'

'You're quite right, Leonard,' Marlowe agreed, suitably chastened. 'I know I can rely on you. Are you in the lead wagon with Tom?'

'No, Master Marlowe. I'm in the rear.' He looked down at his erstwhile employer. 'Don't worry, Master Marlowe,' he rumbled. 'You can rely on us.'

Marlowe smiled and patted an arm like a tree. 'I know I can, Leonard,' he said. 'I know I can.'

And with a cry from Tom Sledd, the first wagon rolled, its wheels crunching over the cobbles on its way to Titchfield and glory.

FOURTEEN

The clash of steel rang below the mellow stone walls of the abbey. Two men of an age with each other faced it out in the meadows, knee high with cornflowers and poppies, the red petals flying like blood from the delicate stems. They wore expensive venetians and silk shirts open at the throat, the rapiers in their hands scraping and sliding together as they circled each other.

Marlowe and Faunt had reined in their horses on the ridge and looked down on the summer scene. The abbey still retained its medieval monasticism, but the reredorter was an empty shell now and a wealthy gentleman's stately home had grown up around it, half-timbering jostling with Italian pargetting and the playing of half a dozen fountains. From somewhere, the melancholy chords of a lute drifted over the river Meon, where the ducks dabbled and the moorhens squeaked their two-pronged cry, like a wet thumb on glass.

'That's him,' Faunt said, 'on the left, with the golden hair.'

Henry Wriothesley was seventeen; already, with his father gone, the Earl of Southampton. He was tall, strikingly handsome, with a mane of flaxen hair that hung over one shoulder nearly to his waist. His eyes were a piercing blue and his chin a touch too long.

'His annual income is ten thousand and ninety-seven pounds, if that kind of thing interests you,' Faunt told Marlowe. 'He's supposed to be engaged to old Burghley's granddaughter, but they say he's none too keen.'

'Somebody else?' Marlowe asked. After all, he knew Henry Percy, who fell in love weekly with a passion only the aristocracy could afford to indulge.

'Yes – Henry Wriothesley,' Faunt chuckled. 'They say there are more mirrors in Titchfield Abbey than any other great house in the country. Besides . . .' Faunt pointed to the fencers below, '. . . Mister HW is not as other peers of the realm.'

As the swordsmen passed each other, Wriothesley pecked his opponent on the cheek and the pair started giggling before coming back to the '*en garde*'.

'There's a clerk in Chancery,' Faunt told Marlowe, 'name of Clapham. He's a poet of sorts. He's just dedicated an ode to the third earl. It's called *Narcissus*. Apt, eh?'

'Does the earl approve?'

Faunt laughed. 'With an ego the size of his, he is no doubt delighted.'

The swordsmen heard the guffaw and broke off the bout. Wriothesley crossed to a table and took a swig from the goat-skin there. 'You, fellow,' he called to Faunt. 'What are you laughing at, pizzle?'

'Oh, dear,' Faunt muttered under his breath. 'I hope this isn't going to end in tears.' He and Marlowe spurred their mounts forward and they trotted down the rise to the meadow.

'I was betting my friend here,' Faunt said to Wriothesley, 'that he couldn't possibly beat the Earl of Southampton in a set of passes. He said he could – hence my laughter, my lord. I'm sorry if it disturbed you.' Marlowe tried not to look at Faunt – the man was a loss to the stage, for sure; he could act all the actors of the Rose off that stage and into the pit when he put his mind to it.

Wriothesley looked at the horsemen. Roisterers both, well mounted and well armed. But he had seen neither of them at Court. In particular, he looked at Marlowe. The man was . . . what? Ten years his senior? Ten years slower. Ten more years out of condition. He would pose no problem.

'Benedict,' he said to his fencing companion, 'come to my chamber at ten. Elizabeth is indisposed and I have need of company.' He grabbed Benedict by the hand and kissed him full on the lips. 'Now, be off with you.'

'Er . . . I think I should stay, Henry,' Benedict said.

'Nonsense.' Wriothesley took up his blade again and stretched his right leg to full lunge, skewering the air with his rapier. 'This . . . gentleman won't detain me long.'

Reluctantly, Benedict collected his doublet from the table and bowed to the company before striding off through the tall grass. Faunt and Marlowe dismounted. 'If he should kill me . . .' Marlowe murmered out of the corner of his mouth.

'Don't worry,' Faunt smiled, clapping him heartily on the shoulder and taking the reins of both animals, 'I'll see you get a good send-off.'

'Gratifying,' Marlowe scowled, unhooking his Colleyweston cloak and flinging it across the saddle.

'Now, sir,' Wriothesley was testing the spring of his blade in both hands. 'If you'd be so good as to tell me your name. I always like to know who I'm killing.'

Marlowe unbuttoned his doublet and hooked it neatly on his saddlebow, brushing out the creases before turning back to his would-be opponent. 'Killed many men have you, my lord?' he asked.

'Enough, you impudent rogue,' Wriothesley lied. There was something in Marlowe's eyes that made him wish he hadn't sent Benedict away so precipitously.

'Very well. I am Christopher Marlowe.'

Wriothesley frowned. 'Marlowe, like the playwright?'

'Marlowe *the* playwright, indeed.' Marlowe bowed to him, unhooking his sword belt and sliding the weapon from the sheath.

'I've heard of you,' the earl said. 'They say you're not half bad, that you have a mighty line.'

'I have a mighty thrust too, my lord, if you'd care to see it.'

Wriothesley had backed himself into a corner. He was vaguely aware of his people creeping nearer to the grassy arena, his woodsmen, his herdsmen, even maids of all work from the house. They were used to seeing the master and Benedict playing swordsmen, but this was different. Even so, witnesses or not, these were the tenants of the Southampton estate. He was their master. He daren't lose face.

'Spanish school?' Wriothesley asked, trying not to squeak too much. 'French? Italian?'

Marlowe smiled. 'The staying alive school,' he said, and launched himself at the earl who parried furiously. Twice, three times, Marlowe beat him back, then he paused, letting Wriothesley catch his breath. 'Good defence, my lord,' he said. 'Have you an attack to match?'

Predictably, the earl attacked in sixte. Marlowe's riposte flashed like fire in the morning sun and Wriothesley dropped to one knee, caught hopelessly off-balance. In a second, Marlowe was standing over him and behind, his sword blade horizontal under the man's chin, tickling his throat. 'First blood to me, I think,' Marlowe whispered in his ear. 'Would you like that to be for real?' He edged the blade upwards until he heard the boy gulp. Then he bent to his ear again, the pearl earring dangling against the sweat-soaked locks. 'We have reason to believe, my lord,' he whispered, 'that your life is in danger.' And he released the blade and the man, watching the young earl collapse in a heap in the grass. Marlowe crossed to his horse and sheathed the sword, collecting his doublet as he did so.

'You've made an enemy there,' Faunt muttered as he passed him.

'With a little help from you,' Marlowe muttered back. He turned to Wriothesley and helped him up. 'My apologies, my lord,' he said. 'We are here on Queen's business.' It was almost unnecessary to flash the cypher, but Faunt did it anyway.

'The Progress,' Wriothesley nodded, scowling at Marlowe and taking a huge swig from the goatskin.

Marlowe kept his voice low. He too had seen Southampton's people standing under the trees, gossiping, watching, a few of the bolder ones exchanging a few coins from their ad-hoc bets. 'There is to be an attempt on Her Majesty's life, we believe. And perhaps yours.'

'My God!' Wriothesley stood open-mouthed.

'Can you think of anyone who would want you dead?'

'Er . . . well,' the earl cleared his throat, anxious to reassert what dignity he could. 'I *am* fabulously handsome, of course, tolerably rich . . .'

'Of course.' Marlowe soothed the man's ego. 'But, specifically . . . Somebody in your past?'

'My . . .?' At seventeen, it was debatable how much of a past the Earl of Southampton actually had. 'Well,' he decided to play the man of the world, 'I am a bencher of Gray's Inn, of course.'

Marlowe looked at Faunt and both men shook their heads and sucked in their breath.

'What?' Wriothesley panicked, staring from one to the other as Marlowe finished dressing. 'Is that a problem?'

'It could be,' Faunt nodded. 'You know what they say about lawyers.'

'I do?' Wriothesley blinked. 'What? What do they say?'

'If you don't know, my lord,' Marlowe said sadly, 'it's not for us to tell you. Who else?'

'What?'

Marlowe frowned, looking into the boy's blue eyes. 'Who else would want to see you dead, my lord?'

'Um . . . well, I graduated from St John's, Cambridge.'

'Oh, bad luck,' Marlowe commiserated.

'Look,' Wriothesley decided to change tack, to see the bigger picture, whatever muddled metaphor his young brain could conjure. 'When did you say the Queen was coming?'

'I didn't,' Marlowe shrugged.

'Sorry,' Faunt pulled the horses forward, 'that's classified information, I'm afraid. Can you put us up somewhere?'

'What? Er . . . oh, yes. Yes, of course.' And, as he walked with them towards the abbey, he called out cheerily, for the benefit of his people, 'Welcome, gentlemen, to Place House. I'm sure you'll be very comfortable here.'

'But I understood there was to be a masque, a ball and a banquet,' Wriothesley complained after Faunt and Marlowe had explained the prevailing situation to him in very simple words and short sentences, so that Benedict could easily follow. 'It was all going to be under the stars. Benedict and I plan to come on as Castor and Pollux, don't we, Benedict?'

'How apt,' Faunt smiled. Benedict said nothing at all. He was looking at himself from a number of angles in the Earl of Southampton's hall of mirrors, turning this way and that to see the effect of the light.

'Tell us, my lord,' Marlowe tried to get comfortable on the low Turkish divan, 'how well do you know His Grace the Earl of Northumberland?'

'Henry Percy?' Wriothesley was sitting in a high chair as his French hairdresser fussed around him, easing his golden locks with a pair of curling tongs. 'Sat in the Lords with him once. Fellow's a bore. Talked about astrolabes and celestial spheres. I'll admit most of it went over my head. Petworth's a frightful monstrosity, of course. Gently, Antoine, we don't want a bald Castor for the great occasion, do we?'

The Frenchman muttered something incomprehensible and continued to curl.

'What about Anthony Browne, Lord Montague?'

'Man's an oaf,' Wriothesley assured Marlowe. 'New money. No class. No breeding.'

'What about the Middlehams, my lord?' Marlowe persisted. 'The late Sir Walter and his family.'

'Never heard of them,' Wriothesley said. He raised a hand to stop the Frenchman curling. 'Look, Marlowe, where is all this going? Are you just name-dropping for the sake of it? Or are you testing my knowledge of the landowners of the south of England? Because if you are, I warn you, I'm not *that* interested.'

'Master Marlowe has reason to ask, my lord,' Faunt thought it was time he chipped in. 'The safety of the Queen . . .'

'Her Majesty will be as safe under my roof as anywhere in England. These gentlemen, Benedict, think that *my* life may be in danger.'

'No! Promise me you'll take every care.' He had clasped Wriothesley's hands in both of his, elbowing the luckless Frenchman aside. Then he scowled at Marlowe and Faunt. 'You sit there, both of you, and you tell me that His Grace is in grave peril and you do nothing about it?' His face had turned purple and a vein throbbed in his forehead.

'On the contrary,' said Marlowe, 'we are doing a great deal about it. Shall we, Nicholas?' and he led the way to the door.

'Give me air!' Marlowe hissed as he reached the roof leads of Place House and looked down on the sunset fields below. A drover, with dog and bells, was bringing the cattle home for milking and a heron dipped its bill into the trout-ringed waters of the lake. Across to the east, somewhere between where he stood and London, a motley caravan of carts and wagons was converging on some open space, to camp, cook, sleep and probably terrify the locals. He hoped that they were still together, that Sledd and Lyttleburye between them could control their rabble which would, all too soon, need to enter in triumph to Titchfield. Norfolk had beaten them to it; not being stage struck like Lyttleburye, he had made his way there straight from Chichester. If there was one skill Norfolk possessed in spades, it was working out a shortcut to avoid too much excess expenditure of energy; he believed in keeping his powder dry against the day, and not working himself up into an unnecessary lather seemed to be the easiest way. He had found himself a comfortable little outhouse with easy access to the kitchen.

'I know what you mean,' Faunt smiled. 'Take a bit of getting used to, don't they, Castor and Pollux?'

'They do indeed,' Marlowe said, 'but are we any further forward?'

'Queen-killing is a complex business, Marlowe,' Faunt told him, crossing his arms on the warm stone of Titchfield's buttress-tops. 'You wouldn't expect it to be easy.'

'Assuming I'm right,' Marlowe was thinking it through, 'that everything is pointing to this place, what can we expect?'

Faunt checked the position of the dying sun and turned around. 'Her Majesty will come from there,' he said, pointing to the north-east, 'along the Hog's Back and through the Vale of the White Horse.'

'Past hedgerows,' Marlowe nodded, looking to the fields that stretched to the horizon, 'ditches, forests, bends in the road. Over hill, over dale, through bush, through brier, over park, over pale – to cut a long journey short, past places of ambush without number. We can't be with her every step of the way, Nicholas.'

'No, we can't,' the ex-projectioner agreed, 'but something tells me there's rhyme and reason to all this. Our man, whoever he is, won't be content with some hole-in-corner murder, a shot in the dark. He's planning something much more spectacular.'

Marlowe nodded. 'You may be right,' he said. 'I'm going to turn in.' He was yawning already, a leather tome in his hand.

'Good book?' Faunt asked.

Marlowe held it up for him to read the title, the setting sun picking out the gilding on the spine.

'*Chronicles of England, Scotland and Ireland*,' Faunt read. 'Ralph Holinshed. Careful, Marlowe, that's subversive stuff.'

'Is it?' Marlowe was surprised.

'The Privy Council demanded the stationers removed certain passages to that second edition. They were offensive to the Queen.'

'Were they now?' Marlowe asked. 'Well,' he tapped the volume, smiling at Faunt, 'the rest of it might just keep her alive.'

The entourage-in-waiting had finally reached its last overnight camp before Titchfield and there was no one who wasn't happy that they were almost there at last. Some were nervous; it had been fun trundling through the leafy lanes of England with their friends, calling out to cottagers who came to their door-steps, curious as to know who it was who was kicking up so much dust, ruining their laundry stretched over the bushes in their gardens. Some passed handfuls of strawberries, raspberries and gooseberries to the passing show; others threw vegetables from the remains of the clamps in their gardens. All were grate-fully received, the former to quench the dusty throats of the travellers, the latter to eke out the few rabbits in their pots at night. The musicians did the best of all; they sang and played as they went and had collected a tidy sum before they finally made camp that night.

Their instructions had been clear; camp tidily and as far from human habitation as possible. Don't make too much noise. Don't annoy – and this was mainly aimed at Alleyn, Burbage and Shaxsper – the fathers and husbands of the locality. Strike camp early and pack the tents well to make it easier when they needed to be put up again. And, despite Marlowe's fears that trying to keep such a motley crew together and well behaved would be akin to herding cats, all had gone very smoothly. Sledd and Lyttleburye checked each night that everyone was still present and correct and, to their combined amazement, they hadn't lost a soul.

Tonight, the camp was on its very best behaviour. They were within a day's walk now of Titchfield and they would not have to travel separately any more. The Queen was joining them and she would ride in triumph on her litter, waving to the crowd that would doubtless throng the verges. They would not be going through any large towns, but rumour travels on swift wings, and so they were all ready for the biggest audience of their lives. Some of them were sick in nearby hedges. Some were simply sure their time had come – royal recognition must surely be around the corner. But if nothing else, in the morning, they could roll up the tents any-old-how and stuff them under seats. Some toyed with leaving them behind, but Philip Henslowe was travelling with them, and he could smell a wasted farthing at a hundred paces, so they all knew that would never work. But even so, it was a happy embryonic royal entourage that finally fell asleep in their field that night. Tomorrow was another day, and what a day!

Dawn came and revealed a camp already up and about. The birds shouted their joy at yet another glorious summer's day as they filled the trees around the campsite, and many of the people sang too, for sheer excitement. The clothes they had been wearing since leaving London needed a brush but also embellishment and the seamstresses unpacked their bags of wonder and the cast lined up to receive their gewgaws and lace. The young lads were grumpy; now was the time that they had to stuff odd bits down their bodices and assume their wigs, hot and scratchy even in the moderate warmth of the start of another scorching summer's day. They grumbled and moaned, but with a lick of powder, a dab of rouge and a talking-to from Tom Sledd, they were soon in character and the air was quickly full of their jackdaw cries and falsetto laughter. The ladies of the court – the real ladies – caught up handfuls of lace and strings of fake pearls and formed a laughing circle to adorn each other and soon looked as near to the real thing as was necessary. Mistress Henslowe, who considered herself to be a cut above the ordinary, had been giving them lessons in deportment, and so now they all sat and stood and walked just like the portly wife of a successful theatrical entrepreneur; but they were none the worse for that.

Behind the line of wagons, Shaxsper's Guard were drilling as if to the manner born, and if not all of the breastplates matched and if some of the morions sounded more like linen stiffened with glue when hit with a careless halberd, then the crowd would not notice. He had drilled them and drilled them and now he was confident that they could pass even under the eye of a veteran. He left them shouldering pikes and wandered off in search of Tom Sledd, who as always was hovering over his people like a dragonfly, darting here and there, eyes everywhere. Finally, everyone was on their carts and, from the rear, Leonard Lyttleburye, in full herald rig with the quartered arms of England and carrying his furled standard as easily under his arm as if it were a walking cane, called the column to advance and, for the first time since leaving London, the Queen's Progress, as yet *sans* Queen, rolled off in festive caravan, some of the men walking alongside, ready to wave at the assembled multitudes as they passed.

Two hours out from their campsite, most of the men had hopped back onto the carts. Walking and waving was all very well and good, but an audience was the only thing that made it all worthwhile and, so far, they had managed to impress two men driving a small herd of pigs, men and swine all encased in a covering of cracking mud. Spirits were sinking, wigs were becoming askew and at least one of the Lovelly maidens had hauled the hose out from the front of her bodice and was having a damn good scratch. Lyttleburye had sent a few runners off ahead to check the road – once a Cecil man, always a Cecil man at some deep level – and now, one of them was running back towards the head of the column, arms waving and face red with the shouting. The leading carter raised his arm and pulled in his horses, who were glad of the rest and stood waiting, ears flicking at the flies which were never far away.

As the lad drew nearer, they could hear what he was shouting. 'The Queen! The Queen! The Queen!'

Mistress Henslowe nudged her husband in the ribs with an elbow surprisingly sharp in so plump a woman. 'Master Henslowe,' she hissed. 'The Queen!'

'Yes,' he said, wearily, 'yes, my love.'

'Well, get down there. You are Sir Christopher Hatton, after all. You should greet her.'

He looked at her as if he had never seen her before. How had he come to marry such a thoroughly stupid woman? How had he not noticed it at the time? Perhaps he had been blinded by the fact that her father was something rather big in rice and she had a dowry as large as the great outdoors. He sighed. If he had his time all over again . . .

'I am only Sir Christopher Hatton for the crowds, my dear. The Queen will be able to tell me from the real one, I have little doubt.' His confidence in his performance had been waning on the journey. He was finding it hard to manage the wig, for one thing, and he had fallen over his rapier more times than he could count. 'But if you think I should be on foot, then so be it.' Anything to get away from the woman and possibly exchange a small squeeze with his little piece from near the Bear Garden. He jumped down and strode off towards the front of the line, remembering to point his toes.

Leonard Lyttleburye sprinted to the front, passing Henslowe easily though not quite as elegantly. He had a turn of speed which had surprised many a malcontent in the past and he was soon looming over the boy with the news.

'The Queen?' he asked. 'Are you sure?'

The lad looked up at the giant and nodded. 'She's up there, just at the crossroads. She's in this . . . thing . . .' he sketched a shape in the air, '. . . a bit like a bed, a bit like a cart . . .'

'Her litter, yes.' Henslowe had caught up with Lyttleburye and gave them all the benefit of his lofty wisdom.

'That's it. And she's got some really pretty girls with her, and some men with swords and that, but that's all. Hardly anybody, really. Dangerous, I call it.'

'Well, she's got us now,' Lyttleburye reassured him. He waved to the carters to move ahead and walked quickly with the leading horse. At the crossroads, there, as the lad had said, waited Gloriana in all her majesty. She was riding in a padded carriage, draped in gold tissue and with a canopy overhead with cooling fringes hardly stirring in the slight summer breeze. She had two beautiful girls sitting with her, one on either side and slightly below her, and they had spread her skirts across their laps, so as to not wrinkle the gorgeous fabric, which was embroidered with seed pearls and gold thread. Her auburn hair was dressed high from her forehead and that too was adorned in pearl and gold. Her face, dead white, was broken only by scarlet lips set in a firm line and two bead-like eyes which missed nothing. The two Guards, one at the front and one at the rear, looked as though they could give the entire company of Shaxsper's men a run for their money, and they sat their horses with impassive faces. Lyttleburye bowed low and motioned the gawping carters to keep moving, breaking the column halfway down to let Gloriana take her place.

At the break for a midday meal, the Queen kept aloof from her subjects and ate alone. The cooks were not at all hurt that she didn't choose to partake of their rye bread.

'She's got no teeth, some do say,' a comfortable matron said, stirring something unspeakable in a pot over a hastily lit fire.

'I heard she's got 'em, only they're all black and rotten. She can't eat nothing more nor jelly and that.'

The comfortable lady guffawed. 'Well, she's out of luck today, then. I've had no call to make a jelly since my old man passed over from . . .'

'. . . eatin' your jelly,' the other one chimed in, the joke being a regular one between them.

'Right enough there.' And still chuckling, the women ladled the food into the waiting plates of the Progress in waiting.

Lyttleburye was going from wagon to wagon and paying off the carters. From now on, there would only be a couple of carts and the Queen's litter. Everyone else would be on foot. Only the most infirm would ride – the whole show could only work if there appeared to be more people than there really were, that everyone danced and capered and waved streamers and garlands to bemuse the people. And even then, he thought with a sigh, it would be a close enough thing. He looked around and caught Tom Sledd's eye. And the look between them said, 'It's a funny old game this theatre thing, right enough.'

FIFTEEN

A hawk, hovering high in the evening air, would have seen it all. She was looking for a harvest mouse scuttling in the golden corn to swoop onto and carry off to her fractious young, squabbling in the nest. But what she saw was a column on the road, like an army of ants far below her. She saw the dying sun glinting on halberd and pike heads, flashing on the jewels of those walking sedately at the column's head. Then the flares burst into light and she wheeled away. There would be other catches, other unsuspecting prey on the south weald, away from all this noise and clamour.

They had lined the road for hours, the great, the good, the unwashed and the lame, waiting for a chance to glimpse Gloriana, the greatest queen of England for a thousand years. Schoolboys in their fustian gowns stood to attention, from their schools in Southampton and Gosport. The scholars of Winchester stood apart from them, as they had for centuries. All of them were under the watchful gaze and the harsh rods of their masters, stern teachers in their long academic robes and their coloured hoods, fluttering with memories of their old colleges of Oxford and Cambridge.

Sailors from Portchester in their scarlet frocks stood to attention, too. These men had faced the mighty Armada of Philip of Spain, stood on their rolling decks as the cannon thundered and death roared through the shrouds. Their Queen had forgotten them, heroes though they were, and had left them to die of scurvy in their hulks. Now, here she was, on her way to honour them at last. They cheered more lustily than any of the watchers as the flames shot towards the sky, thanks to the wizardry of the men of the Rose.

Boatmen in their leather aprons had brought their huge oars and nets to remind Her Majesty that they caught the fish that graced her table and carried her goods all along the south coast, through the Solent and out to the eastern reaches of the

Channel. The shipbuilders from Buckler's Hard intended to be seen by Her Majesty too. They were small acorns as yet, unable to compete with the great shipyards of Deptford and Plymouth, but they knew their day would come.

The merchants of every town within a day's ride had taken up their places on the roadside, their wives, their children, their servants and *their* wives and children. Kit Marlowe, had he been there, would have looked in envy at their sheer numbers. They held aloft their devices, those guildsmen who were the backbone of Gloriana's economy: the Skinners with their crowns and fur; the Vintners with their barrels; the Salters with their cellars; the Goldsmiths with their chalices and leopard's heads, each trying to outshine the rest.

The shepherds and the herdsmen outnumbered everybody. They carried their crooks and wore their smocks, newly bleached and pressed. Could these be the same men who had pointed a cannon at the Bishop of Chichester only days ago? If so, they too had their women and children with them; so, surely, all was forgotten and forgiven? Her Majesty would never allow enclosures to happen, not in Chichester, not anywhere in the southlands. Even so, Wat, trailing the procession as it moved, carried a slim-bladed dagger under his smock and the huge wolf-dog slunk at his heels, snarling and growling at the crowd.

'God Bless Your Majesty!' a woman's voice called from the throng and others took it up. There were cheers and whistles and roars of delight. Doting fathers hoisted their little ones onto their shoulders. Those little ones would go to their graves, long years from now, with this memory in their hearts. The Queen had passed them, close enough to breathe in the wafts of her perfume.

And the gentlemen! The lords and the gentlemen! They paraded like so many peacocks, plumed hats nodding in time to the drums, the hautbois and the flutes from behind. Their backs were ramrod straight, the Queen's courtiers, pearls and diamonds glittering in their ears. Their rapiers swung at their sides. Surely, there was a law about that? The Queen herself had passed it; no sword blade was to be longer than three feet. But these . . . well, obviously, the law didn't apply to the Court – or did they have special dispensation for Progresses?

Behind them, in the royal procession, the ladies of the Court seemed to float, their farthingales gorgeous with gilt, their jewelled skirts sending up little clouds of dust. Pages ran with them, their faces blacked and their eyes shining. They wore silk turbans on their heads and carried rattles, tambours and pipes, keeping perfect time with the musicians at the back.

Will Shaxsper, the glover's son from Stratford, led the whole procession. He was wearing Tamburlaine's breast and back-plate, damascened in mock silver, and his staff of office was an old one pinched from the Lord Chamberlain's Men. His helmet, the Rose's property woman had told him, came from a Spanish hidalgo killed on board the *Concepción de Zubelzu* in the Armada. 'That's easy for you to say,' Shaxsper had told her, and didn't believe a word of it; that said, however, the Spanish whatever-he-had-been had had a very large head, so at least the helmet fitted like a glove.

'Isn't it wonderful?' one of the crowd, for all he was of the Puritan persuasion, nudged his neighbour.

'Well, yes and no.' The man was frowning, looking back-wards and forwards from the head of the column to the back.

'How do you mean?' The Puritan was confused; there were lights, there was music, there were beautiful people dressed in jewelled clothes. Indeed, what was not to like?

'Well, there aren't many of them, are there? I was at Theobalds earlier in the year – haven't missed a Progress in years. There must have been . . . ooh, six times this number.'

'Were you at Kenilworth?' Ingram Frizer had come from nowhere, 'back in seventy-five?'

'Er . . . no,' the perpetual Progressor had to admit. 'Bit before my time.'

'I was there,' Frizer told him. 'Youngster, of course, but I've never forgotten it. Forty-five.'

'Forty-five what?'

'In Her Majesty's entourage.'

'Never!'

'As I live and breathe.'

'No, no,' somebody else had joined the debate. 'That was

the Earl of Leicester's place, Kenilworth. Three days the festivities lasted. Music. Fireworks. Bit with a bear.'

'Were you there?' Frizer rounded on the man.

'Er . . . no.'

'Well, then,' the walking-gentleman-turned-rabble-controller held his ground, 'take it from one who was. *This*,' he swept his arm to the parade passing before them, 'is merely the advance guard, as they say in the army, the Forlorn Hope. The main body – the van, as we used to say in the Queen's Guard – will be along tomorrow.'

The Puritan and the Progressor looked at each other. There it was, then – proof, if ever it were needed. And from a pensioner of the Queen's Guard too, standing right next to . . . oh, no, wait a minute. Ingram Frizer had moved on.

The column had halted, as the dusk gathered and the guttering torches flickered on the travelling Court. Nicholas Skeres got there before Frizer and held his breath. A little nut-brown creature had leapt into the way of the procession, narrowly avoiding the thud of Shaxsper's staff on the ground and nimbly darting to the foot of the Queen's litter. He who jumped out at horses and found hilarious jokes in the most humdrum of things bowed low, like one of the Queen's Fools at the Court. He lifted his head to gaze on his sovereign and his smile froze. Half a dozen halberds were suddenly circling his neck, but Her Majesty clicked her be-ringed fingers and the procession moved on. 'Give that man a guinea,' she called over her shoulder, and the little nut-brown man was rolled aside.

Skeres grabbed his greasy collar and hauled him upright, ramming a groat into the man's palm.

''Ere,' he wheezed, more than a little rattled by the sudden assault of Shaxsper's Guard. 'Her Majesty, God Bless Her, said a guinea.'

'Did she?' Skeres scowled. 'You need your ears cleaned out, Granddad. I distinctly heard "groat".' He twisted the old man's collar so that it cut into his scrawny neck. 'I distinctly remember, because it rhymes with "throat". So, what did I hear?'

'Groat,' the old man squawked.

'Good,' Skeres smiled and smoothed down the greasy collar. 'We can't both be wrong, can we?' And he was gone.

What had worried Marlowe more than somewhat about this Progress that was nothing of the sort, was the chronic shortage of horseflesh. True, the wagons and carts had been pulled by horses of a sort, many of the participants had even ridden the whole journey from London to their last camp. But none of those creatures would pass muster as part of the Queen's entourage. They were poor, spavined creatures at best, with dusty, dry coats and ribs you could play a tune on. So, apart from the four that pulled the Queen's litter, aided by the gentlemen of her court, there were only two outriders, making the most of things by cantering backwards and forwards in a swirl of cloaks and flying horsehair, stirring up dust from the road. Horses were always a problem for the theatre. The rare times they had been used, you could almost guarantee they would misbehave; a steaming pile of shit in the middle of the stage was the least of it.

'Did you see her?' a member of the Worshipful Company of Merchant Taylors asked his neighbour in the crowd after the Queen had passed. 'Her Majesty? It's miraculous, isn't it?'

'What is?' his fellow guildsman asked.

'That Her Majesty looks so radiant, so young.'

'Really?'

'Yes. I saw her last year at Hampton Court. She . . . well, I hesitate to say this, but her teeth were black, what few she had. Her dugs were as flat as any man's and her skin was as grey as—'

'You, sir,' Ingram Frizer had found another mark. 'Did I just hear you disparaging Her Majesty?'

'Er . . . no, I . . .' the guildsman was a little taken aback.

'May I have your name?' Frizer had whipped a piece of parchment from his purse, rolled around a stub of pencil.

The guildsman stood up straight. He was a member of a Worshipful Company, for God's sake. This little upstart couldn't faze him. 'If you give me yours,' he said.

'Certainly,' Frizer smiled. 'Sir Walter Carew, Privy Council.'

The guildsman's mouth hung open.

'Well?' the Privy Councillor was patience itself.

'Thomas Bennington,' he blurted out, 'of the Merchant Taylors' Company.'

'Bennington . . . Bennington.' Frizer ran his eyes down the list of names and underlined one with his pencil. 'Ah, yes. Here we are. Thought so.'

'What?' Bennington frowned, trying to crane his head around to read the list. Frizer snatched it away and returned it to his purse. Amazing how useful an old playbill from the Rose could be.

'You'll find out,' Frizer said cheerily, clapping him on the shoulder as he wandered away, 'you and the Merchant Taylors' Company.'

Kit Marlowe and Nicholas Faunt stood on the leads at Titchfield Abbey. Night was closing fast over the sleepy summer fields and the owls were hunting against the dark woods, gliding like silent ghosts.

'Hear them?' Marlowe asked, half turning his head to catch the distant strains of music.

'I hear them,' Faunt nodded. 'So far, so good, eh?'

Marlowe allowed himself a little smile. 'Indeed, Nicholas,' he said, 'but, by God, it's early days.'

Faunt looked at him. 'When you say anything is "by God",' he murmured, 'it is indeed. It also scares the shit out of me. There!'

He pointed to the horizon where the road snaked white through the woods to the south of Wickham, where the founder of Winchester College had been born back in the Hurling Time, long before anyone had felt the wrath of Nicholas Faunt or heard the haunting, mighty line of Kit Marlowe. They were specks of light at first, like fireflies in the dark. They were the torches of the column, the Queen's procession and Gloriana had come to meet her subjects again. Below the abbey walls, all was in readiness. Her Majesty had commanded, at the last minute, that she spend her nights at Titchfield not in the great house but in a vast tent that would have made an Ottoman Sultan green with envy. At vast expense, using oxen, horses and every available man on his estate, Henry Wriothesley had had the thing erected, a mass of canvas, ropes and awnings, hung with a hundred candles and rich with furs and velvet.

His own best bed had been dismantled, strut by strut, and reassembled at the tent's heart. Circling the tent were two dozen others, smaller, less regal, for the vast entourage the Queen would surely bring. Wriothesley had not been sure of exact numbers, but he was ready for upwards of two thousand. Support for Her Majesty did not come cheap in the year of her Lord 1591.

Marlowe and Faunt watched the earl below them. He had been strapped into his gilded half-armour since noon, his head bare and his ringlets, bright with diamonds, cascading over his breastplate. His squire, a little boy who scarcely reached his stirrup, stood beside him, holding Wriothesley's plumed helmet. Any minute now, Marlowe thought, any minute . . .

On the ground below, Anthony Browne was in his armour too. Unlike Wriothesley, whose hospitality he had grudgingly accepted, he had no magnificent head of hair to show off, so he wore his burgonet with a new plume for this most special of occasions. He had already warned his sons of the proclivities of their host. He hinted darkly at Turkish practices and would say no more; George was puzzled why a liking for preserved dates would mean a man needed to be watched at all times. Sir Anthony's wife, of course, was another matter. She had spent most of her time in the Titchfield kitchens, with the Titchfield cooks, supervising, suggesting and generally getting underfoot. Above ground, she had made a beeline for Master Benedict, he of the calf-eyes and a hint of perfume. He was the perfect chick for a mother hen whose own offspring were about to fly the coop.

The wizard earl was not wearing armour tonight. As promised, he wore his widower's weeds, ignoring the fact that black was the colour appropriated by the Puritans. He had painted his face white, like that of his sovereign the Queen, with glycerine tears running to his jawline. He mourned as he loved, with no half measures. Her Majesty would probably not approve, but what was that to him? Her Majesty could carry on the fine old family tradition of throwing the current Percy into some rat-infested oubliette in the Tower. His heart was broken; she might as well break his body, too.

His once potential brother-in-law, Andrew Gascoigne, barely acknowledged him. He too wore black and had ridden hard from Ashby St Leger to be at Titchfield in time. His beloved sister had died under Percy's roof – no amount of poetic claptrap was ever going to obliterate her.

Lady Blanche Middleham looked radiant under the stars – even Benedict had to acknowledge that. She sat her bay side-saddle, with James scowling unattractively at her side. They had come alone, with no entourage, not even a maid for her or a groom for him. Lady Montague was aghast at this breach of protocol. Henry Wriothesley was not at all surprised; he'd never heard of the Middlehams.

Thomas Brickley had dithered all day about whether to have a crucifix carried behind him for the Queen's arrival or not. Her Majesty's religious leanings were a closed book to most people. True, she had tried to bury the hatchet between Papist and Puritan by her 'middle way', but that was thirty years ago and more. Around her, it was whispered, the Brethren gathered in ever-greater numbers with their low church, their white-washed walls, their lack of music. So, perhaps a crucifix was a little over the top. Then, he looked about him. There was that Papist Anthony Browne; that lackey of Rome, Henry Percy. God alone knew what God, if any, Henry Wriothesley worshipped, but the Bishop of Chichester would not be surprised if he still paid his Peter's Pence secretly to the Holy See. He'd risk the crucifix and be damned for it. And he had just come to this decision, ordering his people into formation like a general of the Lord, when he saw a face he knew in the crowd and his heart stopped. He blinked and looked again. But the face had gone. He looked at the other faces around him, the ones he knew as well as his own, his vergers and his choirboys. They had noticed nothing. They were all looking expectantly towards the woods, along the road where the head of the Queen's procession was in sight. Thomas Brickley could have sworn he had just caught sight of John Simeon, the lawyer; but no, it must have been a trick of the light.

Marlowe and Faunt had reached the ground by now.

'Quite a moment, eh, Norfolk?' Faunt asked Marlowe's man as they stood beside him.

'Indeed, Master Faunt,' the man said.

'Stick close, Jack,' Marlowe told him. 'Anything could happen now.'

Henry Wriothesley mounted his grey and waited. All around him on the sheep-cropped grass below his walls, his people stood with beating hearts and shining faces. Torches guttered in firm hands and formed a funnel curving in to the road. From the saddle, the earl could see the Queen sitting on her litter, the great standard, her *Semper Eadem*, streaming behind her in the torchlight.

'This isn't bad,' Edward Alleyn said to Richard Burbage, outswaggering each other alongside the Queen's litter. 'Look, Dick, quite a crowd. They must have heard I was coming.'

Burbage snorted. 'Keep your feet in, Alleyn,' he grunted. 'You're supposed to be Francis Drake. Can you manage the accent, by the way? The last time I heard you try anything but Dulwich, you sounded like the village idiot.'

'Well, unlace my venetians,' Alleyn growled at him. 'If you look like the Earl of Essex, I'm the Pope's arse. It looks as if you've got a cat hanging out of your mouth; I've never seen such an unconvincing beard.' He stroked his own lovingly.

Burbage clicked his fingers. 'I knew I'd seen that face somewhere,' he said.

Philip Henslowe – *Sir* Philip Henslowe – ignored them both. What had he done to have not one, but two vast egos strutting *his* stage? Why couldn't one of them, preferably both, bugger off to the Curtain . . .? He didn't have to glance back to the Queen's ladies to catch the eye of Mistress Henslowe to answer that one. He knew the answer – loss of revenue. He *did* glance back, however, to meet the grin and the wave of the little piece from near the Bear Garden. To his delight – and horror – she was wearing a gown so low that both nipples stiffened nicely in the cooling night air. He was finding it hard enough to tread as lissomly as Sir Christopher Hatton; now it was nigh on impossible.

*   *   *

Marlowe saw it first and his hand was on his dagger hilt. So was Nicholas Faunt's. Henry Wriothesley had raised his right hand and dropped it and, at his signal, there was a whistle and a roar and a hundred squibs hurtled into the night, to the delighted 'oohs' and 'aahs' of the crowd. The horses shied and whinnied, but all those mounted could control them, and cheering joined the bangs of the fireworks and the whizz of the sparks that illuminated the trees.

Wriothesley urged his horse forward and waited in the path of the procession. Marlowe and Faunt were watching the crowd, waiting for a move. People were edging nearer, gabbling excitedly. For hours, they had waited under a burning sun for this moment. Some, in truth, had waited for years. And now, the moment was here. More importantly, She was here.

Will Shaxsper saluted Wriothesley with his staff, then stood aside. The Queen relaxed on her litter and opened her arms, the ostrich fan in her left hand ruffling in the sudden breeze. The Earl of Southampton leapt from the saddle and dropped to one knee, bowing his golden head.

'Welcome, Majesty,' he said so that all could hear him. 'Welcome to Place House. Welcome to Titchfield.'

Gloriana stirred on her gilded bed and tapped one of the beautiful girls on the shoulder. She immediately rose and folded her Queen's skirt neatly, so she could step down from her litter and not trip; it was one thing to have her crease over laughing when someone else did it, but it didn't look too regal when the Queen herself fell over. People had lost their heads for less.

On the steps of the litter, the Queen paused. Wriothesley and all his contingent had drooping heads and, for all the good they were, they might as well have been so much furniture. She sighed. You just couldn't get the staff these days. Then, suddenly, from out of nowhere, Sir Christopher Hatton, or at least, someone who looked like his rather older, rather uglier brother, was there, hand extended.

'Majesty,' he said, in deep tones, and she took the hand, which felt as safe as the throne itself and she stepped down onto the green sward of Place House.

'Thank you,' she fluted. 'One is exhausted. Is this one's tent?' She swept those who were looking with a blackened smile. 'Such fun.' And, with her two ladies in attendance, she swept inside and the silken door swished down, closing her off from prying eyes. One of the ladies re-emerged after a moment and cleared her throat. With varying degrees of alacrity, the kneeling men all got up and dusted themselves down.

'Yes?' Wriothesley said testily. 'Is that it?'

'Her Majesty is exhausted from her journey,' the woman said, 'and knows that everyone will understand if she now retires. She will see petitioners tomorrow after she breaks her fast and then would be honoured to receive her host and his guests for a private luncheon before the festivities commence.' She turned to Wriothesley. 'I believe we have music in the afternoon and a banquet.'

Wriothesley bowed then straightened up. He didn't have to bow to this chit. 'Indeed,' he said. 'Music, banquet, dancing, a short masque starring my good self and friends and then fireworks.' Henry Percy, even in the depths of his pain, could not suppress a hiss of annoyance. *Nobody* did fireworks like the wizard earl.

The lady in waiting smiled and bobbed her head. Wriothesley sneered inwardly. The woman behaved like a serving maid; really, the riffraff in the court these days knew no bounds. He opened his mouth to speak but, with a swish of silk, the woman had gone.

Marlowe and Faunt had been silently moving through the crowd and were now beside the Earl of Southampton, who looked on the verge of a tantrum.

'What an honour, my lord,' Marlowe said. 'Of all the homes in the south, the Queen has chosen yours as her sole domicile this summer. And the tent was inspired – very clever of you to think of it; she does love novelty, or so I've heard.'

Wriothesley had been under the impression that the tent had been foisted on him but he wasn't going to argue. He smiled vaguely at Marlowe. 'One does what one can,' he murmured.

'And tomorrow sounds like splendid fun,' Faunt chimed in.

'The music in particular; I understand you have had some written specially for the occasion.'

Wriothesley perked up. 'Yes. Someone Benedict knows in London is a composer, of sorts.' He looked daggers at his friend, who was sharing dance steps with the man who looked a lot like Christopher Hatton; it wasn't going well.

'Well, that sounds marvellous. The Queen does love her dancing, as you know. And a banquet, you say. Outside?'

Southampton flung his arms wide. 'Well, we have the room. And the weather, thank Heaven. We're feeding everyone, you know. Servants as well.'

Marlowe blew out his cheeks. 'My word!' he said, and he had never acted better. 'How generous.'

Faunt patted Wriothesley on the arm and the man flinched. 'We must be about our business, my lord. We'll see you in the morning, I hope. Check on . . . measures.'

'Measures?'

Faunt opened innocent eyes wide. 'Measures for the Queen's safety. You have *taken* measures?'

'Well . . . normal measures of course.'

'And I'm sure they will be ample,' Marlowe chimed in. 'I wish you a good night, my lord.'

And they swept away, into the darkness behind the Queen's tent.

'I suppose we shouldn't tease the noble earl,' Faunt remarked as they penetrated the gloom, careful not to fall over guy ropes. As they passed the tents circling the Queen's they could hear desultory snatches of conversation and the occasional raised voice. Eavesdropping was bred in Faunt's bones, but he walked on, reluctantly; a man could learn a lot outside a tent.

'Perhaps not,' Marlowe agreed with a smile. 'But we've had a hard few weeks, Nicholas, we must get our pleasure where we can.'

'True, very true.' Faunt was peering into the dark. 'Did Sledd say he would meet us here?'

'Yes, I did,' a voice said at Faunt's elbow, and the ex-projectioner jumped. It wasn't often he was taken by surprise. 'We'll make a spy of you yet, Master Sledd,' he said, to cover his confusion.

Marlowe clapped the man on the back. 'Tom,' he said, 'you've done us proud. It's all going like clockwork. Is the Queen abed?'

'Sleeping like a babe,' Sledd assured him. 'I must give the girls their due, they played the part of ladies of the court to perfection. Where did you find them, again? And the costume? Marvellous; just like the real thing.'

'Nicholas got the dress.'

Faunt put a finger to his lips.

'But he isn't saying how. As for the girls, they're just a couple of Winchester Geese,' Marlowe admitted. 'New to the game, so they still look . . . well, let's say fresher than the others.'

Sledd shook his head slowly. 'It makes me wonder sometimes why we don't have women on the stage, you know,' he said. 'They can act the spots off Alleyn and Burbage.'

'Oh, be nice, Tom.' Marlowe laughed. 'I think they're doing a really good job. No one out there is any the wiser that they are not entertaining Drake and Essex.'

'I wish Dick Burbage would stop fiddling with that beard, though,' Sledd said, ever the stage manager. 'If Shaxsper has told him once—'

'Don't worry too much about that, Tom, Marlowe said. 'It's nearly over and no milk spilt; all will yet be well. We just need to see it through. There is a tide in the affairs of men which, taken at the flood, leads on to fortune. Omitted, all the voyage of their life is bound in shallows and in miseries. On such a full sea are we now afloat. And we must take the current when it serves, or lose our ventures.'

The stage manager and the poet looked at each other.

'Yes, Tom, if you have a moment, jot that down. Now, to bed, everyone, tomorrow is going to be another busy day.'

SIXTEEN

I t was all agreed. Or at least, Henslowe as Hatton as Court
Chamberlain had told the Earl of Southampton and all and
sundry that the Queen would spend the morning meeting
petitioners, the great and the good who had a special request
that only Her Majesty could answer.

Southampton's musicians were already warming up in the
sunny fields around the abbey, eyeing with suspicion the
Queen's music-makers who, frankly, left a little to be desired.
They looked – and sounded – more like the ragtag fiddlers
who accompanied the wandering theatre troupes. For their
part, the Rose orchestra had never heard such a lot of
discordant rubbish as Wriothesley's musicians were turning
out. As the sackbut player was heard to remark, he had heard
more tuneful utterings from a couple of cats fighting in a
barrel. The music composed by Benedict's friend had been
described even by those who loved him most as 'challenging'
and the orchestra leader would have agreed with that, with
certain other more descriptive words thrown in. Fortunately,
his style depended on quite a few meaningful silences, and
the audience would learn in time to be grateful for that.
Meanwhile, anyone standing in just one perfect acoustic
place in the grounds could hear both sets of musicians at
once, and so no one stayed there long; the contrapuntal
result could turn a man's bowels to water quicker than the
threat of the most hideous torture; if Richard Topcliffe ever
thought of it, there wouldn't be a secret left undiscovered
in the land.

Her Majesty had slept in. The journey had been gruelling,
Henslowe explained, and the Queen's ladies had much to do
in preparing Her Majesty to look her best for her subjects.
A trumpet fanfare announced, at shortly after eleven of the
clock, that she was ready, and Leonard Lyttleburye stood in
front of the great tent swirling the *Semper Eadem* over his

head, the dragon and the greyhound shifting and snarling around the leopards and the lilies.

The handful of petitioners allowed in to the tent's ante-chamber gasped collectively as the curtain was drawn back by Southampton's people to reveal Elizabeth, in majesty, on her dais. They stared in awe, eyes wide, pulses racing. Here she was, in the flesh. Some of them had waited all their lives for this; others thought the great day would never come. It was difficult to know exactly where to look to take in the wonder of what they saw. Ropes of pearls hung over her stomacher, bows of pale pink festooned her farthingale and her wide sleeves. An ostrich-feather fan dangled from her left wrist and her ruff, of finest Nottingham lace, radiated from her exquisite neck. The petitioners' eyes were drawn upward, from the oddly large feet to the face. Her Majesty's eyes were a piercing blue, her nose narrow and hawkish. Her high fore-head, a sign of intelligence as all men knew, was as white as the horse she often rode – they had heard – on her Progresses. The thin lips were smiling at them and huge pearls glowed with an underwater pallor from the vivid red of her hair, topped by a tiara that could have bought Southampton's Titchfield three times over, the diamonds catching the light filtering through the canvas and returning it tenfold to the dazzled eyes of the petitioners.

Henslowe cleared his throat, puffing out his chest so that Christopher Hatton's garter chain reimposed his presence. At the signal, the petitioners dropped to the ground, some on one knee, some on two, a couple of them lying face down with the emotion of it all, spread-eagled on the Turkey carpet brought down from the house to shield the foot of Gloriana from anything as common as grass. All of them, no matter what position they adopted, were agreed – she looked just like she did on her coins.

There was a pecking order of sorts, and the first to petition Her Majesty was Lady Alice Peake. The old girl, having dropped to her knees, had to be helped up, and she hobbled forward into the royal presence. Whatever complex legal issue she had to present went unheard, however, because there was a commotion outside. Marlowe and Faunt, behind the dais and watching carefully, both stiffened. Anything sudden, anything out of the ordinary, might be the signal. A young man burst through the still kneeling throng, batting old Alice aside and dropping to one knee. It was James Middleham.

'A thousand pardons, Majesty,' he said, jerking his head up to face his Queen, 'for this untimely interruption, but your time has come. *Loyaulté me lie*,' and he lunged forward, a dagger in his right hand. The Queen batted aside the blade with her fan and kicked Middleham in the chest. He reeled back, but the dagger was still in his hand and he tried again, the tip slicing through the Queen's sleeve and flicking aside the pearls. Gloriana ducked sideways and her knee came up but Marlowe and Faunt were on the attacker, spinning him round to face the terrified petitioners and pinning him to the ground. There were screams from the women and a babble of voices all at once. Behind the struggling trio, as Faunt took the dagger from the boy and Marlowe wrenched his arm firmly behind his back, the Queen stood there, tight-lipped and furious. Her stomacher was hanging open to reveal a scrawny, finely haired chest and she tore off her tiara and wig in a burst of fury. The screaming and the hubbub stopped abruptly and an eerie silence descended on the Queen's tent. They were all staring at the wronged monarch, standing in a state of undress before them.

'Well?' Tom Sledd snapped, dragging the stomacher back into place and holding it there with as much dignity as he could muster, 'what are you all looking at?'

Before anyone had a chance to move or react, Jack Norfolk dashed across the space below the dais. He pushed past Marlowe and threw his right arm back slightly. There was a spurt of blood and a gurgling sound as Norfolk's dagger blade severed Middleham's artery. The boy's eyes rolled in his head and he went down. Marlowe grabbed Norfolk's arm. 'Why did you do that?' he asked.

'The man's an assassin, Kit,' Norfolk said calmly. 'I was merely saving the headsman a job.'

'The Devil you say,' Faunt snapped.

'You've over-reached yourself, Norfolk.' Marlowe had grabbed the man's sleeve while keeping hold of the fallen boy.

Norfolk closed to him. 'For all I knew,' he hissed, 'that was the Queen herself. I didn't know it was Tom? Why didn't anyone tell me? Why didn't either of you finish the job?'

Before he could answer, the noise and the screaming began again and Marlowe called over a couple of the Rose lads to drag the body of the dead Queen-killer behind the arras. 'Nothing to see here.' Henslowe was still in his Christopher Hatton persona, holding his head high and strutting like a peacock. 'It's a Lovely day out there,' he waved his staff of office towards the tent's entrance. 'Go and listen to some nice music. I'm afraid Her Majesty is rather indisposed.'

'Indisposed?' Sledd was incandescent. 'Indisposed? Her Majesty is bloody furious!' He rounded on Marlowe and Faunt. 'Where the Hell were you two? "It'll be all right, Tom" you said when you bludgeoned me into taking on this part. "There's absolutely no danger. We'll be by your side the whole time."'

'So we were,' Faunt pointed out.

'Yes.' Sledd wouldn't let it go. 'You were by my *side*; but not in front, were you? Not in the direction that madman's knife was coming from?'

'All's well that ends well, Tom,' Marlowe said. 'And he *was* masterly, wasn't he, Nicholas?' Marlowe had seen men who had stared death in the face before. Anger always came first. Then the euphoria of denial. Then, hopefully, acceptance, but just as often, a collapse so total they were never the same again. If he could get his friend to acceptance as quickly as possible and help him stay there, it would be a mercy.

'I've never seen anything like it,' Faunt nodded. 'Her Majesty to the life.'

'Really?' Sledd asked. There were signs that his fury was abating.

'You know Her Majesty, Nicholas.' Marlowe looked at the man earnestly.

'Perfect,' Faunt said.

'How?' Sledd wanted to know, curiosity beginning to take precedence. 'In what way "perfect"?'

'Well,' Faunt frowned. 'It's the little things. The costume was excellent of course, as it should be, coming straight from the Queen's own wardrobe.'

Sledd's eyes widened and he made more fruitless attempts to keep the stomacher in place. 'Really? The Queen's own wardrobe?' The stage manager wouldn't know a real pearl from his left tit.

Faunt nodded. 'But then there was the way you tilt your head. The smile. Even . . . and this is remarkable . . . that little quiver of the nostrils. You *must* have seen Her Majesty to get that right.'

'No,' Sledd assured the ex-Projectioner. 'No, I never have. I just felt, instinctively, that that's what she'd do. You know, Kit,' he turned, beaming to Marlowe, 'I thought I was tired of playing women, that all that was behind me once my voice broke, but now, well, I'm not so sure. A thought suddenly occurred to him and he flashed his blackened teeth. 'I wonder if old Henslowe might consider putting on a masque at the Rose – you could write it, Kit. The story of the attempted murder of the Queen. Sounds good, eh?'

'Better than anything Robert Greene's written, that's for sure,' Marlowe said, seeing euphoria sweep across the stage manager's face.

'Well, we'd have to change the ending a bit,' Sledd said, embracing acceptance with both arms. He hauled up his farthingale and stomped off to find the man. 'Master Henslowe . . . Master Henslowe . . .'

Sir Christopher Hatton ignored him.

Marlowe, Faunt and Norfolk slid behind the arras and looked down at the body of James Middleham.

'Well, that's that,' Norfolk said. 'Clever ruse, to put Tom on the throne.'

'I don't think that's that at all,' Faunt said. 'It's too pat. In the end, too easily stopped.'

'You expected something like this?' Norfolk asked.

'We did,' Marlowe said. 'What did he say, as he stabbed the Queen? Did either of you hear?'

'Sounded like "loyalty" . . . something. I didn't quite catch it,' Faunt admitted.

'I didn't hear it at all,' Norfolk said. 'Look, gentlemen, I may have been a little precipitate there, with my dagger,

I mean. I didn't think . . . the heat of the moment . . .' He looked down with regret at the still form at their feet. 'Now, we'll never know why he did it.'

There was a scream and a woman rushed through the tent, hauling the arras aside and throwing herself onto the body in the grass. They let her stay there for a moment, then Marlowe gently pulled her up. 'Mistress Blanche,' he said. 'I am so sorry.'

Her face was deathly pale and her eyes red and brimming with tears that splashed onto her cheeks. 'It wasn't supposed to happen,' she said. 'Not like this.'

'Madam . . .' Norfolk moved towards her.

'Not now, Jack,' Marlowe said. 'Nicholas, find Southampton. We owe him an explanation. The rumours will be flying already out there and we've got to establish some sort of order.'

Faunt nodded and took Norfolk with him, clapping his hands and bringing the Rose people together. Petitioners, honoured guests, hangers-on without number were all numbed by the passage of events, if they had witnessed any of it, and agog to know exactly what had happened if they hadn't. Many of them saw the weeping woman being led into the house by that dark-haired roisterer who had turned up a couple of days ago, but then, there were several women weeping that morning and several roisterers, too, most of them enjoying the Earl of Southampton's wine and flirting with his ladies. But mainly, the talk was of the Queen – who would have thought the old dear would have a kick like a mule? And the hairy chest? That had surprised no one.

Marlowe found Southampton's solar and settled Blanche Middleham down on the divan. He offered her the claret that was on the side table, but she shook her head. He gave her a moment, then said, 'How *was* it supposed to happen?'

'What?' she sniffed, as though she didn't understand the question, wasn't even sure who Marlowe was.

'Do you have a lady with you?' Marlowe asked. 'A maidservant?'

'No,' she told him. 'No one.'

'Why is that, Mistress Blanche?' he asked her.

There was no answer.

'Is it because the Middlehams aren't from round here? That in fact, the Middlehams don't exist?'

'What are you talking about?' she frowned. The sudden loss of her brother was one thing, but now the conversation was taking a sinister turn.

'When Leonard Lyttleburye brought you my invitation,' Marlowe said quietly, 'he was surprised to find no servants at Farnham; just you and your brother. That struck him as odd.'

'I would give no great moment to anything from that oaf,' she said. 'He attacked my poor James.' But she had nothing else to say.

'It was because you and your brother had merely moved in to Farnham temporarily, hadn't you? Oh, yes, it was your grandfather's home back in the day, but you live now in the north, don't you, Lady Blanche? Barnard Castle? Richmond?'

'Not any more,' Blanche said sadly. 'Once, but not now.'

'And your name isn't Blanche Middleham, is it?'

She looked levelly at him, her hopes fading in the gentle eyes of the man she had once taken for the Master of the Revels. 'You're the clever one,' she said, her head held high. 'You tell me.'

'Well, I may be wrong of course, and tell me if I am, but my guess would be Ratcliffe,' he said. 'Middleham is a castle in Yorkshire. Blanche? Well, that means white, doesn't it? As in a herald long years ago, Blanche Sanglier; the white boar.'

'How did you find out?' There was little now of her previous strength; somehow, in a matter of what was still only minutes, her brother was dead and now this man stood before her, seemingly knowing everything. She had known their plan had risks and she had made plans to hedge them about, to keep James safe, as a big sister should. But . . . he was dead. Every thought came back to that one fact. And James should not be dead.

'That does not matter,' he said. 'When Sir Robert Cecil sent me to you, he knew that something was afoot, but he didn't know what. I don't know whether something about your invitation to the Queen piqued his interest, but something drew you to his attention. He – and I – assumed it was another outbreak of the Papist violence against the Jezebel of England. You told me yourself that that was it, didn't you? That the Middlehams were of the old faith and you hoped that I could keep that to myself. *You* were the clever one there. You thought I'd look no further. There are a number of titled families who still follow Rome and they are no threat to the Queen or to England. But the *Yorkist* cause, something we all thought was dead and gone – *that* Cecil wasn't expecting; and neither was I.'

She sat defiantly, her eyes dry now and smouldering. 'Yes, she told him, 'My name is Ratcliffe, Margaret Ratcliffe, the great-great-granddaughter of Sir Richard, who died fighting at Bosworth, when so many noble lords deserted their true King.'

'After all this time?' Marlowe shook his head in disbelief. 'Bosworth was over a century ago. There has been so much blood since then. The world has moved on.'

'So much blood,' the woman agreed. 'All of it on the hands of the Tudors, the descendants of a renegade outlaw and usurper who had no more rights to the Crown than that theatrical misfit playing the Queen this morning. Elizabeth is the Jezebel of England, all right; not merely the bastard daughter of Harry, but the bastard granddaughter of the first Tudor, may he rot in Hell.'

'And *your* grandfather?' he asked her.

Her face fell slightly, then she recovered herself. 'He had to go,' she said. 'I realized that he was becoming a liability. As a Ratcliffe, he had sworn to uphold the family honour, but his mind was going. My elder brother died, shot by accident in the hunt, and it turned his brain; he had relied so much on him, you see, to bring the family back to where they should be. James and I scarcely counted with him. He rarely knew where he was or who he was talking to. He muttered nonsense about rats at the dinner table and gave that ludicrous toast to our friends in the North.'

Marlowe had not even thought that the rat comment had any significance; the hare was of very dubious origin and there couldn't have been a soul around the table who had not had a similar thought. The toast he and others *had* noticed, however. 'I took the toast to refer to the Rebellion of 1569, not the powerhouse of York. Tell me, do you have an army readying itself up there? Was the murder of the queen supposed to trigger a mass rising in the North?'

She spat in his face and he recoiled. 'I'll tell you nothing else, lackey,' she said. 'When the Day dawns, you'll be the first to feel the headsman's axe.'

Marlowe wiped his face with his sleeve. 'Won't you even tell me who killed the old man?' he asked. 'I can see that you had to shut him up, but was it you or James?'

'Neither of us,' she said, defiant. 'We don't kill our own kin, no matter how dangerous they might be.'

Marlowe smiled. 'I thought not,' he said. He stood up suddenly and gestured towards the door. 'Leonard,' he called to the man he knew would be waiting there, 'Lady Margaret Ratcliffe here is guilty of treason and conspiracy to murder. Take charge of her, will you? I'm sure the Earl of Southampton has a lockable room somewhere where she can cool her heels. Then, I think, she has an appointment with Sir Robert Cecil.'

Lyttleburye nodded and lifted the woman as gently as he knew how. 'And maybe Master Topcliffe,' he said, a little sadly. He knew what Richard Topcliffe could do to women and it was never pretty.

Marlowe paused on his way to the door, looking Margaret Ratcliffe in the face. 'I hope not,' he said softly. 'For her sake, I hope not.'

Marlowe collected Nicholas Faunt as he crossed Southampton's courtyard. The sun was at its height and Southampton's people, not to mention the company of the Rose, were still buzzing with the events of the day. Tom Sledd, back in his working clothes, and with only a hint of dead white makeup clinging around the hairline, was a little disappointed not to get the odd plaudit. All right, a bouquet of flowers was unlikely, but the occasional 'Astonishing', 'Brilliant', and 'Well done' wouldn't have come amiss. In the kitchens, Southampton's cooks and servants milled around, uncertain what to do. The earl himself had ordered a halt to proceedings, waiting to see what Marlowe would do. An ox still rotated untended in the fireplace; as the cook had said to all and sundry, a half-cooked ox was good for nothing; a cooked one, even an overcooked one, could feed the estate for days. As it was, it was food for the heavy flies of summer, landing on the luscious juices that trickled slowly down its flanks to hiss unheeded into the fire.

What Marlowe would do would be to check outbuildings, stables, yards and pigpens. Faunt took the knot garden and jogged around the lake. Nothing. It was well over an hour later that they saw him, standing half hidden by the willows that trailed their pale branches in the river. And he was not alone.

'Well, Jack,' Marlowe saw the pair spring apart guiltily at his approach. 'Here's someone I wouldn't have thought would give you the time of day after Chichester. Good afternoon, Master Simeon; offering your legal services to a servant, now?'

The lawyer shifted uneasily, but bluff was, after all, his stock in trade. He could out-argue a mere playwright any day.

'Who I talk to, sir, is none of your business. Master Norfolk here was telling me of the extraordinary events of this morning.'

'Extraordinary, indeed,' Marlowe said. 'Not as extraordinary, though, as a man escaping from a mob with a few cuts and bruises.'

'You've lost me,' Simeon said, with a puzzled smile and a raised eyebrow.

'I thought I had,' Marlowe said, pleasantly, 'but you came back, like a bad groat. Considerate of you, Master Lawyer. Oh, but I forgot – you're not a lawyer, are you?'

'Of course I am,' Simeon snapped. 'Gray's Inn.'

'That's right!' Marlowe clicked his fingers. 'You know, Nicholas, I had quite forgotten how sloppy the bookkeeping is at the Inns of Court. When I sent Leonard Lyttleburye to check on Master Simeon here, he couldn't find the name in any ledger. All he found was Simeon Levelle. And, of course, he had unwittingly found pure gold. You should have changed it, Simeon.'

The lawyer exchanged a glance with Norfolk. 'I don't know what you're talking about,' he said.

'Yes, you do.' Marlowe took a step towards him. 'Who's got it now? You, or Jack here?'

'Got what?' Simeon frowned.

'The wolf-dog, a perfectly hideous heraldic design, the crest of Francis, Viscount Lovell. The knight of the ancient armour carried it at Cowdray when he had a damned good try at killing the heir to Montague. Somebody helped themselves to it from the body of the very late Viscount Lovell from his tomb under the stones of Minster Lovell in Oxfordshire. It was a symbol, wasn't it? A totem of your insane cause.'

'Who is this Lovell?' Simeon was brazening it out to the end.

'Francis Lovell,' Marlowe sighed, 'fought for his king at Bosworth and got away, barely, with his life. He tried to organize a rebellion against Henry Tudor in the North, but that failed. He tried again in Ireland – no luck there either. He was wounded at Stoke and died later of those wounds. Legend has it that he sits in a once-sealed room at Minster Lovell, waiting for the day when his liege lord's heirs should have need of him again. Isn't that so, Jack?' Marlowe's smile had vanished and he looked hard at the man. 'Jack Norfolk,' he said. 'That was clever.'

'Was it?' Norfolk asked, his face, as ever, a mask. 'How so?'

'There's a book I always meant to read,' Marlowe said, 'and I finally did, only a few days ago. It's Ralph Holinshed's *Chronicle.*'

'Never heard of it,' Norfolk shrugged.

'That's a shame.' Marlowe folded his arms. 'Because you could have read there all about your cause, your family – you, in short.'

'Really?'

'Really,' Marlowe nodded. 'Holinshed writes that on the eve of the Battle of Bosworth, King Richard found a note pinned to the tent of one of his followers. It was an omen, a warning – "Jack of Norfolk, be not so bold, for Dickon, thy master, is bought and sold." Richard ignored it and charged to his death the next day. Couldn't help having your little joke, could you?'

'This is preposterous,' the lawyer interjected.

'Shut up, Simeon,' Norfolk growled. 'He knows; don't you, Marlowe?'

'I think so,' the projectioner-playwright said. 'You two – and the so-called Middleham children – are the descendants of the fellowship of steel around King Richard. Holinshed quotes something else – a piece of doggerel that appeared in London during Richard's reign; doggerel for which a man died. It read, "The rat, the cat and Lovell our dog rule all England under a hog." The hog – the white boar, Blanche Sanglier. But that – and the white rose of the Yorkists – was a badge too obvious, wasn't it? Lovell's wolf-dog, now; that was more obscure, but would be known to the fanatics who would follow your cause.'

'Do you always rely on a book-bound scholar to answer your conundrums, Marlowe?' Norfolk asked.

'I am a book-bound scholar myself, Jack,' Marlowe said, and Faunt snorted. 'You were too pat, weren't you? The mercurial Jack Norfolk with no past and no roots. Jack Norfolk who saved my life with the dice players at the sign of the Sun. Jack Norfolk who saved all our lives by putting out the culverin's fuse at Chichester. All put-up jobs, of course.'

'Of course,' Norfolk smiled. 'The lads at the Sun came cheap enough and I had to win you over somehow. As soon as we found out the Queen's itinerary, we guessed that Cecil would send someone to scout out the ground. In case we could reach the Queen at Farnham, the Ratcliffes became the Middlehams and moved into their abandoned house there. Simeon here pulled various legal strings in court – it wasn't difficult. Cecil fell for it like the intellectual cripple he is. Then you came along. And then I had to keep the subterfuge going, to find out exactly what you knew. So, tempted though I was to let Gottlieb the gunner blow a hole in you at Chichester, I held him back. A couple of punches and a cut lip was painless enough in the scheme of things.'

'And what is the scheme of things?' Faunt asked. 'Just what are you planning?'

'A rising, of course,' Norfolk said. 'A rebellion. The restoration of the Yorkist cause. There are dozens of Gottliebs, foreign mercenaries in the North, just waiting for the word; exactly as there were foreign mercenaries at Bosworth the day God ceased to smile on our house.'

'Your house?' Marlowe raised an eyebrow.

'Of course. You're right, Marlowe. My name isn't Jack Norfolk. It's Plantagenet. Arthur Plantagenet, right-wise born king of England – not that I'd expect any subservience from either of you two, lackeys of usurpers as you are.'

'"*Loyaulté me lie*",' Marlowe clicked his fingers.

'You know my great-great-grandfather's motto,' Norfolk said. 'I'm impressed.'

'Don't be,' Marlowe said. 'Young James Ratcliffe shouted it as his dagger missed Tom Sledd.'

'Yes,' Norfolk nodded. 'That, I admit, was inspired. Part of your little act you didn't let me in on. Oh, I had a few doubts – the Queen turning up with so small and false a train. But I had to take my chances. Unfortunately, James was an idiot. Too young, too stupid to understand the niceties of assassination. Stabbing the Queen of England in broad daylight in front of a hundred or so witnesses is all very dramatic, but it doesn't do the business, does it? And I had to shut him up, of course. He would have blabbed it all. Never mind; I always had a fall-back position.'

'I don't think you understand the situation, Master Plantagenet,' Faunt said. 'It's over. We know.'

'Oh, yes,' Norfolk smiled. '*You* know; you and Marlowe. But I'll wager you are the only two who do. I can bide my time. There've been attempts on the Queen's life before and there will, of course, be one more – one that will succeed. And the only two who can prevent that are you two.' He took a step backwards and drew the schiavona hanging at his hip. '"The rat, the cat, and Lovell our dog,"' he quoted, the blade glinting in the sun, '"rule all England under a hog." Well, Marlowe,' he crouched low, 'from today, the hog's back.' And he lunged, the steel ripping Marlowe's doublet.

'Take the lawyer, Faunt!' Marlowe shouted and stumbled backwards, clawing his own sword free.

'My pleasure,' said Faunt, and drove the hilt of his dagger into Simeon's face. The lawyer squealed, his nose broken, the blood pouring into his mouth and over his chin. In seconds, he was lying flat on his face in the tall grass, Nicholas Faunt sitting on his back watching the day's sport.

No one wandering at a loss in the abbey grounds was

remotely alarmed at the scrape and clash of steel. The earl and his ingle, Benedict, were always duelling on some part of the estate. Lord Montague had two lusty sons who no doubt crossed swords from time to time. There may even have been a few of the Queen's Guard, or whoever they really were, who might partake in a few passes, so the only two who came to investigate the noise along the river were two of the walking gentlemen, bored with the ease of catching conies among Southampton's people.

'Three guineas says Marlowe,' Frizer said.

'Don't be a silly bastard, Ing,' Skeres said. 'There's no sport in that.'

'All right, then,' Frizer said. 'Let's do it by time, then. Three guineas says Marlowe in three minutes.'

'How can we possibly time that?' Skeres sat on a tree stump on the far bank to the duellists, circling each other in the sun.

From nowhere, Ingram Frizer had an expensive pocket watch dangling from a chain in his hand.

'Nice,' Skeres acknowledged. 'Provenance?'

'Earl of Northumberland. Heartbroken bloke. You've probably seen him about the place. Black clothes. Face like a wet Sunday. Never saw me coming.'

'Hang on,' Skeres frowned. 'Whoever that bloke is with Marlowe, he's pretty good.'

He was. Arthur Plantagenet was as far removed from Henry Wriothesley as it was possible to be. He was fast and deadly in his attack, clever and resourceful in defence. Marlowe slashed high and Plantagenet ducked, hacking with the heavy Italian blade against Marlowe's buskin. The leather ripped and the playwright's leg gave way. The man who would be king still had it all to do. Not only had he to dispatch this upstart Machiavel, he had the other one to deal with, the one sitting on Simeon Lovell enjoying the bout. Marlowe caught the next attack, the quillons locking as the pair struggled. Plantagenet was half a head taller and his cause, he knew, was just, and he drove Marlowe back.

'One minute,' Frizer called.

Again the blades rang, once, twice, three times, four as the pair moved along the river bank. Plantagenet drove Marlowe back, then Marlowe took the advantage and returned the compliment.

'Two minutes,' Skeres was peering at the dangling watch-face. 'Get ready to hand over, Ing, me old lad. Like taking sweetmeats from a baby.'

Marlowe lunged for all he was worth, but Plantagenet's footwork caught him off balance and he went down heavily. Faunt half rose but he sensed Simeon trying to struggle and sat on him again. Plantagenet banged the sword from Marlowe's grip and raised the schiavona to finish the job.

'*Loyaulté me lie!*' he roared, but he had barely finished the battle cry when Marlowe thrust the dagger in his left hand upwards, under the doublet and shirt to the stomach beneath. He twisted the blade and raised his arm to deflect the falling sword blade. For a second, Plantagenet held on to Marlowe's dagger arm with both hands, then his eyes crossed and he slid sideways, splashing into the running waters of the river and gliding away downstream, slipping over the trailing weeds, heading effortlessly to the sea.

'Thank you, Nick, my boy,' Frizer pocketed the watch and held out his hand. 'I make that two minutes and forty-nine seconds.'

Southampton's own physician tended Kit Marlowe's wounds that night. The bewildered visitors, invited by the playwright to catch a killer, decided to leave the next day. There had been a plot, they understood, an assassination attempt on Her Majesty. But all was well and somewhere in England, the Queen breathed yet. Henslowe's wife, Henslowe's people and Henslowe's little piece from near the Bear Garden were packing up to go home, loading costumes onto carts, bidding farewell to the greatest show of their lives. Henslowe himself would miss being Christopher Hatton, but neither Alleyn nor Burbage minded too much. Alleyn had never *quite* got under the skin of a salt-caked sea dog from Devon, and Burbage had had *such* trouble with that ludicrous beard. He really must try harder to grow his own.

'Here's to the Queen,' Nicholas Faunt raised a goblet to Marlowe in the seclusion of Southampton's solar.

'God bless her,' Marlowe said, raising his cup. His leg hurt, his arm hurt, his best doublet might as well be consigned to the Rose's costume department for all it was wearable in polite society again.

'There's one thing I don't follow, though,' Faunt said, gazing out of the window as the sun died again in the west, dusting the fields with its golden magic.

'What's that?' Marlowe asked. The divan, too low for normal use, was bliss to his tired bones.

'The rat was the Ratcliffes – Blanche, Margaret if you will, and James. The dog was Lovell. The hog, of course, King Richard, was Norfolk. What happened to—?'

The door crashed back and Andrew Gascoigne stood there, a wheel-lock pistol in his fist, staring at them both. 'The cat?' he asked. 'That would be me. Andrew Catesby of Ashby St Leger.'

'. . . whose great-great-grandfather William was executed immediately after Bosworth,' Marlowe remembered his Holinshed.

'Correct,' Gascoigne said. 'I was just going to walk away. I was part of it all, all right – the conspiracy. But I only agreed to rid the world of that bitch, Elizabeth. The rest of it was Arthur, and I realized at Petworth that he was mad.'

'He killed your sister,' Marlowe realized.

'Yes, and with my own gun,' Gascoigne grated, 'this one. All that theatrical nonsense with locked doors and the cat. Always a showman, was Arthur.'

'You can still walk away, Gascoigne,' Faunt said. 'Your cause has gone, man. Your King is dead. Again.

'I was tempted,' Gascoigne said, 'but it was you, Marlowe, who actually caused it all.'

'It was?' Marlowe had been accused of all sorts in his lifetime and nothing surprised him any more.

'You were sniffing around the Ratcliffes and they knew the old man had to be silenced.'

'Arthur,' Marlowe said.

'Of course. Lured the old fool up onto the battlements and threw him over. Then, he performed that piece of costumed nonsense at Cowdray. It was symbolic, he said, wearing the armour that our forebears would have worn at Bosworth, challenging the aristocracy like that. But, Barbara . . .' his voice broke, 'that was a step too far. She never did anything wrong, unless you count falling in love with that mooning fool Northumberland. I should have killed Arthur then. Wanted to kill him, then. But you see, Marlowe, without your snooping, none of this would have been necessary.'

'Nice-looking weapon,' Faunt waved a hand carelessly in the direction of the wheel-lock, 'but it only fires one ball, Master Catesby. And there are two of us.'

There was a crash as the wheel-lock bucked, the shot going wide and crunching into Southampton's plasterwork, a little above his Italian fireplace, imported at almost ruinous cost from the workshops of Carrara. Andrew Gascoigne toppled forward, senseless, and a grinning Leonard Lyttleburye stood in his place. 'Make that three,' he said. 'I just came to tell you, Master Marlowe, that the lawyer's under lock and key, waiting for his journey back to London.'

Marlowe crossed the room and shook him by the hand. It was like grasping a ham. 'And may I say, Leonard, that your timing is immaculate?'

'Well,' Lyttleburye dipped his head and looked awkward. 'All right then. Go on. If you must.'

SEVENTEEN

Larks, ascending on the morning air, would have seen it all later that summer. Gloriana, in all her glory, sitting on her litter at the head of a glittering procession. Robert Cecil, Lord Burghley, the ailing Christopher Hatton, and all the rest of her court who were not travelling with her, held their collective breath and prayed. One attempt on the Queen's life had been thwarted; would that be the end of it?

The Queen's Spymaster was busy that summer, crossing the t's and dotting the i's of prosecuting traitors – Lady Margaret Ratcliffe and Simeon Lovell, formerly of Gray's Inn. And Andrew Catesby of Ashby St Leger. And both Marlowe and Lyttleburye breathed a sigh of relief when they heard that Richard Topcliffe was not involved with any of them.

The larks sang their songs above the Queen's people that summer's day as they lined the route; they threw flowers and sang for her, dancing by the roadside. At Cowdray, she knighted the sons of Anthony Browne who both rode before her in the tilt yard, and she complimented Lady Montague on the wonderful banquet spread out on forty-eight yards of table. The fireworks dazzled over the towers at Petworth. The wizard earl excelled himself and wrote a masque, complete with music, for Her Majesty. She, in turn, was pleased to present to him a new face among her ladies in waiting, Dorothy Devereux and the earl found himself wearing bright clothing again and taking to poetry once more. At Titchfield, where her double had so nearly met his death, the Queen was prompted, over a sumptuous banquet, to tell the Earl of Southampton how the Order of the Garter, which she might bestow, would look fetching just below his left knee, nestling above the curve of his calf; its velvet would match his eyes.

Summer along the Thames brought its usual problems. No larks for them, but the seagulls screamed, harsh and angry as they swept above the river, flowing brown and sluggish as always until it roared and crashed its fury around the buttresses of the bridge. At low tide, the bones of caravels showed, rotting in their muddy graves. The stench was unbearable and knights of the shire, forced to attend Parliament or the Queen's offices, sniffed their pomanders more fiercely than ever and left Town as soon as they could.

One man who could not leave, perhaps ever, was Kit Marlowe, all fire and air. He had an appointment in the Queen's Palace of Westminster with a curiously short man who owed him not one, but several favours.

'If you're waiting for an honour of some kind, Marlowe,' Cecil said, sprinkling sand onto the letter he had just dictated and affixing his seal, 'I think you'll find Hell will freeze over first.'

Marlowe was not waiting for an honour. He had served the Queen's first Spymaster, Francis Walsingham, and none had been forthcoming then. Why should anything change now? He knew how thankless was the job he had undertaken and knew that its achievement must remain unsung. If they still quoted Christopher Marlowe five hundred years from now, that would be gratifying. But if they still talked about his backstairs intrigue and the lightning thrust of his dagger, that would be nothing short of a miracle.

'You'll be pleased to know,' Cecil went on, passing the letter to a uniformed lackey who bowed and left, 'that I have found no evidence of another rising, not in the North or anywhere else. If the German gunner was ever real, he has no counterparts waiting to blow us all to oblivion. We can, for the moment, rest easy in our beds.'

Marlowe nodded. 'Was there anything else, Sir Robert? I have a play to write.'

'Really? Oh, yes, of course.' Cecil racked his razor-sharp brain and remembered. '*Ralph Roister Doister*, wasn't it? A revival?'

'Something like that,' Marlowe smiled. He rose to go.

'Just one thing,' Cecil said. 'A little bird told me that that troublemaker Nicholas Faunt was in on this Progress business with you. Is that right?'

'Nicholas Faunt?' Marlowe frowned. 'I haven't seen Nicholas Faunt for . . . oh, it must be the best part of two years.'

'Right.' Cecil looked at the man, trying to read his face. 'Right. Oh, and what about Leonard Lyttleburye? He seems to have gone to ground somewhere. I don't like to lose a good man like that; he took some training, but he'll be hard to replace. Any ideas?'

'Leonard is indeed a useful man to have at your back.' Marlowe smiled. 'The last time I saw him, he was dragging a rather worried lawyer in the direction of the Tower. But don't worry – I feel sure he'll soon turn up.'

Leonard Lyttleburye sat on the edge of Master Sackerson's Pit that afternoon, outside the Rose. On his arm, he carried little Tom junior, carefully shielding him from the sun with his cloak. His left hand was engaged in stopping the baby's sister from lolling over too far in her attempts to get at the bear; throwing buns was all very fine and well, but she wanted to *stroke* the animal. Master Sackerson could take as much of this treatment as they cared to give out, catching the cakes with a moth-eaten paw before shoving them into his toothless mouth.

Meg Sledd quickened her pace just a little when she took in the scene. Her daughter was in no hurry to run to her. In fact, she was rather annoyed that the visit had been cut short. She clung to Lyttleburye's ample leg and stared with a look that could freeze Hell at her approaching mother.

'Thank you, Leonard,' Meg said, 'for looking after them for me. Tom said you wouldn't mind.' She took the baby from the giant and his little lip quivered as the great arm released his precious burden.

'Any time, Meg,' he said. 'Well, I've got a palace to build. Inside,' and he jerked his head in the direction of the theatre. She smiled and walked on, past the bear and the gardens and the tenter-grounds dazzling white in the sun.

'Hello, Meg.' A fresh-faced blonde girl hailed her. Her gown was cut low and her nipples poked out just above the linen.

'Hello, Jacinta,' Meg smiled.

'Have you just come from the Rose?' Jacinta chucked little Tom under the chin, but kept her distance. Her old grandame had always told her babies could be catching.

'Just went up to take Tom his bread and cheese. When they're busy, he'd forget his head.'

'Seen my Phil anywhere?' the girl enquired.

'Oh, you know,' Meg said. 'You'll always know where to find Master Henslowe – anywhere Mistress Henslowe isn't.'

And the two pretty women leaned against each other and laughed in the sunshine.

Inside the darkness of the theatre, Will Shaxsper was poring over some scraps of paper. He'd found them lying about during that ridiculous mock Progress earlier in the summer and they appeared to be in Tom Sledd's hand. They weren't Tom Sledd's words, though. They were poetry, pure and simple. Rhyming iambic pentameter. They *could* be . . . come to think of it, they *had* to be Kit Marlowe's. Shaxsper stuffed them into his leather satchel; you never knew when things like that might come in handy.

He heard footsteps along the passageway and recognized the shape making for Henslowe's chamber under the eaves.

'Oh, Kit,' he called, 'there you are.' He picked up a leather-bound tome. 'Do you know this?' he asked, showing it to the playwright. 'Ralph Holinshed's *Chronicles*?'

Marlowe shrugged. 'Never heard of it,' he said.

'Only, it's a history of the country. And there's some bloody good stuff in it too. Some of it would make brilliant material for a play. I can almost feel the words clamouring in my head, trying to get out, and I've only dipped into it as yet.'

'Really?' Marlowe was already climbing the wooden stairs, his back to Shaxsper.

'Yes. I was particularly struck on this bit. Listen. "The rat, the cat and Lovell our dog, rule all England under a hog". Good stuff, isn't it, Kit? And I was thinking, why don't I write a play about Richard III?'

Nothing.

'Richard III, Kit. What do you think, eh? Kit? Kit?'